YEARS

SIMON &
SCHUSTER
PAPERBACKS

ALSO BY RAFAEL FRUMKIN

The Comedown

Confidence

Bugsy & Other Stories

Rafael Frumkin

SIMON & SCHUSTER PAPERBACKS

New York   London   Toronto   Sydney   New Delhi

An Imprint of Simon & Schuster, LLC
1230 Avenue of the Americas
New York, NY 10020

First Simon & Schuster trade paperback edition February 2024

SIMON & SCHUSTER PAPERBACKS and colophon are registered trademarks of Simon & Schuster, LLC

Simon & Schuster: Celebrating 100 Years of Publishing in 2024

For information about special discounts for bulk purchases, please contact Simon & Schuster Special Sales at 1-866-506-1949 or business@simonandschuster.com.

The Simon & Schuster Speakers Bureau can bring authors to your live event. For more information or to book an event, contact the Simon & Schuster Speakers Bureau at 1-866-248-3049 or visit our website at www.simonspeakers.com.

Interior design by Carly Loman

Manufactured in the United States of America

10 9 8 7 6 5 4 3 2 1

Library of Congress Cataloging-in-Publication Data Control No. 1982189762

ISBN 978-1-9821-8976-1
ISBN 978-1-9821-8977-8 (ebook)

For Doris McHenry
1925–2020

"We must cultivate our garden."

—VOLTAIRE

Contents

Bugsy

I DROPPED OUT OF COLLEGE at twenty. I got so depressed the words blurred on the pages of the PDFs I was supposed to be reading, even when I printed them out. Books were out of the question: I read the same sentence over and over again and got through a thirty-page chapter in a week and a half. All food tasted grainy, mealy, gray. I stopped going to the dining hall and ordered pizza instead, which tasted the same as the food in the dining hall. I emailed professors saying I was sick and they responded kindly, offering to set up meetings during their office hours. My philosophy professor said she'd meet me at the local coffee shop over the weekend if that was more convenient. She added that "we all run into hard times, especially in college, when we're away from our support systems," and that I should please let her know if I needed to be connected with a counselor at the student health center.

Soon I was too broke to keep ordering pizza so I stopped eating. I let the professor help me set up an appointment at the student health center, where I saw a therapist named Dr. John Neely, PsyD. Dr. John Neely asked about my childhood trauma and I told him I had none. He said to be honest with him, everything I said was confidential. So I told him that both my parents had cheated on the other. He asked if they were divorced and I didn't want to disappoint him but I told him the truth, which was that they were still together.

"All mental illness stems from childhood trauma," he said. "You have to understand that."

He told me to come see him the next week but I didn't. I didn't get out of bed for a week. All the professors emailed me. I had more than one email from the same professor, the French one I had five times a week, with the words *How are you doing?* and then *Where are you?* and then *This many unexcused absences is going to result in a failing grade.* I looked up at the ceiling of my dorm room, which I shared with a girl named Abby who stuck little plastic diamonds around the contours of her eyeliner. She didn't talk to me much but she didn't seem to mind me. On the ceiling was a crack that made me think of a single vein traveling the length of a body. I followed the crack from where it began above my bed to where it ended above Abby's bed. I thought of blood moving through a body. I thought of the fragility of bodies. A body crumpling to the ground from a blood clot in the brain. A body crushed under a fallen tree. All the ways a body could kill itself or be killed.

I didn't shower for two weeks. Abby started staying over at her boyfriend's on the weekends, and then during the week. I got out of bed twice a day to pee. The rest of the day I watched Netflix on my parents' account, shows I couldn't remember watching minutes after finishing them. My mom called me and I didn't pick up. My dad called me and I didn't pick up. Eventually Abby told someone—I have no idea who— and a "wellness check" was performed. Campus security with chunky belts and walkie talkies. But by then the semester was over and I'd already failed all my classes.

I was placed on academic probation. I lost my partial scholarship. I told my parents I didn't want to go back and my mom told me that was OK and my dad said, "Why are you saying that's OK? What are you teaching her?" And my mom said, "She's clearly suffering." And my dad said, "She's already cost us a small fortune." And then he looked at me and said, "If you drop out of college, you can't come back home, do you understand? We're not going to support you anymore." My mom cried and begged him not to be so harsh with me. My dad shrugged and said, "Play it as it lays."

I wound up in Chicago, two hours north of my college. Someone I kind of knew from college named Jules had an apartment in Uptown that she was sharing with four people. I had a "room" in the living room created by hanging bedsheets for walls, with a mattress on the floor. Jules had been two years ahead of me in college, graduating around the time I flunked out. I knew her from a production of Edward Albee's *Seascape* the drama department had put on where she played one of the lizards. I had done some tech for the play but didn't really like it and never did it again. Jules wanted to get famous doing improv in Chicago and so did all her friends. Instead, they were all nannies or dog walkers, making googly-eyed gourds and SMASH THE PATRIARCHY needlepoints for Fiverr and Etsy while working as "teaching artists" in after-school theater programs. I got a job at Oly's, an all-night burger-and-quesadillas-and-gyros place on Granville. I made $11 an hour. My mom texted me every day and my dad every week and I sent the shortest responses possible. At night when Jules and her friends were out or asleep, I made little welts in my arm with a pocketknife. I grew my nails out and scratched into my wrists, seeing how close I could get to a vein. I figured that one day I would be all alone, my phone turned off and the door locked, and I would finally get close enough.

I was a virgin. I had never even kissed anyone of any gender. One time in high school a guy tried to finger me in his car and I punched him in the head and ran home. He never said anything about it because he was the kind of guy who'd be embarrassed about being beaten up by a girl.

When she did talk to me—or rather, at me—Abby had described how big her boyfriend's dick was and how great it felt inside her. She had a nickname for his dick: Dwayne Johnson. She'd asked me how many dicks I'd sucked and I lied and said twenty-four. She'd looked worried and told me she could tell I was lying. She'd said that if I stopped dressing like the guys in *Pineapple Express* maybe I'd get some. She'd said, "I honestly think you might be too messed up to fuck. You need to get that fixed."

Jules had a boyfriend who lived in Pilsen, which took hours to get to by train, but she had threesomes all the time, sometimes with her friends, sometimes with other people she knew from her improv classes. The living room was next to Jules's bedroom, and I could hear her through her wall and my bedsheet. If the noise of the fucking made me feel bad, I took the pocketknife to my arm. Sometimes I took it to the tops of my thighs.

One night I got off work early and Jules was in the apartment alone. All her friends were at the screening of an independent film. They all knew the director but Jules was in a fight with him so she'd stayed home. Jules was sitting on the couch looking at her phone. She was wearing a tartan crop top and black jeans with a hole in the right knee. Her hair was up but a strand had fallen loose and hung next to the curve of her jawline. I hadn't noticed her jawline before, but now I couldn't stop looking at it.

"Hey," she said. "You busy tonight?"

It was nice of her to pretend I was ever busy. "No, actually."

"Do you know what a speakeasy is?"

"Like, in the twenties?"

She laughed, so I laughed too.

"Yeah, I mean, that's sort of the concept behind them. Except we don't need them for alcohol anymore."

I nodded.

"There's this one in Albany Park. You can only get into it if you know someone who's already in. And you can only bring one guest." She looked at her phone and began texting, briefly absorbed in some drama. Then she looked back up. "Wanna be my guest?"

The speakeasy was underneath a boring-looking liquor store on the block across from a bunch of slate-colored townhomes. Jules knocked and waited to be assessed through the peephole. A guy who was maybe in his forties opened the door, the kind of guy who would roll into my place of work around 3 a.m. after a Weezer show, and Jules said, "Kenny," and then she said, "Don't water the flowers," and the guy nodded and stood aside.

Inside was what looked like a garden apartment made into a performance space: there was a three-person band playing in one corner, high-quality photos of oiled bodies having sex in another. People were walking around drinking and talking. There was a couch and two easy chairs in the center where people sat and smoked, and on the coffee table were massive, purplish nuggets of weed. The walls had been painted with Day-Glo paints: flowers and dinosaurs and elves and hairy monsters.

"Oh my god, machine elves," Jules said, pausing at a scene of squinty-eyed elves piecing together a human body out of gears and electric wire.

"Yeah," I said.

"Do you know what those are?"

I shrugged and gave a half nod, trying not to lie without revealing my ignorance. She smiled.

"You see those when you do DMT," she said. "God, I wanna do DMT."

A guy in black glasses and a T-shirt with what looked like a demon making out with a '50s housewife came over to us. Jules hugged him and said, "Kenny!"

"Who's this?" Kenny pointed at me.

"Oh, this is my roommate. She moved here a few months ago."

The two of them waited for me to introduce myself, but I just nodded and half-smiled.

"OK. That's cool," Kenny said. "You know, everything here's free. Like, literally. Whatever you can get your hands on, you can take."

"Even the photos?" Jules asked.

Kenny smiled and puffed out his chest. "Even the photos," he said. "I took them, actually." Then he grabbed Jules's hand and pulled her close and whispered something in her ear.

"Hey," she said to me. "Kenny needs to show me something. Are you gonna be OK on your own for a minute?"

I worried I wasn't going to be, but I nodded anyway.

"Cool," she said. "I'll be right back."

I watched Jules and Kenny disappear into the crowd. I decided to do what I had done at parties before, which was get a drink. It was harder to get into awkward situations when you were drinking something.

The kitchen was just behind the weed couch. It was packed. The island was completely covered with liquor bottles, and people were taking and leaving them at a steady clip. A girl in a dress made of newspaper gave me a cup of what she told me was hot buttered rum. An inch of newspaper on her left boob had gotten wet and the ink was starting to run. I sipped the rum, unafraid of roofies because a girl had given it to me. It tasted thick and sweet. I stood against the wall and nodded back when people smiled at me in passing. I began to think then. I thought of drinking moonshine and going blind. I thought of drinking so much my organs would begin to shut down. I thought of getting my stomach pumped and choking on my own vomit. I drank faster.

Then there was a woman leaning against the wall next to me. She looked older than everyone else there, and her face was thin but in a glamorous way, with smile lines like Charlotte Gainsbourg. She wore a maroon velvet jacket and metal bracelets on her wrists that disappeared beneath her sleeves and reappeared as she ran her hand through the un-combed length of her hair or raised her mug to drink. Her legs were wiry and crossed at the ankles, and she wore leather shoes with massive buckles and low heels, the kind that belonged in the nineteenth century. I wanted to look at her for hours.

"Do you like it here?" she asked.

"Like, at this place?"

She tilted her head to one side. "No, like Chicago."

I became anxious that I'd already messed up the conversation. "Yeah," I said.

She smiled and I looked straight ahead. I could feel her gaze traveling from my feet to my face.

"I'm Vanessa," she said.

I told her my name.

"You ever see someone and like them instantly?" she asked.

I wanted to say that I just had but instead I stayed silent and downed the last of my drink.

"Of all the people here"—she wagged her index finger across the length of the room—"I think you're the most interesting."

I swallowed and then barked out a laugh and then got embarrassed. I rubbed the rum from my lips with the back of my hand. "OK, well, that seems wrong."

Vanessa smiled. "Why's that wrong?"

"Because I'm a fuckup."

She laughed.

"I'm going to get another drink," I said.

"You're very beautiful," she said.

I felt my heart begin to race. "Are you hitting on me?" I asked. "Is this a trick?"

She shrugged.

"I'm not beautiful," I said. My hair was boy-short, shaggy, my legs thin and my stomach thick enough that I had a small belly. I wore sneakers and skinny jeans that were too tight at my waist and, over my long-sleeved shirt, a hoodie for a mediocre metal band that Abby's boyfriend had discarded in our dorm room.

"You are, but I'm not going to sit here arguing with you. I can't convince you of anything. I'm just some idiot in a drug basement."

I didn't know how to preserve my dignity. "I am, too," I said.

She brought the mug back to her lips. "Sure, and you're also beautiful."

I drained my drink. "I'm gonna go find my friend."

She grabbed the sleeve of my hoodie and pulled a flash drive out of her back pocket. It had what looked like her name and number taped to the side. "Take this home and tell me what you think. It's my work. Or, at least, some of it. If you like it, give me a call."

I put it in my pocket. She looked down at my shoes, Timberlands my mom had gotten me for my nineteenth birthday.

"Do you lace those up every time? Or slip them on?"

I looked down with her. "I slip them on."

"Yeah," she said, and grabbed my hand and squeezed it. "I could tell."

Kenny and Jules had taken molly and were making out in the Lyft. They made me sit in front with the driver, who tried to talk to me about how he never went south of Roosevelt because "thugs live on the South Side." When we got home, Kenny and Jules tore off their clothes in the hallway and he started fucking her against the wall, his pants at his ankles. I watched for a minute, my hand around the flash drive in my pocket. It was like a video of praying mantises I'd seen in the fifth grade, the male's body bobbing a little up and down while the female stayed relatively still before biting his head off. Jules's face screwed up when her eyes met mine.

"What the fuck?" she said. "Stop looking, seriously."

I stopped looking and went into my room, where I could hear Jules moaning. Eventually they went into Jules's room and the moaning got a little more muffled. It felt like the barometric pressure had suddenly dropped in my head. Involuntarily, I imagined Kenny stabbing Jules, Jules stabbing Kenny. I imagined stabbing myself, stabbing them both. Was it possible to accidentally stab someone? Was I someone with such awfulness inside of me that I was capable of accidentally stabbing someone? I used the pocketknife to make a little slice in my forearm. I took off my pants and made another one on my thigh. I felt sick and restless, like a swarm of bees was pressing to be released from under my skin. I got a knife from the block in the kitchen and brought it back to my room and set it next to me. The blood from my forearm and thigh was starting to drip. I didn't do anything about it. My mom had texted me *I love you sweets. I hope you're having a good night.* I turned my phone off.

I opened my laptop. I had watched everything on Netflix. I had streamed every movie and show that wasn't on Netflix. There was nothing left. There was no use for my laptop. Might as well infect it with the malware that was probably on Vanessa's flash drive. The laptop would make screeching dying-robot sounds that would hopefully drown out the noise of the fucking.

The flash drive was called OPUSES and there was one folder inside: TO WATCH. I clicked on it and the thumbnails of a bunch of mp4s showed up with names like TheInquisition.mp4 and AnInquiry.mp4. I thought about Vanessa again, thin in her velvet jacket, and imagined her filming a beheading like ISIS. I pressed my thumb into the knife and drew a little blood. I felt disgusting, like the kind of person who would lie about being pregnant or steal change from a homeless person. I decided I would watch one video and then try to find a vein.

I chose NotesFromUnderground.mp4. The screen read **VANESSA REDWIRE PRODUCTIONS**. There was the thick staticky sound of video without music. Then the title screen vanished and Vanessa was sitting on a folding chair in shorts and a tank top in a room with soft white light. Behind her was some kind of metal frame, like a medieval torture rack but friendly looking. Vanessa was beaming. She crossed and uncrossed her legs.

"How are you feeling about this?" said a man's voice behind the camera. It, like the rack, was friendly.

"Amazing," said Vanessa without hesitation.

The man laughed good-naturedly. "I'm glad to hear that."

Vanessa adjusted the straps of her tank top. She was acting at least ten years younger than the woman I'd met at the speakeasy.

"Can you tell me when this started?"

"Well, as a kid I always wondered what it would be like to be tied up. And then as a teenager I wanted the room quiet and dark while I made myself come. And then in my twenties I bought a sex swing to use with my boyfriend but . . ."

They both laughed.

"I'm guessing that didn't work out so well?" the man said.

Vanessa grabbed the edges of her seat and rocked back and forth. "Obviously not."

Then there was a cut and Vanessa was in a full-body black suit made of what looked like latex. Something about her bare head made me feel like I was watching an explorer-queen, someone beautiful and regal who didn't care about her beauty when she was cutting through thickets in an uncharted wood. The creases at either side of her mouth were softer in the white light. A black-haired woman in a shiny latex dress and very high heels was standing next to her holding a leather hood with buckles on all sides and a hole for the mouth. Vanessa stood still as the woman put the hood over her head. The woman had a hard time getting it on, and Vanessa, the woman, and the man behind the camera all laughed. Once the hood was on, the woman began to buckle the buckles and asked repeatedly if the buckles were too tight or too loose. Vanessa directed her and the woman responded promptly to her direction, a look of worried compassion on her face. Then the hood was secure and Vanessa was giving a thumbs-up to the camera.

Another cut, and Vanessa had been tied to the frame and was completely suspended. She pretended to be struggling. She made moaning noises as she struggled. The woman had gone off-screen but now appeared on-screen again. She was holding a vibrator bigger than the one I'd seen on Abby's nightstand. She asked Vanessa if Vanessa liked being tied up and Vanessa nodded. She asked Vanessa if Vanessa wanted to come and Vanessa nodded again. The woman held the vibrator to Vanessa's crotch and Vanessa's muffled moans intensified. Then the woman took the vibrator away and said, "Not yet," and Vanessa whimpered. The woman laughed. She turned the vibrator on again and traced Vanessa's breasts over the latex. She traced the inside of Vanessa's thigh. She teased her like this for a few minutes. Then she pressed the vibrator to Vanessa's crotch and Vanessa's muffled voice said, "Oh, oh, oh!" and I didn't really notice what happened next because I was feeling better than I'd felt in a long time, something bright and colorful was flooding my brain, and there were stars on the ceiling, and my whole body was shaking.

I watched all twenty-four videos in the TO WATCH folder that night and then started watching them again and fell asleep to the fifth. I had seen porn before: on my parents' computer as a kid, when TorontoDude87 sent me a picture of a woman licking an erect dick on AOL Instant Messenger. When my friend Trish had dared me to google "hardcore porn" sophomore year of high school and we'd watched a video of a man thrusting into and choking a woman who wheezed, "Thank you, daddy" after she'd swallowed his cum. When Abby showed me her "dream," which was a video of a woman on all fours with one guy's dick in her mouth and another guy's dick in her ass. I didn't understand porn, and on the rare occasion that the subject of porn came up in my parents' house, it was referred to as "degrading" and "obscene." I decided not to watch it because, I told myself, I didn't want to be involved in something that was degrading and obscene, but really it was because I didn't like it. The women always acted scared and worshipped the men. There was always a close-up shot of the man coming on the woman's stomach or boobs or face. Sometimes the women would come and scream and the men would put their hands over the women's mouths and tell them to be quiet, especially if it was one of those storylines where the woman was cheating on her husband while he was in the next room.

Trish had told me she could make herself come without touching herself. All she had to do was think of her boyfriend naked and cross her legs together really tight. A lot of people's boyfriends made them come multiple times in one session: the highest count I'd ever heard was thirty-one, which I didn't believe. At night while my parents watched PBS, I lay in my bed wearing the oversized T-shirt I'd gotten from sleepaway camp and no underwear and I'd rub myself, thinking of Jake Gyllenhaal and Channing Tatum. When they first appeared in my mind, they were fully clothed. I tried to undress them but for some reason I couldn't imagine them without clothes. Sometimes they had my dad's upper body when he walked around shirtless in his towel after a shower (in which case I stopped touching myself immediately and pulled the shirt over my knees), and sometimes they had the oversized biceps and thighs of bodybuilders. They were usually in midconversation with me when I imagined them saying their lines from *Prince of Persia: The Sands of Time* or *Magic Mike XXL*, and I felt rude for interrupting them. So I tried to imagine Trish's boyfriend instead, his peach fuzz and high-tops, but that was somehow worse than imagining my dad's shirtless body. Then I tried imagining erect dicks, but whenever I tried that I'd start laughing because I'd be thinking of bratwurst or elephant's trunks. By the time I left for college, I'd stopped trying altogether.

Vanessa's videos were different from anything I'd ever seen. The women had ideas and Vanessa let them act the ideas out. Rope, leather, buckles, straitjackets, Lycra, latex, gas masks, ball gags, rubber gloves, hoods, vibrators, swings, Saran Wrap. And when the women came, no one told them not to make noise. And other women made them come. And they talked to each other, told each other their ideas, said they were feeling great about each other's ideas.

For a few days, I woke up, watched the videos, went to work for nine hours, came home, watched the videos. I felt sick and dizzy when

I was away from the videos. I felt like I was falling in love. I barely saw Jules and her friends—I barely took the time to take my shoes off in the hallway before running to my room, closing the bedsheets around me, and watching the videos. Sometimes I would come up for air—get a glass of water, pee, change from my work clothes into my pajamas—and wonder what it meant that I liked the videos. Before I could draw any conclusions, I'd whisper *You like the videos because you like the videos*, and then I'd plunge back in again. I came constantly, involuntarily.

I read an article online about a serial rapist and pedophile who remembered being five years old and fantasizing about the way Jabba the Hutt put Princess Leia in shackles. "When you're five and already thinking about shackles, where do you go from there?" the article asked. I thought about destroying the flash drive. I thought about telling Jules and asking if she could help me. But ultimately I made an incision in my left forearm and told myself to stop thinking about it. When I couldn't stop thinking about it, I decided I owed it to myself to call Vanessa.

I called on a Friday, my only day off, in the morning. When she answered, her voice was foggy and tired. She had either just woken up or been up all night. I told her I was the girl from the speakeasy.

"Beautiful girl," she said. "How are you?"

I told her I was fine.

"Did you watch the videos?"

I told her I had.

"Very nice. What did you think of them?"

I was silent. I had no idea how I could begin to say the things I wanted to say.

"Well," she said dreamily. "I know you did, because you're calling. I don't give flash drives to a lot of people. If I did, people would think I was a pervert."

She laughed but the word destabilized something in me and I felt myself beginning to sweat.

"I'm guessing you want more of them," she said.

I could barely say yes, but I did. She gave me an address. I promised I'd be there next Friday.

* * *

The house was in Humboldt Park, a Chicago Greystone with a neon-pink-and-green palm tree filling a corner of the lower left-hand window. Someone was smoking on the porch, a blond girl in a striped hoodie. She was frowning at her phone. When she turned so I could see her face, I recognized her from Don'tKnockItTilYouveTriedIt.mp4, in which the blond girl wore a latex catsuit and put her feet up on the back of a woman in a full-body cast who was serving as her ottoman. In the video, the blond girl wore full makeup and what you could see of her hair was shiny and thick. Now she wore smudged mascara, and strands of her hair stuck out from under her hood like straw.

I was worried the blond girl would see me and think I looked suspicious, so I checked my phone, too. I had no new messages and no new notifications on any social media app. I scrolled through my own camera roll: covert pictures of other people's dogs, a poorly lit picture of some plastic-wrapped food lump whose label read HAM AND RESINS, a picture I'd taken of my arm right after a fresh cut. The blood had swelled to the surface and begun to trickle out the edges, which was always something I liked to watch. I looked at it for too long and then, feeling as though I was about to be found out, put it away.

"Hey!" the blond girl was shouting. Her voice was hoarse and deep, not at all how I'd expected it to sound. "Are you watching me?"

I shook my head and halfway raised my arms as though I was about to be arrested. "I'm here to see Vanessa," I said, quieter than I probably needed to. I crossed the street and stood in the front yard and pulled the flash drive out of my pocket, my hand shaking as I did. "She gave me this."

The blond girl looked at me skeptically. She extended her arm and I gave her the flash drive. She looked it over, rubbing her finger over Vanessa's name and number.

"Who are you?" she asked.

I said my name.

"That's a horrible name," she said. "I've never heard of you."

"I'm sorry."

She smiled and then wheezed out a laugh. "Thanks for apologizing. Vanessa's not here right now."

This sent an explosion of adrenaline through my stomach and chest. The buzzing beneath my skin picked back up in full force.

"I'm Andie," she said. "Spelled with an *i-e*."

"Nice to meet you."

"Yeah," she said, and took another drag on her cigarette. "Do you want to sit inside and wait for her? She'll be back in twenty."

The walls of the living room were crowded with photos of women tied to beds, gagged, wearing collars. They were all tamer than much of what I'd seen in the videos. The couch was large and stiff and obviously expensive, and I more balanced myself on it than sat on it. In front of me was a photo larger than a TV of a woman in Lucite heels and a latex bodysuit with a circular cutout in the chest that showed her cleavage. She was standing facing away from the camera but turning back to wink at the photographer. In her right hand she held a riding crop.

Andie went into the kitchen and left me sitting there, surrounded by the pictures of beautiful women. How could Vanessa possibly find me beautiful when she had so many pictures of women like this— well-proportioned, with perfect hair and teeth, capable of holding your gaze even in a photo? I began to feel self-conscious. I was here because I wanted more videos. I wanted them so badly that I was willing to be humiliated by these photos of beautiful women to get them.

Vanessa came in through the front door wearing jeans over a leotard patterned with images of outer space. When she saw me, she ran to sit on the couch next to me and held my face in her hands.

"Beautiful girl," she said. "I'm so glad you came."

We went into the kitchen where Andie no longer was. Vanessa made me tea and pulled a bottle of Miller High Life from the fridge for herself. She slouched against the counter as she drank, squinting up at the ceiling. I looked up with her and saw only drywall and a few light fixtures.

"I'm so glad I found you," she said. "I think I'm a fairly good judge of character, but I didn't know quite *how* good until I took a gamble on you."

"I really liked the videos."

She nodded. "I know you did. I knew you would."

"They were like my favorite thing I've seen all year."

"My videos? Really? I think that's one of the highest compliments I've ever been paid."

She rubbed the back of her long neck and looked at a point on my face just below my eyes. She was thinking, and it felt strange that I'd inadvertently become her focal point. She raised her eyes to meet mine.

"Have you ever had a boyfriend? A girlfriend?"

I shook my head.

She frowned. "Have you ever had sex?"

I shook my head again, slower this time.

"Been kissed?"

"No."

She clucked. "My poor beauty." She got out her phone and began texting. I looked away, as if texting were as private a thing as getting undressed. She put her phone back in her pocket and a woman appeared in the doorway. She was the most beautiful woman I'd seen in my life, and not because she was wearing silver gradient eye shadow or a shiny latex halter and miniskirt. There was a softness about her, a fullness, a warmth—the way her thighs pressed together, the way her bangs fell so close to her eyebrows, the way she ran an index finger over the edge of her shining lower lip before smacking both lips together. She tilted her head and looked at me as though I were an interesting toadstool she'd found in the woods.

"This is Stella," Vanessa said. "She's taking her fifteen. Right, Stella?"

Stella smiled and nodded. "Davey treats me well."

"Yes," Vanessa said, assessing me from the ground up as she had the first time we met. "We all love Davey."

Stella took a step closer to me, then another. Her face was inches from mine. I could feel her breath on my chin.

"Hi," she said, and grabbed my hand.

My first instinct was to pull my hand from hers, but I didn't want to disrespect her or Vanessa, so I squeezed her hand instead. She laughed.

"You're cute," she said.

And then suddenly Stella's tongue was in my mouth. I felt panicked at first, suffocated, but as her lips folded over mine, I started to shiver. I kissed back, wanting to be soft, too. I got her lip gloss on my own lips. I grabbed her other hand.

"Very nice," Vanessa said. I'd forgotten she was there.

Then Stella was holding the back of my neck and I was leaning deeper into the kiss. Heat flushed my cheeks, my hands, my chest. There was a tightness in my crotch, the kind I'd felt while watching the videos. Then Stella's hand was on my breast. She pulled her lips away from mine to kiss my neck, my collarbone. She pulled down my shirt collar and kissed the tops of my breasts. I felt dizzy. I felt warm. I grabbed her by the waist.

"Well done, beautiful girl!" Vanessa said.

I should have been bothered that Vanessa was still there, but I liked it. I wanted to be watched. I wanted someone to bear witness to what we must have looked like locked in that kiss. I had no comparison, but Stella must have had one of the softest mouths in the world. She pulled her lips away from my chest and said, "Is this your first time?" I told her yes and she grabbed me by the waist and guided me onto the counter. Then she was unbuttoning my jeans and pulling them down to my shoes and pulling down my underwear and I didn't even think about the cuts on my thighs because I was holding onto the knobs on the cabinets and her tongue was inside me, and Vanessa was saying with a little laugh, "I'm going to leave you two to your business."

The new flash drive of videos was somehow better than the last one. I watched them every moment I was awake and not working. I thought about Stella, too. The way she had electrified me and then come up from between my legs and put her forehead against mine and said, "You're wearing my lip gloss all over now. It's peach." And we'd laughed and I'd put my pants back on and she'd poured me a glass of water and we'd talked about Illinois winters and growing up with dogs and then

she'd told me that I was welcome at Vanessa's house anytime. I composed questions for her in my head. *Do you like getting your arms tied up
behind you? Do you like the way Vanessa laughs? Do you like me?*

I typically worked the night shift at Oly's, and the guys working
with me were both in their midtwenties and had been there for years:
Miguel and Dustin. Miguel, solidly built and bearded in a Cubs snap-
back, led and Dustin followed. If Miguel wanted to talk about girls,
Dustin talked about girls. If he wanted to talk about baseball, Dustin
talked about baseball. I usually stayed quiet. Sometimes they called me
Lil Sis and made jokes about me burning my hand off in the deep fryer.
I laughed along even though they weren't funny. The night after I got
the second flash drive was slow, and Miguel was asking Dustin if he'd
seen a Reddit thread called r/unspeakable.

"Yeah," Dustin said, clearly a lie.

Miguel snorted. "Yeah, man, there was this fucking pervert on there.
He fucked his dog, apparently."

"No shit."

My head pulsed.

"Yeah he like, was so in love with his dog that he fucked her and she
got pregnant."

Dustin paused, the limits of his understanding tested. "I think that's
impossible?"

"Well, yeah, but he like put dog semen in his dick. So like the puppies aren't his but he did the fucking."

I dropped a basket of cheese curds into the deep fryer. They hissed
and bubbled.

"That's fucked up," Dustin said.

Miguel nodded an exaggerated nod. "I mean *yeah*. There are people
who do all kinds of sick shit out there."

Dustin considered this. He put a pasty flour tortilla—the only kind
we had in stock—on the stovetop and sprinkled some cheese on top.
"I saw this one movie where this woman wanted to get fucked by a
mechanical dick."

Miguel laughed, childishly high-pitched. "Yeah, man. A *movie*."

"No, for real! It was like a movie in theaters. Like a mainstream movie. She wanted to replace her husband with this, like, machine. And then in the middle of the night her husband leaves because he's been cucked by this machine and this other guy breaks in and like blindfolds her and tapes her mouth shut."

I retrieved the cheese curds and let them cool on the counter. I tried to think of Stella. Miguel wasn't saying anything.

"So like," Dustin persisted, "this guy uses the mechanical dick to fuck her but she can't say yes because she's blindfolded and gagged so he's just raping her, and then he basically makes the thing go so hard it kills her."

"Sounds like a bullshit movie."

"I swear I saw it in theaters."

"Yo, Lil Sis," Miguel said, and tossed me a loaf of frozen garlic bread. I caught it close to my stomach like a football. "You OK with this? We being too weird for you?"

"I'm fine," I said.

"Because we can stop. We can stop talking about this fucked-up pervert shit."

I involuntarily thought of Stella's tongue while looking at Miguel and my face flushed.

"Aww shit, you're blushing! Listen, we don't have to talk about this. But, OK, this is the last thing I'll say. You need to be careful."

"Yeah," Dustin said. "These streets are dangerous."

"Like, seriously. This girl who lives a block down from me on Argyle got raped two days ago. By some random dude she didn't even know." He lowered his voice. "And they found a *child pornographer* in Uptown."

"Fuck!" Dustin spat.

"Dude, fucking be quiet. We're gonna have customers in like six seconds and you're up in here screaming FUCK like an idiot."

Dustin shook his head.

"This dude was doing shit to *infants*. We're talking like some kind of Hannibal Lecter sicko. He was tying kids up."

I swallowed and put the brick of garlic bread in the oven.

"So I just want you to be safe, OK?" Miguel's baritone came from behind me. "I think of you as a little sister. Just carry your pepper spray or your brass knuckles or whatever. There are too many messed-up people walking around this city."

When I got home, I didn't go straight to my room. I sat on the couch and dutifully sent my mom a picture of a new pair of shoes I'd recently gotten. She wrote right back *Wow! Looking good!* Getting such an earnest text from her made the skin on my hands prickle. Jules wandered into the living room with a bowl of ramen and asked me if I wanted to watch some old *Sailor Moon* episodes with her. We sat on her bed and I tried to focus on the screen, on Sailor Moon's ribbony hair and pink mouth, but I kept on feeling sick. Maybe I was a bad person. Maybe all the things I did and said were wrong. I imagined Jules taking a sledgehammer to my head, my skull breaking apart in pieces, frothy spumes of blood. I told her I was getting tired and went back to my room.

I made a cut I had to really focus on this time, testing to see how deep I could go without opening a vein. I never cut when there was a risk of someone seeing my silhouette against the bedsheets, but I wanted to get this one in really quickly, because I was going to be sick if I didn't. The blood came up fast and thick. I panicked. It was dripping on my sheets, the floor. I tried putting a towel over it, then a pillow. Five minutes in and it looked like someone had been killed in my bed. Crying, I ran to the kitchen and twisted a rubber band around my arm below the cut. I pressed a wad of paper towels against my forearm and looked out the window. In the building across from ours, a graying man in a green sweater was drying dishes. I was pathetic. I was so fucking pathetic. The sound of Sailor Moon paused in the next room and Jules was in the doorway, looking at me, her mouth open.

"Oh my god. Do you need any help?" she asked.

I shook my head, still crying.

"What happened?"

I didn't know what to say. There was no way to explain it. Blood dripped on the floor.

"I did it," I said.

Jules's eyes widened. "Seriously?"

I nodded.

"OK," she said, backing away, her fingers curled at her sides. "Feel better."

I couldn't go to the ER. Bad things would happen if I went to the ER, because they'd see the other cuts. I got out my phone and called Vanessa.

"Beautiful girl," she said liltingly.

By then I was crying so much I could barely speak. "I had an accident," I managed. "I'm bleeding a lot."

Her voice sharpened. "What happened?"

I made a mewling noise.

"Where are you?"

I gave her the address.

"I'll be right over."

I was waiting on the front steps, my arm swaddled in paper towels, when Vanessa pulled up. She got out of her car, saw me, and then went back and came out again with the kind of rubber tie phlebotomists tie around your forearm to make your veins pop. She tied my arm off and sat next to me while we both watched the bleeding stop. Then she wrapped me in what felt like yards of gauze and told me to get in the car with her. We sat parked in front of my building, both of us staring ahead. Snow began to fall around us, smudging my view of the streetlights.

"You have a lot of scars on your arm," Vanessa said. "Show me your other."

I rolled up my sleeve. She ran her fingers over the bumps.

"I saw some on your thighs, too. The other day." She sighed. "We can't have this, beautiful girl."

I began to cry again. "I know," I said.

"What makes you do this?"

I shook my head. "I don't know." It was the last thing I wanted to say to her. Now she'd know beyond a doubt how grotesque I was.

She put her arm around my shoulders and pulled me into a hug.

Shocked, I cried into her chest, which was moist and warm and smelled like rosewater. "I'm going to be seeing a whole lot more of you, I think," she said.

What happened next happened fast. I went to Vanessa's that night and met Davey, who was thin in a button-down and tight jeans and thick glasses. As we shook hands and he said, "Pleasure to meet you," I recognized his voice from the videos: the man behind the camera. When I told him my name, he shook his head.

"I'm sorry," he said, "please don't take this the wrong way, but that's an awful name. It doesn't suit you at all." He turned to Vanessa. "Do you see her hair right now?"

Vanessa collected a few loose strands and tucked them behind my ear. "Yes," she said.

"Short and slicked back like that, doesn't it kind of look like Warren Beatty?"

Vanessa burst into an awkward caw, but quieted quickly when she looked at me. "I mean, it kind of does."

"You're probably too young to remember any Warren Beatty movies, hon," Davey said to me. "But right now you kind of look like Bugsy. I was so into Bugsy when I was a kid."

Vanessa clapped her hands. "Oh my god, Bugsy!"

Davey held my chin and gently swiveled my head back and forth. "You look like a gritty gangster lesbian. Like a dykey Al Capone."

"I love it," Vanessa said. "Can we call you Bugsy?"

"Sure," I said. I had no idea who Warren Beatty was.

The rest of the house was dark. As we walked through it, Davey kept running ahead of us to flip on lights. Here were the wooden stocks in which the girl in the sensory deprivation hood had been locked. The frame from which Vanessa had been suspended. The table to which the girl in the full-body Lycra suit had been strapped and tickled. There were tons of cameras, high-quality cameras, and boom microphones, and the kinds of lights I'd seen in pictures of movie sets.

We stopped upstairs, in a completely bare room with nothing but white sheets hanging from the walls. "We still have to light and stock this one," Davey said, hands in his back pockets. "Vanessa tells me you've been liking our videos."

"I have."

"Well, I knew she would," Vanessa said. "I know a freak when I see one."

I wanted to ask her what she meant by that, but I didn't want to ruin things.

"So, I'm the producer," Davey said. "But really the girls and Vanessa are the directors. And actors."

"Davey's an aromantic asexual," Vanessa explained, moving to put her arm around him. "He feels neutral-to-negative about sex and he doesn't get off on anything we do. But he does like filmmaking."

Davey smiled and shook his head at the floor in an enough-about-me way. "Have you seen our page? It's called Our Hands Are Tied."

Vanessa tsked him. "Why would I make her go to our page? There's a paywall. She's a kid working a minimum-wage job."

"Maybe when you get a raise you can become a monthly subscriber."

Vanessa shook her head and slid her fingers through my hair. "Bugsy's not going to lose money to us. She's going to *make* money from us."

I stayed there that night, on an inflatable mattress in what I'd come to think of as The Bare Room. The next morning, Vanessa woke me up with black tea and a croissant.

"We need your help, Bugsy," she said. "Have you ever operated a boom?"

I shook my head.

"Would you like to?"

"Yes," I said, trying not to sound too eager. In that moment, it was the one thing I wanted most in the world.

I wore headphones in which I could hear the amplified sounds of the girls moaning, putting on latex mittens, wrapping each other up in chains. I stood by Davey while he sat behind the camera, stepping closer to or farther from the scene as he wished. After that, I thought I'd never feel the buzzing under my skin again.

Vanessa cut me a check for $120 at the end of the day and told me she was paying me $15 an hour. I went home that night and could barely sleep from excitement. I went back the next day to be the boom operator, and the next. My supervisor at Oly's called to ask what was wrong with me. When I called back, it was to tell him I was quitting.

I saw Stella again. She lived in the house, along with Andie and three other girls: Dolce, Lea, and Missy. I memorized their names and how they looked wrapped up in straitjackets, taped to poles, suspended from racks. I learned what fetish objects were—girls who were immobilized and deprived of sight and sound and forced to orgasm repeatedly—and what chastity belts and orgasm belts were and what it meant to top and to bottom. Andie, who had grown up the daughter of mechanics, looked babydollish during shoots, with red cheeks and full lips, and preferred to be enclosed in cages with her head mummified so only her nose, lips, and ponytail stuck out. Dolce was the smallest of the group, a former nurse, and liked to be suspended in the air, blindfolded, tickled, and fingered. Lea had been a runner in college and loved anything that tested the limits of her physical endurance; she would be taped to wooden crosses or hung upside down, or forced to stand for hours with her legs apart as she was edged by a vibrator on an orgasm belt. Missy had escaped a Mormon family in Utah and loved to wear the kind of leather hoods with metal-ringed mouth holes that allowed dildos to be slid down her throat and showed the full edges of her lips as she sucked on them. And Stella did everything: scenes where she was hog-tied, scenes where she was a helpless gagged fetish object, scenes where her legs were spread apart with clamps and one of the other girls fingered her. After we filmed a scene and Davey let us take a fifteen, Stella and I would go into the upstairs bathroom and make out. Sometimes she'd have rope burns on her arms or imprints on her forehead from tape or a gas mask, and that would make it hotter.

I slept on the inflatable mattress more often than I slept in my old apartment, and I'd arranged the few belongings I had around my new bed. I went to sleep looking at the soft white sheets around me and thinking of the sky, or of outer space. I always woke up feeling better rested than I had since before going to college. One morning Davey was standing above me, pushing his glasses up his nose and saying, "Bugsy, if you're gonna sleep here every night, you might as well stop paying rent at the other place."

When I told Jules I was moving out, she told me that wouldn't be possible, because I was paying one fifth of the rent and there was no one to replace me.

"I didn't sign a contract," I said. We were standing on the front steps and Vanessa was in her car next to the curb, smoking and watching us.

Jules crossed her arms. "You signed, like, an emotional contract. You moved in with me at the beginning of the year and promised you'd still be here when we renewed the lease."

I looked at Vanessa and then back at Jules.

"I'm breaking that promise," I said.

"Fuck you!" she spat. "You can't just break promises like that! I tried to make you my friend!"

I stood back, watching her. She was small and furious in the cold.

"God, you psycho bitch. This is because you cut your arm open, isn't it?"

"Fuck you, too, Jules," I said. I felt as good as I did making out with Stella, but in a different way.

Slowly, Stella told me about herself. She was six years older than me. She had lived in Chicago most of her life. Her father was a county judge who drank and beat her mother. He'd recently ruled in favor of a cop who'd shot a Black teenager from Altgeld Gardens eighteen times, continuing to fire bullets into his back long after the teenager was lying facedown on the pavement. Stella hadn't spoken to her father in ten years. Her mother, who had wanted only to be a well-treated and well-kept woman, had done sex work—that was how she and her father had met—and had died of brain cancer when Stella was fourteen, long before Stella had known she'd wanted to go into the business herself. But she'd always known she wanted to do something that would make people stop what they were doing and watch her. She wanted to be on people's minds even when they weren't looking at her. She'd read that scientists had discovered that people have whole clusters of neurons dedicated to recognizing a single face. "You could go inside people's heads," she told me, "and point to the cluster of Lady Gaga cells, or the cluster of Rihanna cells." She wanted people's brains to have a cluster of cells for her. She decided that changing her name to Stella Hardwycke would be a good start.

The thing about Stella, though, was she didn't want to be famous. At least not Lady Gaga- or Rihanna-famous. She wanted to be known and worshipped by people she didn't know, but she didn't want to be what she called "sugarpop," which meant that the threshold for loving her would be so low that virtually anyone walking around in Target or in line at the McDondald's drive-thru could clear it. She wanted her people to have to find her. She graduated high school in Oak Park and went to New York for a few years, doing scenes in straight porn for $1,000 each and escorting on the weekends. In the scenes, which were elaborate, she was dressed in tartan skirts and given a girl to act with, the producer's twentysomething girlfriend who had no industry experience and whom the producer constantly referred to as "pure." Stella and the pure girlfriend would pretend to be gossipy teenagers texting on the girlfriend's bed when Rico or Shane or Johnny would appear in the doorway and summon Stella to him by saying, "I don't think you're a very good influence on my daughter." Ignoring the girlfriend's protestations, Rico or Shane or Johnny would take Stella into his room, rip off her skirt and tights, and spank her. Oftentimes there'd be a close-up shot of Stella's squealing face next to a bedside picture of the spanker and his wife and daughter. Then Rico or Shane or Johnny would pin Stella to the bed and fuck her from behind, saying, "I don't want you in my house, you filthy little slut!" There were several variations on that scene, some of which involved the wife watching and insulting Stella, too. The scene work came regularly for a year but then started to wane when the producer's eye wandered to different girls. Stella was not deluxe enough an escort to be able to afford her Brooklyn studio without the scene work. She moved back to Chicago and got a job as a server at a steakhouse in River North. On weekends, she saw shows at a place in Humboldt Park called the Empty Bottle. It was there during a noise show that she met Davey, who happened to like the same band. He gave her his card in case she ever wanted work.

I told her I'd met Vanessa at a speakeasy and Stella laughed.

"I swear those weirdos always do their talent scouting in the grodiest places. Who do they think they'll find?"

I snuggled up closer to her. "Well, they found us," I said, and she kissed the crown of my head.

Before I spent my first night in her bed, Stella told me we weren't going to be exclusive. She didn't believe in monogamy. She'd tried it too many times and it had been stupid every time. I told her I didn't believe in it, either, even though I'd never done it. I was embarrassed when her room started to smell like me, but she didn't seem to mind. Sometimes after we'd had sex for hours, she would hold my forearms in her hands and rub her thumbs against the scars. Sometimes she was quiet when she did this and other times she said, "Shit," and other times she said "I've been depressed, too, but it's never been like this." Sometimes we strayed from the strap-on and going down on each other and did different things, the kinds of things I'd seen her do in Vanessa's videos. She wrapped me up in tape. She tied my arms behind my back in a binder. Once she tied me to the bed and made me wear a leather hood that blocked out all light and let her lips hover above mine, breathing her Listerine-and-Mountain-Dew-and-cigarettes breath into my mouth, and then denied me kiss after kiss. She ground up against me while I was tied down and I felt a pressure welling in me, an incredible pressure, and saw flashes of light behind my closed eyes and felt my legs begin to twitch and then in my brain every single Stella Hardwycke cell lit up, all cells were Stella Hardwycke cells, all cells were exploding. She took the hood off but left me flush and tied up and kissed me on the cheek. She asked me why I was so cute. I didn't tell her I was in love.

On weekends, I played Catan with Lea, Andie, and Dolce. I ran errands for Davey, to Ace Hardware for a special type of screw whose name I would have forgotten had I not written it in my phone, or to Target to get Lysol or a broom for a scene in which Vanessa was going to buzz Missy's head. In the credits for each video I was listed as "Bugsy . . . Gaffer, Key Grip, and Best Boi." It was some film joke Davey was very pleased with that I didn't get, but I never asked about it.

Sometimes Stella and I went on long walks through the park, or to Garfield Park Conservatory to look at plants. She told me about monocots and dicots and how bivoltine bees were her favorite pollinators. She said in another, quieter, less interesting life she would have been a botanist. Sometimes we went to Wicker Park to get tacos at Picante Taqueria and talk about how the earth was created and why we're all here and what emotions are made of. She called me Little One, which bothered me, but I didn't stop her. When my parents texted, I told them how much better I was feeling working my job and living with Jules and that I might even consider going back to school. My dad made it clear I'd be paying for it this time. I told him sure, that was fine.

We were set up for a scene in which Vanessa was going to seal Lea in a vacbed and take a vibrator to her clit. I was in my bulky headphones wearing my toolbelt and holding the boom when Vanessa came up behind me and hugged me around the waist. I jumped and set the boom down as carefully as I could.

"You scared me," I said.

She laughed in my ear. "I'm always scaring you, Bugsy. I'm scary, you're jumpy." Then she let go of me. "Do you want to do this scene and I'll hold the boom?"

"Like, do your part in the scene?"

She nodded.

"I'm—"

"Say yes," Vanessa said. "You know you're beautiful."

"I have a potbelly," I said.

She shook her head. "Doesn't matter. It's better that way, actually."

"Are the subscribers going to want to see a potbelly?"

"Yes," she said, without hesitation. "*Our* subscribers will."

It should have taken longer to convince me but it didn't. I got into the latex, which stretched and wrinkled in places it maybe wasn't supposed to, and sat on my knees with a big smile on my face as Lea breathed audibly through her tube. Davey asked me if I was excited and I told him I was and bounced on my heels a little.

I did the scene, giggling the way Vanessa and the other girls did while they were domming, watching Lea writhe. Occasionally I pinched her nipples, hard beneath the black latex, and she squealed and shifted and Davey said, "Good, good!" When I had made Lea come a few times, Davey stopped rolling and everyone clapped for me. Vanessa depressurized the vacbed and Lea slid out and wrapped her ropey arms around me and told me she'd never had better. Vanessa proposed we all go to Picante Taqueria and then go dancing to celebrate my debut.

I wore three-quarter length sleeves without even thinking about it. I sat next to Stella and we all laughed when she dribbled sour cream down her chest. In the club I danced with all of them, even Davey. Stella and I snuck into the bathroom and did bumps of coke and my head felt clear and my ideas were coming fast: We should recruit in coffee shops and boba places, where the hot queers go to mope. We should film a scene where Lea's hog-tied and suspended from the ceiling and there's a dildo in her mouth and Stella slides it in and out and denies her any pleasure. We should lower the subscription rate so more people working at Whole Foods or Petco and making zines could have the money to see our content—more subscribers over time would recoup any losses from lowering the rate. We should make Davey dress as Elton John for Halloween and we could all go in drag as his lovers, except Vanessa could stay female and go as his beard. Stella kissed me and told me to stop talking. She wanted to have sex with me in the bathroom stall. She locked the door and pressed me against the wall and shoved her tongue in my mouth. I had never been happier in my life.

Then he showed up. He was just at dinner one night, in jeans and a pink hoodie that read MY MANTRA in a blocky mauve font. He had a sprinkling of acne at the base of his chin. I could see very clearly at least one whitehead that hadn't been popped. He wore a double-undercut with his hair slicked back on top, which reminded me of the Hitler youth. He kept complimenting the food, which no one had made: we were eating Chinese takeout. He sat in between Stella and me. When he made a joke—an unfunny joke—about trying to pop and lock as a white fourteen-year-old, Stella laughed and laid her head on his shoulder. The old buzzing started beneath my skin again.

Vanessa told us that she'd met Cody at an "art party" in Wicker Park. He was doing some kind of web development at Venmo and wanted a part-time gig on the side. He was going to redesign our website and boost our social media presence. He was going to fiddle with the SEO so we would be the first or second hit when someone googled terms like "forced orgasm" or "multiple forced orgasms" or "lesbian BDSM." Vanessa tilted her head and smiled and said Cody had big ideas for us and was going to make magic happen. Cody deflected her praise with his brittle-looking hands and said he was no magician, he was just a nerd who believed in sex positivity.

That night, Cody slept in Stella's room and I slept on my neglected air mattress. I hated the sound he made when he came: a strangled, breathy noise that would have been good as a soprano but was disgusting as a baritone. I hated the little murmurings they did in between rounds. I hated seeing him walk out into the hallway in his pink hoodie and polka-dot boxers and look my way, staring long as if he could see me in the dark, as if I was a dormant threat that could spring to life at any minute. I hated when he showed up the next day and the next. I hated the way Stella checked her phone, waiting for his texts. I hated how Stella and I could only have sex during our fifteens, or in the mornings, and how distracted she was, how fast she made it. I hated his jokes, the way his ugly haircut grew out, the way one night he taught Vanessa how to Lindy Hop, saying he'd learned it in college because he was such a huge nerd and beer made him break out in hives so he'd found other ways to pass the time, and I hated the way everyone applauded them as they Lindy Hopped and

Davey said, "I didn't realize teaching a girl to Lindy Hop was the new spitting game."

I asked Vanessa if maybe it was distracting having Cody around, citing the fact that Missy, Lea, Andie, and Dolce never invited the people they were sleeping with to dinner or to shoots. For the first time since I'd met her, Vanessa seemed annoyed with me.

"Unlike those people, Cody's working for us."

I told her I knew that, but maybe it would be better if Cody got some perspective on the whole thing. He was too close to it.

"Bugsy," Vanessa said. She was chopping carrots, and she quickened her pace. "Stella likes to mix work and play. You of all people should know this. Do you think maybe you're a bit jealous?"

I said I could never be jealous of Cody.

"Why not?"

I didn't know how to respond.

"Maybe you're too *close* to it, Bugsy. Maybe you need some *perspective*."

I wanted to be better than Cody but I had no way to be. I worked diligently on set, setting up key lights and fill lights before Davey could ask me to, helping the girls apply their hair and eyelash extensions, buying organic makeup remover for Dolce, who was convinced that carcinogens were seeping into her skin at all times. We filmed what Vanessa called a Solo Series, where the girls were just alone onscreen being tortured by someone holding a magic wand off-screen. Sometimes I was holding the magic wand, but most often it was Vanessa. In one video, Stella was cuffed to a suspension bar with a full Lycra bodysuit and I was supposed to wear black—not even latex, just clothes—with my back to the camera and rub the magic wand against her clit. The goal, according to Vanessa, was to give the impression that the girls were getting off on the efforts of a nameless, faceless torturer who could very well be the viewer.

As the camera began rolling and I knelt in front of Stella and turned the vibrator up to its highest setting, I could've sworn she stiffened. I jammed it against her clit and she moaned and flinched.

Davey told me to go easy so I turned it off altogether and waited a few seconds while Stella whined and twisted back and forth. Then I set the vibrator to its lowest setting and traced semicircles around her upper thighs, listening to her muffled gasps. I thought of Cody. His skinny legs. His stupid jokes. I thought of her in bed with Cody, his dick inside her, her arms wrapped around his back. I thought of him breathing into her hair. I switched the vibrator up to high again and circled her labia, teasing her clit. She moaned, deeper and less self-conscious than she usually did on-screen. She had moaned like that before, but it had been for me only. I felt a pressure behind my eyes and blinked out a few tears. I made her come once, then again, then again. I thought involuntarily of the Garfield Park Conservatory and then of how raw her clit must be and made her come a fourth time, a fifth. Davey told me I'd done a great job.

That evening, she texted me to meet her on the front porch. When I came out to see her sitting alone with a blanket over her lap, her face pale and scrubbed of makeup, I was excited. I thought maybe she'd dumped Cody and I'd be the first person to learn about it. I thought maybe we'd kiss.

"Hey," she said as I sat down next to her. "You were savage on set today."

"Thanks."

"You're just savage all around, aren't you?"

I shrugged.

She tilted her head and looked at me like my mom used to when she was worried I was coming down with a cold. "How are you doing?"

"Yeah, I dunno, I'm fine," I said. "Making money. Living the dream."

"Are you taking any time for yourself?"

"I guess so, yeah."

"Can you take my advice? As someone who cares about you a lot? I think you need to tell Vanessa and Davey that you need a few days off. I'm worried you're not sleeping enough."

There were pins jabbing the lining of my stomach. "I'm fine," I said.

"OK. I'm just worried."

We both looked ahead at the house across the street. I counted the cars as they went by. Four until she talked again.

"It's getting serious with Cody," she said, not looking at me. "I think I'm going to try and be exclusive with him."

I coughd hoarsely. It felt like I'd just been given a diagnosis of stage four cancer. "I thought you hated monogamy."

"I know, I know." She looked me in the eyes, putting a hand on mine. "I feel like everyone says that until they've found the right person."

"It's kind of traditional, don't you think?"

She laughed. "Little One, things change when you get into your late twenties. You start to want stability. You get it, right? He's smart, he's got a nice job, he's cute. He makes me feel good about myself."

I nodded shakily.

"And seriously, you need to sleep with more people besides me! There's a whole world out there." She nudged my shoulder. I was rigid. "You gotta get that bang count up."

"OK."

"You get what I'm saying? No hard feelings, right?"

I shook my head. I felt like I was underwater. "No hard feelings."

That night, the house was silent. My room was no longer The Bare Room: Vanessa and Davey had gotten me a cheap full bed and some plastic shelves from IKEA and hung a few old movie posters on the walls. My favorite was *Who Framed Roger Rabbit* because I loved the way Jessica Rabbit looked in her sparkling dress and blue eye shadow with the sultry curtain of hair over her right eye. I lay in bed looking at Jessica Rabbit, feeling the buzzing behind my skin and imagining for the first time in a long time the ceiling collapsing in on me, a single point of drywall becoming knife-sharp and stabbing me in the chest. It would be better to be stabbed, I thought, than crushed, because a stabbing would preserve my body and Stella would have to see my body when they all heard the crash and came running. She would have to think about how my dead fingers had once been inside of her and my dead lips had once kissed her all over. And the next day Cody would try to comfort her but what would he know about death? Some rich tech dude who cares about a website's SEO? If we were living in purgatory and the only way out was suicide, Cody would be the last to catch on. He would be the last person left on Earth. The sun could collide with the Earth and he'd be sitting at his ergonomic desk playing *League of Legends*.

I felt as if all my energy was being directed to maintaining my corporeal form. There was nothing left inside of me, no guts, no brains, no emotions. There was a void, and that void was hurting me physically, as if I'd ripped a tendon in half but all over. Lying on my back hurt and so did sitting up and so did lying on my side. My head and feet were so heavy that it became difficult to change positions. My eyes throbbed. My wrists throbbed.

I lurched from my bed, making my blocky feet step painfully one in front of the other. At one point in the hallway, I had to lean against a wall to catch my breath. The stairs took a long time—I had to sit down repeatedly—but eventually I got to the kitchen and then the laundry room, where Vanessa kept the first-aid cabinet. I shook out my hands, thinking I'd be better able to use them if they were "looser," whatever that meant, and opened the cabinet. There was a bottle of sixty capsules of aspirin. I opened it up and saw that not all sixty were left, but there were certainly enough. I took it and staggered into the kitchen and then swung open the fridge, where Missy kept a bottle of Smirnoff. Gulp by gulp, I swallowed a quarter of it and the entire bottle of aspirin. Then I slid to the floor and blinked.

Next, Davey was looking into my eyes and there were bright lights behind him. I couldn't talk because my throat felt torn apart and full of something thick. My stomach was cold; I was cold. I discovered I could breathe out words, so I asked him why he was here.

"Why I'm here?" he asked, and he sounded angry. "Because it's the hospital, Bugsy. Why would I not be in the hospital if you are?"

Vanessa was next to him, crying, asking me why I'd done what I'd done. I could see Missy next to her, texting, looking up at me and then down at her phone. She said something about Dolce and Lea taking the next train they could from Hyde Park, where they had apparently been at a party, and Andie getting someone to take her shift at Strange's so she could meet us as soon as she possibly could. Then Stella and Cody were at the foot of my bed, and Stella's face was round and wet, and she was grabbing my ankles and saying "Jesus, Bugsy," and Cody was holding her around the shoulders.

I had to stay in the hospital for a week. I sat in groups with other people in hospital gowns who wanted to talk about their cheating spouses or their theories about the president's methods of mind control or their hatred of the other people in hospital gowns. I ate roast beef slathered in gravy that looked like frosting. I got up at 6:00 a.m. so a nurse who called me by my old name could take my vitals. When I told her my name was Bugsy, she told me that's not what it said in my chart. I took 200 milligrams of Zoloft every morning out of a paper cup. When I was released, I was told to keep taking the Zoloft or else I'd end up back in the hospital.

When I got back home, Vanessa told me I wouldn't be working on shoots for a few weeks but she would keep paying me anyway. My mom was anxious that I hadn't called or texted in a week, so I spent hours on the porch telling her made-up details about my life: how I was applying to office jobs, how I was looking into taking a few classes at DePaul, how I had just been taking a "tech cleanse" for a week and I was sorry I hadn't warned her about it beforehand. I avoided seeing Stella as much as I could, only spending time in the house at night or when I knew she wouldn't be home. I ignored her texts. I spent time in coffee shops reading books I had been assigned but hadn't read in college: *Madame Bovary* and *Written on the Body* and *Swann's Way*. I got myself cheap dinners at McDonald's or Taco Bell and ate under bright lights, reading the news on my phone. Sometimes I looked at social media and saw pictures of Jules—she hadn't blocked me for some reason—at parties or music festivals or improv shows, her face painted with Day-Glo paint, flowers in her hair, a cigarette between her lips. The Zoloft made me feel cocooned. I could think about the videos I'd watched or help shoot, or I could think about Stella naked, and I still wouldn't want sex. My potbelly got bigger.

I spent enough time at the Taco Bell that I began to recognize the regulars. There was a couple, a man and a woman, who came in almost every night I was there, sat a couple booths away from me, and argued. The woman sat with her back to me, so I saw only her shoulders in her red pleather jacket and her green hair, roots growing out at the top. The man wore plugs in his earlobes and black-framed glasses and had a full beard. I listened as the woman said, "I just think we should try," and he said to her, "No, babe. I'm sorry, but it's fucked up. It's against my personal morals." One night I moved booths to be closer to them and they didn't notice me.

"Seriously," the woman said, "it can't be so weird if other people are doing it."

"Rule thirty-four," the man said sternly.

"What's rule thirty-four?"

He rolled his eyes. "If it exists, there's porn of it."

The woman's shoulders slumped. "I just think it would be cool if we could use some toys."

He raised an eyebrow. "*Toys?*"

"Yeah."

"What kind of toys?"

"I don't know."

"So my dick's not enough for you?"

"No, babe! No, I'm not saying that."

"Lesbians use toys," he said. "We're not lesbians."

"I'm just saying I saw this video. Just hear me out."

He opened his hands, encouraging her to go on.

"There was this girl and she was, um, tied to like a wooden cross. And someone came in with a riding crop and was like, slapping her on the breasts."

He gave an exaggerated nod. "Right. That's porn. Not what we do."

Then they started talking about how hard a time he was having at work, how he had all these ideas but his boss wasn't listening to him. A thought entered my head: Andie was supposedly twenty-two, but she could've been seventeen. What if she was lying about her age? What if she was younger than me? What if we were technically making child porn?

I lay in my bed that night thinking about it, running through my head every single time I'd seen Andie and what she'd been wearing and how she'd been standing and what I'd thought about it. I asked myself several times whether I'd been attracted to Andie and the answer was yes, I had, I had definitely found Andie hot. If Andie was seventeen or sixteen and I found her hot, then I was attracted to a child who couldn't give her consent. What if she was fifteen? She had sometimes looked very young in videos. Even worse: What if Vanessa and Davey knew about this and were employing her anyway?

At 3:30 a.m., I knocked on Andie's door. When she didn't answer, I knocked again. I heard a whine of complaint and footsteps and then she opened the door, blinking herself awake.

"Bugsy, I went to bed like half an hour ago," she croaked. "What do you want?"

"Are you twenty-two?" I asked.

Her eyes were suddenly wide, which sent ice down my spine. "Of course I am."

"Why are your eyes wide?"

"Because I can't believe you're asking me this at three thirty in the morning."

"But it looks like you're surprised. Or guilty."

"Fucking A. Go to bed."

She tried to shut the door but I held it open. "Show me your driver's license."

"Are we really doing this?"

"If you're under eighteen, we're making child porn."

"*You're* younger than me. Maybe *you're* the reason we're making child porn."

"I never said we *were* making child porn. I said *if*—"

"Jesus Christ!" She stumbled back into her room and emerged carrying her purse, which she fished around in until she'd found her wallet. She opened it to show me her ID.

"See there? Born December 27, 1997. Are you happy?"

It occurred to me that it was a fake ID. "Is it a fake ID?"

Her face soured. "What the fuck is wrong with you?" Then she closed the door in my face.

I lay in my bed but I couldn't sleep. I knew Andie had shown me a fake ID. Why would she try to deceive me like this? When it was light outside, I tried to wake Vanessa up. It was entirely possible that she was knowingly making child porn, but I still cared about her. What did that say about *me*, that I cared about a child pornographer?

I pounded on her door and listened. No noise. I pounded again. She was probably out. I texted her *We need to talk.* I waited a few seconds, then a minute, then five. No response. Davey wasn't home, either. I didn't try to text him, though. It felt more heinous to talk to a male child pornographer than a female one.

I spent all day at the Taco Bell, waiting for the couple. When they didn't show up, I went to Myopic Books, where one of the workers, obviously genderqueer, started following me. They wore aviator glasses and a chunky black-and-white sweater and had a round, red face. I disliked them instantly. Luckily, I was able to move quickly to avoid them. And as I moved, I was reading: a paragraph from Marcus Aurelius's *Meditations*, a poem from *The End of the Alphabet*, six pages from a book about an angry lion tamer who's lost in another dimension. I felt myself becoming stronger, smarter, increasingly prepared to fight a life-defining battle.

"You'll have to put those back," the worker said.

I told them I would and then didn't. They watched me run out of the store. The fact that they cared about the arrangement of books in a store was sad to me, and I felt bad for them.

I didn't sleep the next night, or the next. Colors were brighter. Cars seemed to be moving faster. I started a group chat with Vanessa and Davey, telling them I knew about Andie and just wanted to take measures for everyone's protection. They sat me down at the kitchen table and asked me why I was making false accusations. I told them I was trying to be protective of the empire they'd built. Davey sputtered a laugh and asked what empire. I told him to take what I was saying seriously, that Cody had made us bigger than we ever were before and if he didn't understand that then I was just going to have to take matters into my own hands.

"What matters?" Davey asked. "Have you been blowing rails of someone else's coke?"

Vanessa looked worried. "Bugsy, honey, I know it hasn't been an easy month for you—"

"It's been a fine month for me," I said. "You're either with me or against me."

I didn't sleep the next night. I avoided Andie, which meant I was avoiding both her and Stella, which was difficult to do with all of us living in the same house. I homed in on the Taco Bell, which was open twenty-four hours. Finally the man and the woman were back, the man in a black hoodie and the woman in her same pleather jacket. They sat down so the woman was facing me, and I noticed she was beautiful: round-eyed, with black lip liner and thick red lips, a slim nose, a mole on her right cheek. I took her beauty as a sign.

They weren't talking, just eating their Supremes. I moved into the booth next to the woman.

"Sorry if this is awkward," I said. "But you were talking about porn a few nights ago."

"What the fuck?" the man said.

The woman laughed. "I remember you," she said. "You're the girl who's like always here."

I nodded. "I happen to be in the industry and I'm trying to clean it up."

"Get the fuck away from us," the man said.

"No, no, no," I said. "I mean, I realize that child pornography is an

FBI risk and I want to make sure we're not creating the potential for a major sting, as all our names are attached to everything we make."

The woman frowned.

The man said, "Are you a *child pornographer?*"

A few people looked over at us. I ducked my head.

"Can we speak in private?" I asked.

"If you don't leave this table, sicko, I'm going to call the police on you," he said.

I left. I felt the woman's eyes on me. I felt she might be falling in love with me as I had fallen in love with Stella.

It occurred to me that maybe the FBI was monitoring my bedroom because of what I'd said and done in the past few days, that my laptop was being keystroked and that the authorities had already found all of the videos Vanessa had given me. I stayed out all night, wandering around Humboldt and Wicker, giving what little change I had to homeless people, blessing them back when they said *God bless you.* I was the most afraid I'd ever been, since I was a felon, but also the happiest I'd ever been, since I didn't need to sleep anymore, since I was smarter than everyone, since I could solve perhaps the greatest problem that was hanging like a specter over the industry, the problem of child pornography. I could outsmart the FBI. I was going to outsmart the FBI.

After five nights of not sleeping, I began to notice giant security cameras on every building. These cameras seemed to have the ability to see that I was a freak, that I liked "unnatural" sex. If I didn't have missionary sex with a man in twenty-four hours, I was going to be arrested. It would of course be better to be arrested for being a freak than for being a child pornographer but to be arrested at all was a bad thing. I had accumulated tons of missed calls and texts from everyone during my nights out. I ignored them all and called Vanessa.

"I need a car," I said. "I need your car."

"Bugsy! Where are you? What's wrong?"

"Don't ask. Please, for your own safety."

"Tell me where you are. I'm coming to get you."

"No!" I shouted so loudly that people on the street were looking at me, and I realized that maybe they were spies, too. That maybe it wasn't just the cameras. "Just, please, no. My phone's being tapped. My laptop's being keystroked."

"What are you talking about?"

"What we're doing is illegal and I need to leave town. We should all leave town."

Vanessa started to say something else but I hung up. She was useless. I would take the bus to the Metra and then I would take the Metra to a different part of the state.

I was riding the bus downtown, avoiding calls from Vanessa for her own protection, searching how to stop my phone from being tapped on my phone that was being tapped, when Stella got on the bus and sat down next to me. She was more beautiful than I had ever remembered her being. There was actual light coming off her body. I had never believed in god, but she looked like god. I realized she was god. She was god living under the same roof as me, pretending to be a human woman. I'd had sex with god.

"Don't let any of them tell you what you're doing is wrong," god-Stella said.

"But what I'm doing *is* wrong," I said. "It's very wrong."

She shook her head. "Don't be scared."

I stood, edging closer to her. The closer I came, the farther away she appeared to be. "Stella," I said.

She raised her glowing head. "Yes?"

"I love you," I said. "I've been in love with you for a long time."

The bus screeched and I jolted forward and god-Stella walked through the wall of the bus and I stood at the bus's pressurized doors, waiting to be let out, waiting to follow her, and I yelled at the driver, "Open these doors, shithead! You're keeping me from the fucking love of my life!" And then I was in an ambulance.

* * *

It was the Zoloft's fault, apparently. They gave me a pill they told me was an antipsychotic and they changed my diagnosis. More nightgowns, more frosting-gravy, more boring groups. Vanessa and Davey came to visit me every day. The girls were all working during visiting hours, which were typically at night. After a week, my parents showed up. My dad had grown a beard and couldn't bring himself to make eye contact with me. My mom hugged me, but her hug was tense and resistant.

"We got a phone call," she said, sitting down across from me. "We came here as soon as we could, sweetie."

My dad screwed up his face. "Are you doing drugs?"

I told him I wasn't.

"Then what's going on?"

I told him I didn't know.

"Sweetie," my mom said, "We got a phone call from a woman named Vanessa Redwire. We looked her up."

My dad's eyebrows arched. A look came across my mom's face that resembled the looks lawyers in TV shows give to clients who they know aren't telling the whole truth. "Are these the people you're associating with?"

I looked down at the table. My dad grunted.

"You're my only child," he said. "And you've flunked out of college and started hanging out with pornographers. How do you think that makes me feel?"

My mom put her hand on his. "We just don't want this for you. These people are dangerous, and what they do for a living is immoral. We want you to come live at home until you get back on your feet."

My dad withdrew his hand from hers. "I never agreed to that."

"Kevin," she hissed. "If the options are live with us or make pornography, then what do you think we should choose?"

"Make pornography," I said, raising my eyes to meet hers.

"No," my mom said. "Sweetie—"

A nurse came in to announce that visiting hours were over. My parents tried to linger, but she told them they needed to leave or she'd have to call security.

"Think of your future," my mom said.

I told the nurse to take them off my visitors list. I ignored their calls and texts when I got out, responding only to say I'd made my choice. *I don't consider you my daughter anymore*, my dad wrote. My mom fell silent.

Every day I took three pills in the morning and two at night. I went to yoga classes with Vanessa. I ate a spoonful of peanut butter and drank a glass of milk before going to bed so I wouldn't wake up hungry. My sleep was important. Seeing a psychiatrist was important. Davey found me someone I could talk to, a counselor who worked in West Lakeview. The counselor was named Randy: he was thin and knobby-jointed with a lilting voice and an eyebrow piercing and told me within the first ten minutes of meeting me that he specialized in LGBTQ issues. I talked to him about college, and the buzzing beneath my skin, and the pocketknife, and how the videos changed my life, and how I'd fallen in love with Stella.

After a few months, I started doing shoots again. The girls threw a party to welcome me back. Stella baked a cake for me. Cody, who was apparently a hobbyist cake decorator, wrote *Our long national nightmare is over* in green frosting on top. He had done something to the SEO to make us the first result for "girl-on-girl bondage," the third result for "forced orgasm," and the second result for "forced multiple orgasms." Subscribers were coming in by the hundreds, then the thousands: at the end of three months, we'd netted a little over three thousand. My hourly rate went up to $20, then $30.

On Sundays, Vanessa and Davey would do something called Girl of the Week, where they'd film a live scene with one of the girls for the "Diamond Club" subscribers. They usually let me sleep in during Girl of the Week, deputizing whoever wasn't in the scene to do the gaffer work. Once I woke up early to find Stella sitting on my bed in the same latex bodysuit and Lucite heels the woman in the giant photograph in the living room was wearing. The one difference was Stella's bodysuit had a hood, with cutouts for her eyes and mouth.

"You look good," I said.

She laughed. "I know. It's a classic look."

"Are you Girl of the Week?"

She nodded. "They're setting up now."

She gave me her hand and I took it, sitting up.

"I feel like I haven't been able to talk to you in a long time," she said. "Like, really talk to you."

I shrugged. "I haven't really talked to anyone."

She put a finger under my chin, her eyes blinking in their cutouts. "You know I love you, Bugsy."

My heart swelled. "Yeah."

"And I know you love me, too."

I nodded.

"But you understand why maybe you've got to live a little more life before you've decided I'm the one you need to be with, yeah? Like, I don't even know what *I'm* doing."

I nodded again. She took her finger from my chin and held my hands in both of hers. "I talked to Cody, though. A girl gets tired of monogamy all the damn time."

"What do you mean?"

She kissed me, the same way she'd kissed me in the kitchen when we'd first met. Then she pulled away, her lipstick smudged. "He wants me to be happy. And he thinks you're pretty cute, for what it's worth. Would you do it with a man?"

I laughed and looked at my hands.

"No pressure, of course. He's getting used to everything, too." She kissed me on the cheek, and I could feel the imprint she'd left. "Don't forget about me when you and your wife get rich and famous, OK?"

"I won't."

"Promise?"

"I definitely won't."

"Get some rest, Bugsy."

Then she went downstairs, her heels clunking, and I heard Davey's muffled voice cracking a joke, giving her directions. I lay back down and listened through my pillow: Stella saying, *Hi everyone, I'm Stella Hardwycke and I'm your Girl of the Week!* And then buzzing, cooing, moaning. Sounds I'd heard so often they'd become background noise, as much a part of my daily life as a spinning ceiling fan or falling rain.

Fugato

I

TO ALL THE PEOPLE WHO had ever insulted or belittled him he could now claim (if he ever met them) that he was an expert in his field. This on face value would mean nothing to them, being the kind of people who insulted and belittled, but at some point in their small lives they'd find themselves in some vulnerable position where he held all the power, and they'd be kicking themselves for having ignored him at a party or punching him in the stomach or implying once that his mother (who had done her very best every day to keep him and his sister fed and clothed and cared for, who had come to America to give them a better life) had sex with anyone who wanted her. And even more humiliating for them would be the fact that he wouldn't be vengeful: he would show them compassion and forgiveness and leave them no opportunity to smart at his totally justifiable opprobrium. They would come away from their brief, formal interaction with him feeling that the world was bigger than them and their petty psychodramas, bigger and more complex than what they thought it to be when they tried to lord their strength or knowledge over him, and they would learn far too late something he had always known, which was that you had to make peace with your insignificance in order to become someone of significance.

He sat in a chair in the visitation room at Cook County Jail, the plexiglass reflecting his diminutive form by virtue of the fluorescent lights and dark opposing wall. When he wore short sleeves, it was easy to see his muscle tone and conclude that he was strong, but when he wore a suit, as he did now, it could only be concluded that he was small and athletic—in truth, his body had been heavily disciplined by half-marathons and morning strength training. At his side was a briefcase, and from that briefcase he withdrew a neat stack of papers across which he'd written notes in medical shorthand.

On the other side of the plexiglass, Archer Armour took his seat. In his regulation jumpsuit he looked like another nameless victim of the state. The news had barely mentioned that he owned a Zagat-rated restaurant in Greektown. The eyes in his grayish-tawny face seemed to be taking in his surroundings, but his features did not suggest he was registering any visual input. He picked up the receiver to his left.

"You Dr. Lihn?"

Dr. Lihn nodded. "It's nice to finally meet you, Archer. Do you want to call me Leo?"

Archer looked down and then back up. He shook his head. Behind him, a guard shifted his belt under his paunch.

"That's fine," Leo said. "So I think you've been told by your lawyer that I requested this interview. I'd like to get to know you a little better before I give you what's called a Structured Clinical Interview. This is like a pre-interview interview, just to get the jitters out."

"It's fucked up," Archer said, his voice almost a keen. "It's fucked up what happened and what's going to happen."

Leo could tell this was not how Archer normally spoke, but maybe it was how he used to speak at moments of peak frustration during his adolescence. It was the kind of desperate, emotional speech that somehow required a freshly minted baritone.

"We'll see about what's going to happen. What I want to do right now is get more information from you, OK?"

Archer sighed and nodded.

Leo flipped over the first few pages of the stack, preliminary notes to himself, landing on a page with Archer's mug shot and the words

ARMOUR, ARCHER, 41 printed beneath. The rest of the page was blank. "Do you ever see things other people can't see?"

Archer's nostrils flared briefly. His pupils might have constricted, or that could have been a trick of the light. "No," he said.

"Do you hear things other people can't hear?"

"No."

"Do you ever experience periods of heightened energy: grandiose moods, racing thoughts, decreased need for sleep?"

"No."

"What about periods of decreased energy: isolation, lethargy, suicidal ideation?"

Archer blinked and laughed curtly. "I've got a family and a business. I own my house. Why would I want to kill myself?"

"What about desires to harm others?"

It took a moment for the question to land, then Archer blanched. His hand tightened around the receiver. "What are you trying to do here?"

Leo allowed a five-second silence and watched Archer move back in his chair and sit up straight. In that moment he resembled a classmate of Leo's from grade school, a boy named Max whom bigger boys tortured but who was big enough to torture Leo. Max had an excess of norepinephrine such that his eyes were always wide and panicked during class time. Unlike the other unintelligent kids, who did what they could to ignore their surroundings, Max would jerk his head in the direction of whomever the teacher called on for an answer, nervously awaiting the moment when his own ignorance would be exposed. When he was called on and inevitably didn't know the answer, he'd emit a low whine and pound his thighs with his fists, inspiring laughter from the bigger boys. Girls ignored Max, which Max didn't like. Sometimes he would find Leo on his way home from school, trip him, and kneel across his back, pressing Leo's face into the grass and dirt as he called him a fag.

"What are you trying to do here?" Archer repeated with more urgency.

Leo made a note: *Plans to harm others: fear, disbelief, dissociation. Highly lucid.*

"Are you trying to set me up?" Archer asked. "Whose side are you on? I don't have to talk to you about anything."

"I'm not trying to set you up," Leo said, and smiled tensely. "Your lawyer has asked me to testify about your case in court. I'm sure she told you that."

"She told me a psychiatrist was coming to talk to me. That was it."

"Archer, you believed that man was Donald Trump, right?"

"I don't know what I fucking believed, man."

"You believed a man was Donald Trump who was not Donald Trump. You know that."

Archer's shoulders slumped and he exhaled loudly into the receiver. Some overextended band of resistance had finally snapped in him. Leo made a point of not holding his receiver away from his ear.

"I've never taken drugs in my life," Archer said, his speech pressured. "I know you people probably think I have after what happened, but I never have. Not even marijuana. I was a straight-A student in college. I'm a good husband and a good father. I swear to god, nothing unusual happened that day except I woke up with this voice, high-pitched like a demon girl's, telling me I was going to die. It was all I could hear. And I thought I saw Donald Trump with a gun in my front yard and I thought that was the demon girl's prophecy, that he was the one coming to kill me."

Leo wrote: *Hallucinations, psychosis, schizotypy. Insight to a moderate degree.*

"It sounds crazy, but I swear to god that's what happened. That's all that happened! I didn't want to hurt anyone except if they were going to hurt me!"

"I know. I can tell from talking to you that you were acting in self-defense."

The storm behind Archer's eyes cleared. He nodded, his mouth open in a grateful half smile. "Yes, thank you, doctor. Thank you."

They spoke until the guard sauntered up behind Archer and told him his time was up. Archer held the receiver with both hands when he said goodbye.

On the way to the train, Leo turned his phone on to find that his sister Grace had sent him a picture of her husband sitting on their ratty sofa in a pair of cutoffs, cradling their two massive cats in either arm. He wore a T-shirt that read KILL ME, KILL YOU, under which the decapitated head of Shaggy from Scooby-Doo appeared to be in midspin. *They turn two today!* Grace had written.

What's his shirt mean? Leo wrote back. He had sat on that couch just last week, dialing Grace's husband over and over again while she sat in the adjacent armchair with her knees to her chin, crying.

It's a band. He used to roadie for them.

Leo struggled with what to send next. He settled on *How are you?* And then, *Call me?*

The text bubble appeared promptly and he watched it for a full five seconds. Then it disappeared. He spent another minute staring at the screen, waiting for a response. Then he put the phone back in his pocket.

II

Because Richard freelanced from home, Leo was accustomed to him sleeping in on weekdays. On this morning, however, Richard woke up and leaned over the side of the bed to watch Leo do pushups.

"You're a morning addict," he said.

Though it compromised his form, Leo raised his head to watch Richard walk stiffly from the bedroom through the living room to the kitchen and then disappear behind a wall. There was the sound of running water. The French doors between the living room and the bedroom bobbed up and down in Leo's vision. In the mornings, Richard moved with the shuffling circumspection of a man twenty years his senior. He spoke differently in the mornings, too, as if he were practicing lines of dialogue without a scene partner.

"Shall I try the new beans?" he asked, and before Leo could answer there came the chaotic whir of the coffee grinder.

He decided to skip his morning run and stood, shook his arms out, and went through the living room to his office, where he opened his laptop. There were three emails from clients, all about recent changes he'd made to their medication regimens. He answered them all quickly but thoroughly: *Hi Renata, The prior authorization for the Vraylar went through, so you can check with your pharmacy now; Hi Jeremy, You should be fine if you stay the course with the Paxil; Hi Lou, If the agitation persists, you can go up to 2mgs of Rexulti, but no more.* Each note ended in his signature:

Dr. Leo J. Lihn
Professor of Professional Practice, Feinberg School of Medicine
The Lihn Group, 750 N. Dearborn St., Chicago, IL 60654

He checked his phone. A text from Ellen, the other Lihn Group clinician, who was wondering if he would be willing to assess a twenty-seven-year-old patient who had been referred by a well-regarded therapist. She totally understood if Leo didn't have time for this, and would normally do it herself, but her son was home sick with what appeared to be chicken pox and she would have to leave by noon.

Leo wrote back: *OK.*

In the kitchen, Richard was pouring the coffee into a NORTHWEST-ERN UNIVERSITY mug and another that had a silhouette of a cardinal on it. He gave Leo the cardinal mug and then brought his hand to the small of Leo's back and pulled him in.

"How do you feel this morning?" he asked, lips to Leo's ear.

"Fine."

Richard kissed his ear, then his cheek. The kisses made him shiver.

"Just fine?"

"Good! I feel good."

Richard made a scoffing noise. He went to the kitchen table, where

Leo had left his Archer Armour file after studying it for two hours the night before. He made a show of carefully leafing through it. Leo felt a flood of warmth in his face, the way he remembered feeling whenever his mother brought him along to a parent-teacher conference and she and the teacher spent an hour discussing how exceptional he was. He laughed and made a halfhearted effort to snatch the file out of Richard's hands. Richard jumped away.

"Archer Armour *c'est moi*," he said.

"Archer Armour? I think he has schizoaffective disorder, probably bipolar type. You're nothing like him."

"Well, I want to kill Donald Trump," Richard said, and spun around to open the refrigerator. "And I'm not a to-the-manor-born white man."

Leo finally grabbed the file back. He opened it to make sure all the papers were in order. "But you wouldn't do it. Not even if the opportunity presented itself."

Richard unscrewed and sniffed a jar of sauerkraut, wrinkled his nose, and set the jar down. "How do you know? You've only known me two years—you didn't see me on election night. You don't know what I'm capable of. I don't know what I'm capable of."

"What did you do on election night?"

"That's my secret," Richard said, smiling a pointed, impish smile. His eyes darted to the left, then the right. "I might very well have spit at a cop."

Leo pecked him on the cheek. "We're all very proud of you."

On the way to the office, he checked his phone for texts from his sister. None. He composed one: *You probably know what I'm going to say about going to group, so preempt me by actually going to group.* It was harsh. Grace had once told him he acted like a Bond villain when he got angry. He deleted the message and wrote instead: *Call me after 4 today?*

His least favorite of the three secretaries was working on her own that day, by some wretched scheduling logic known only to the three of them. She wore a turtleneck sweater despite the 73-degree heat and gave him a wide smirk as he unlocked the door. When she stood—and he hated when she stood—she had at least three inches on him.

"Hi, Dr. Lihn," she said.

"Hi, Marsha," he said. "That's a nice sweater."

She took the edge of the left sleeve in her hand and nodded.

He passed Ellen's office in the hallway and she rushed to her door. She, too, wore a sweater, but it was cable-knit and the sleeves gaped at her wrists like loose skin. Her concealer flaked in the wrinkles at the corners of her eyes. Leo remembered without wanting to that, when he was a teenager, his mother had worn concealer to hide a sudden-onset case of rosacea. She was working in a restaurant then and told him very solemnly that if the server's face was dirty, then the customers thought the food was dirty, too.

"Thank you so, so much for covering for me today! I told the patient she'd be seeing you, at least for the intake, and she seemed fine." She held his hands in both of hers. He felt suddenly grateful to Ellen: for her goofy expressiveness, for all the times she told him not to be so hard on himself in that stale-smelling break room during their residency at Northwestern, for that Fourth of July when she let Grace read tarot for her.

"It's really no problem," he said, regretting his simple *OK* text. "Matthew needs his mom."

Ellen rolled her eyes. "What Matthew really needs is his dad. If I could get Matthew Sr. to take off work like I do, maybe we'd be in business."

Leo nodded, not wanting to even begin to imagine that family dynamic, and excused himself with the promise that they would get lunch later in the week. For the rest of the morning he updated charts and listened to Ellen's patients—most of them the well-dressed women he often saw in the waiting room picking at the stacks of old magazines—sobbing in the next room. At 2:30, Marsha buzzed him to let him know the twenty-seven-year-old patient had arrived.

She was tall, much taller than him, and wore a striped tank top and owlish glasses. Her hair was Annie Lennox short. Her jeans buttoned high at her waist and were nearly bleached white—"mom jeans." She shook his hand limply and took small steps as she walked to the couch, her shoulders hunched. She moved with the attitude, long familiar to Leo, of a young woman who has spent years of her life loathing her body. She said her name was Dillon Halliday, spelled D-I-L-L-O-N.

"Is that a Southern name?" he asked.

She shrugged. "My mom's from Texas."

He asked Dillon to tell him a little bit about what had brought her in today. She said her therapist had recommended the Lihn Group because they were supposed to be the best in the business, and she had problems with sleeping and remembering things and often wanted to kill herself and couldn't stop thinking that she might be straight even though she knew she was gay. He recorded all this on his laptop and then looked up at her.

"Any other symptoms of OCD?" he asked. "Repetitive behaviors? Intrusive thoughts about taboo subjects?"

Her eyes widened. "How did you know?"

"How did I know what?"

"Did my therapist tell you? That she thinks I have OCD?"

"No, you would have to sign a release of information form for me to talk to her. It was just clear from what you were saying that you're presenting with something we call pure OCD, possibly coupled with depression and anxiety."

"But I didn't even tell you about any of the big-ticket items," she said. "Like the cutting and the picking, or the thoughts that I might be a pedophile."

"All OCD," he said, and tried to maintain the lilt in his voice that would keep her from feeling like just another chart on his laptop. "And fortunately, it's highly treatable."

She flashed him the same stunned open-mouthed smile Archer Armour had. She scooted forward on the sofa. At this point in his career—he was forty-three and had been practicing for thirteen years—he could feel when transference was occurring: it happened the quickest with young millennials, impressed with his speed and accuracy and willingness to listen as they spoke about themselves. Kids whose futures had been mortgaged by the generations ahead of them, who were working in food service chains like Starbucks with horrible pay and so-so health benefits (the ones without insurance never saw him, of course), saddled with student debt, with scars on their forearms and bad dye jobs, accustomed to bingeing Netflix shows about serial killers or female friendship, mumbling about how rising sea levels and melting ice floes were "good news for my depressed ass." Kids who identified so strongly with their diagnoses that Leo was like a monarch knighting them, inducting them into the realm of the Mentally Troubled, where they could find relief in an explanation for their abnormal psychologies, where they could indulge in the comforting language of destigmatization and self-care.

"Why don't you tell me in a little more detail about the other symptoms you mentioned?"

Dillon sat forward in her seat. She was looking at him in the way she probably should have looked at her parents as a child, her face aglow with wonder, admiration, and unconditional trust. She began telling him about a day at the beach during which she'd abandoned her friends to cut the soles of her feet with a shard of glass. While she spoke, he imagined the apartment she probably shared with three roommates: the common area a hodgepodge of roughly assembled Ikea furniture, her room barely big enough to fit her bed, a flimsy bookcase full of radical literature from the women's and gender studies courses she'd taken in college. He imagined that she went home to that room every night and picked furiously at the skin on her arms and hands (he could see the scars from seven feet away), trying to stave off thoughts about her insignificance. Maybe she held a lighter under her thumb like Grace had when their mother went out grocery shopping and left her to watch Leo. She'd hold the lighter close until the pad of her thumb grew coarse from exposure to the flame. Then she'd move on to her index finger, then her middle finger. She'd keep her hands out of reach of Leo and keep burning her fingers while he whined *Stop it! Stop it!* and jumped up and down, trying to grab the lighter.

He let Dillon talk for the rest of the session and then told her he would prescribe 100 milligrams of Luvox to be taken daily in the morning. He said, "Do you have any questions for me?" and reread her chart instead of looking at her.

From Dillon's direction came a throaty growl: "Fucking faggot loves killers."

He looked up. Dillon wore the same grateful smile she'd worn moments ago.

"What did you say?" he asked.

She looked confused. "Sorry—I didn't say anything?" She shifted around on the couch and looked down at the cushions, as if between them lay a viable explanation for his question.

"You didn't say anything?"

"No, I didn't. I'm still thinking of questions. Did you hear something? Sorry, I'm really hard of hearing. I think it's from going to shows?"

He looked right at her and heard the growl again, this time with no words.

"It must be the building," he said, trying to keep an even tempo to his speech. "It's an old building." He wanted her out of his office.

She stood up and lingered by the couch, then the door. He told her that next time she would be seeing Dr. Ellen Mirsky and not him—he would make sure Dr. Mirsky got her chart.

"Oh, but I want to see you, if that's OK?" she asked. "You're probably the best psychiatrist I've ever seen."

He thanked her and told her he would be able to see her again in two weeks.

It was 4:03. He was alone in the office with Marsha, who was probably moving glacially around the little alcove where she sat behind the sliding glass window, gathering her phone and crossword puzzles and stress ball made to look like an alien's head before she left. He sat still, waiting for the growling to begin again. It had been a feral dog's growl. He went to the window and looked down into the street. No dogs, and he was too high up to hear them even if there had been any. It could be an auditory hallucination, for which he typically prescribed risperidone, aripiprazole, olanzapine, ziprasidone or quetiapine. When those drugs failed, clozapine or haloperidol.

The colors in the room went suddenly bright and electric and then desaturated again. He blinked. He couldn't tell if he was hearing the growl or an echo of the growl.

"What do you mean I'm a faggot who loves killers?" he asked the room. He received no response.

His phone buzzed and he had the thought that maybe whatever had been growling was now calling him. His tongue cottoned. Whenever they watched a horror movie and Richard noticed him lingering on a particularly gruesome scene, he would jokingly tell Leo not to let himself be scared for a second longer than he needed to be, or else he'd be scared forever. Heart flapping in his chest, he reached for the phone and saw that it was Grace.

"Hey," she said. "You told me to call you."

He held the phone in his right hand and worried a shirt button with his left. He asked her how her husband was doing after his bender last week.

"Fuck," she breathed. "This is what you wanted to talk to me about?"

He told her it wasn't what he wanted to talk to her about, he was just worried.

"No, you're not *worried*, Leo. You're all superior and trying to parent me from your little office downtown. You're trying to run my life."

He wasn't trying to run her life. Also, she sounded drunk.

"Fuck you, Leo," she said, and hung up.

III

He had a light teaching load that semester at Feinberg, just a lecture course called Special Topics in Medical Literature: Psychotic Disorders. He assigned two tests and the department assistants graded them both for him. That afternoon he had to deliver a lecture called "DAOA (G72) Polymorphisms and Heritable Psychosis."

He checked his phone on the train. Archer Armour's attorney had written with the information that the warden would allow him to conduct a psychological evaluation in the medical examination room, if that was of any use to him. The attorney wanted a report from him in two weeks at the latest—she hoped that didn't inconvenience him. Richard had texted him about possibly getting a guest membership at the gym. Ellen had texted him thanking him again for yesterday, including a picture of her red-pocked son giving the camera a thumbs-up. Leo wrote back to her: *No problem, although I think the client wants to stick with me.*

There were no texts or emails from Grace.

He looked up and his heart began to flap again. Dillon was somehow sitting across from him. As if she'd sought him out. Today she wore a jean dress with ruffled sleeves, loose even on her frame, and a pair of clogs.

"Hi, Dr Lihn!" she said.

"Hi, Dillon," he said, and looked back down at his phone.

In the upper periphery of his vision, he watched her shift uneasily on the train seat as she had on the couch the day before. She had the height of a Marfan sufferer.

"I just wanted to say that you really helped me out yesterday," she said. "I really, really feel a lot better because of what you said."

The rule was you did not engage a client about their case outside of your practice unless they engaged you first.

"I'm glad," he said.

She smiled. A feeling of urgency swelled in his chest, as though he had just realized he was about to get mugged. He wanted to turn to the woman sitting next to him—middle-aged, wearing a papery raincoat and playing *Candy Crush*—and tell her that he was in grave danger.

"So are you from here?" Dillon asked.

"No, um, not exactly," he said.

"I'm not either."

"This is my stop."

He waved a curt goodbye and got off the train. He was twelve blocks from Feinberg. As he walked he heard an officious baritone not unlike Alex Trebek's say "People die because of you."

He shook his head and checked his watch. 7:46. *No one dies because of me.*

"But they do," Alex Trebek responded.

Time moved faster than he was accustomed to. His students' faces were blank, featureless, their questions inane or possibly nonexistent. He wondered on the train back home whether something unfavorable might be happening with the dopamine receptors in his brain. What were his symptoms? He thought of being six or eight and having to jump over the small oval rug in the bathroom an even number of times or his mother would die. He thought of when his mother actually did die, how he overworked himself in his residency and didn't take any of Grace's calls. His boyfriend at the time, a fellow psychiatry resident with an attractively crooked nose, had given him a copy of *Modern Man in Search of a Soul*, which Leo had read in twenty-four hours. When the boyfriend gave it to him, he'd said, *Leo, don't hide your grief.* He had one patient ten years ago, a particularly neurotic teenage boy, who had not cried when his sister died of bone cancer and was consumed by the thought that his grief had instead manifested as a tumor in his brain. He was prescribed Paxil and Xanax. That had been a clinical error, Leo realized later, because the boy ended up becoming addicted to the Xanax and overdosing.

When he got home, he found a bean casserole in the fridge with a note taped to it: *Dig in, dearest.* He cut himself a big square and brought it into his office, where the Archer Armour file sat on his desk.

He flipped past the police report, his own cursory notes, and a news clipping ("Mailman Slain by Suburban Restaurateur"), to a scanned page of a diary from Archer's teen years that his mother had given the attorney. The entry was dated March 8, 1994:

There are two voices, a little one and a big one, and they're both telling me to kill myself. I'm not going to because I love my parents and I can't put them through that, but that doesn't mean I don't want to. It would be worth it just to get the voices to go away.

If anyone ends up reading this, don't worry—I turned out OK. Everything went fine for me.

Leo didn't read the rest. He stood and listed to the couch in the living room. There he checked his phone again, seeing his ghostly features emerging from the lock screen photo of him and Richard skiing in Colorado. He was needed. He had a place in the world, unlike so many of the people who relied on him. Plus, he had been through enough humiliation in this life, taken enough gut punches for himself and his mother and Grace and sometimes even Richard, that this, whatever it was, was entirely unnecessary. That is to say, if there was some kind of codified karmic justice at work, it would be a huge error to strike him now.

He recalled, unbidden, that the worst part about getting his face rammed into the ground by mean Max in grade school was that he'd actually liked it. The humiliation, the dirt smeared across his cheekbones and lips, Max's bony knees in his back. Back then he had, in fact, departed from his body and viewed the scene from above and stiffened a little with pleasure. Of course he would never tell anyone that. Not even Richard.

"Filthy slut," Alex Trebek said. "Kill yourself."

He sprang from the sofa and began a text to Ellen: *I'm having symptoms of . . .*

He deleted the message and tried again: *I was wondering if you could give me an evaluation?*

He deleted that, too, and sat back down, biting his lower lip. The room was expanding and contracting as though he were in a lung. When Richard met with his editor, he was usually back by 6:15. and it was 5:46. Twenty-nine minutes to go. Leo had probably seen hundreds of clients like Dillon, hundreds of broke twentysomethings dogged by thoughts of suicide. Why was he having these symptoms after seeing her, on this day? What about her had triggered him? What made her so special?

Suddenly it was morning and he was lying down somewhere and there was a loud beeping coming from behind him. Richard was standing over him, and when they made eye contact, he smiled and said, "You're awake, my love!" And then, "Grace, come here!"

Grace's sallow, bone-thin face appeared over him. She wore a small smile.

"The idiot's awake," she said, and shook him softly by the shoulder.

Richard's face was gone and then back again. He proffered a cup of water, which Leo found himself wanting desperately. He drank and then sat up. He was in a hospital bed. There was a pulse oximeter on his right finger. He took it off.

"Don't take that off!" Richard said, waving his hands. Leo ignored him.

"Did you ever come home?" he asked. "Why are we here?"

Grace and Richard looked at each other. Leo could feel his pulse in his right forearm, and noticed that the entire thing was wrapped tightly in gauze and tape. "What's this?"

Grace turned to him, her face taut. Her expression was the same dour expression he himself wore whenever he had to tell a client bad news. Richard put one hand on Leo's thigh, the other on his shoulder.

"What do you remember?" Richard asked.

Leo shook his head. "What do you mean, what do I *remember*? I was at home eating the casserole you made and waiting for you and now we're here."

"On what day were you home?" Grace asked.

So now Grace was asking the clinical questions. "Thursday," he said. "June sixth."

"It's June eighth," said Grace.

Leo shook his head. Grace pulled her phone out of the pocket of her tiny tight jeans and showed him the lock screen: Saturday, June 8, 3:12 p.m.

"Let me see my chart," Leo said.

"I—I don't know how to do that," Richard said. "What I know is I saw you walking down Clark with a massive gash in your arm on Thursday night as I was coming home. People were scared. I got you in the car and you passed out on the way to the hospital. You've been in and out of consciousness since then."

"People were scared?"

"You weren't yourself," Richard said gently.

"Can you go find someone who will let me see my chart? Is this Northwestern?"

Grace and Richard both nodded.

"OK, see if Dr. Reddy is still the attending," Leo said. "She taught me in med school. Can you do that?"

Richard sighed. "I'll try, love."

He stumbled out of the room and Grace took a seat. Leo made to swing his legs over the side of the bed but she stood to block him.

"You're in the hospital," she said. "You're here for a reason."

"I feel fine."

"You always 'feel fine.'" She rolled the sleeves of her sweatshirt up: he saw now that it had been screen-printed with the same spinning Shaggy head as her husband's T-shirt.

"That shirt is grotesque," he said.

She narrowed her eyes at him. "You're grotesque."

Her face was pitted with acne and a tangled clump of hair rose asymmetrically from the back of her head. She seemed to feel his gaze on her, because she raised a hand to smooth the hair back down. She was unsuccessful.

"You went crazy," she said. "You carved like a four-inch gash into your arm. Richard found the knife in the kitchen."

His forearm pulsed again. He felt his cheeks redden and his mind speed up.

"How's the restaurant?" he asked.

"You just woke up in the hospital and you want to talk about the Hard Rock Café?"

"Getting any big tips?"

She put her arms on her hips and exhaled, a gesture from her teenage years meant to communicate that whomever she was speaking to had completely exhausted her reserves of patience. "Come on, Leo."

"Your young husband disappears for four days and comes back missing a tooth, I talk to you on the phone and you sound drunk. You expect me to just ignore all that?"

"I'm *staying sober*," she hissed. "My life is my life. How can you manage to make a crisis about you into a crisis about me?"

"There is no crisis about me," he said. "I'm fine."

"You were raving in the street!" She threw her hands up in the air as if to solicit a witness to his unreasonableness.

"I'm under a lot of stress," he said slowly. "People under a lot of stress are prone to breakthrough moments—"

"Break*down* moments."

"—where the fabric of reality twists and bends for them. It's completely normal. If this were a legitimate clinical issue, I'd still be exhibiting symptoms." He was lying to her, he knew, but he wasn't sure to what extent. "Really, whose opinion are you going to trust? Mine or Richard's, who writes magazine copy for a living?"

"Richard's, because he wasn't the one who dug into his arm with a knife."

Every time she mentioned the arm, it felt worse. He tried to raise it and it was log-like, heavy.

Richard came back into the room, a look of benign confusion on his face. "I don't think Dr. Reddy's here anymore," he said. "I asked everyone. They thought I was a madman." At the pronunciation of this last word, he inhaled quickly and looked cautiously at Leo as if he'd said something unforgivable. "You know, Leo, Grace and I had a little bit of a conversation. About where we'd go from here?"

Leo scowled and picked at the gauze. His arm was beginning to throb. Whatever they'd given him was wearing off. Was he not worth a morphine drip?

"Since you were a bit erratic on Thursday, we'd, um, like to do something for you. And I know you, I know you definitely *don't* want to do inpatient. They didn't have any beds. And in any case, no one—not me, not Grace, not any of the staff here—is going to make you do it."

"Doing inpatient" was a term Richard had learned from Leo. He hated it being weaponized against him. "Why would I need to do inpatient? I was momentarily stressed. I've had clients go through a lot worse and come out fine."

"You did carve up your arm," Grace said. Richard made a little waving gesture to quiet her.

"We were thinking that Grace would try and rearrange her schedule this coming week to be with you after work, during that time after you get home from the office and before I get home from my meetings."

"Just this coming week. I'll be gone after."

Leo could feel something hot and bilious rising in his stomach. "No, I don't want you gone, Grace, remember? Right before she died Mom told me I had to keep an eye on you. I don't want to be derelict in my duties."

Grace huffed and looked up at the ceiling. He knew she didn't believe him because she hadn't been there. She had been off in Tucson getting married to her first husband while Leo was twenty-two and headed to medical school. The car was packed full of his belongings—in the morning he and his mother planned to drive from the south suburbs to his dormitory at Northwestern—and they were sitting at the kitchen table eating spaghetti dusted with Parmesan. Leo's mother had placed her hand on Leo's wrist and said, *Your sister is wild. I need you to watch after her.* He had looked up from his spaghetti to see that his mother's eyes were watering and her lips were screwed up in a diagonal line. *Of course*, he'd said, and grabbed her searching hand in his own.

"I think this will be good for everyone," Richard said, his eyes darting between Leo and Grace. "I think we all stand to benefit from this."

IV

Even when he wore his suit jacket with the slightly long sleeves, the gauze was still visible. He had been lazy about redressing it, partly because he didn't believe he was the one who'd injured himself, partly because he didn't want to believe it was even there. It was possible—distinctly possible—that someone had attacked him and Richard and Grace were protecting him from this knowledge. The stitches hurt.

"I want you dead," Alex Trebek growled, and then said something inaudible that sounded like it had been distorted by wind. He flicked at his ear as if to brush the sounds away. He had written himself a prescription for 100 milligrams of tiapride—ethically ambiguous, but then who abused tiapride? He had picked it up at Walgreens with Richard, who had made him promise to "do something." In the Lyft on the way to Cook County Jail, he shook out a pill from the bottle and took it with a gulp of coffee from the thermos Richard had prepared for him. The coffee burned the back of his throat.

As he was given his visitor's badge and taken past the security barrier, he had the feeling that his brain had been sliced diagonally and a magnet of an opposing pole placed in each half, so that trying to get the halves to cohere in his skull was extremely painful. He wondered if he was developing an aneurysm just by trying to keep both halves of his brain in his head. Everything around him—the walls, the floor, the swaying shoulders of the prison guard walking ahead of him—seemed bright and unreal, as if his faculties were set to peel off into insanity, and he wondered if there would ever come a time again when he was just sitting at home with Richard watching a dumb TV show and feeling bored. The idea that he might have permanently lost boredom and all its beige normalcy, its safe uneventfulness, struck him as profoundly sad and a little scary.

Archer Armour was already waiting for him in the medical examination room, flanked by two guards: a stocky one with a shaved head and another who very conspicuously wore a gun on his right hip. Archer had gotten a haircut since Leo's last visit. The gray showed more obviously at his temples. Leo felt Archer's eyes travel to his gauze.

"What happened, doctor?"

Leo shrugged, the halves of his disintegrating brain banging around in his head. "Nothing, just an accident in the kitchen."

"It's at a weird angle to be an accident in the kitchen," Archer said. "Usually those happen on the hand, not the forearm."

"Quiet," one of the guards said.

"No, it's fine." Leo opened his briefcase and withdrew a binder containing the Structured Clinical Interview for *DSM-5*. "I don't care if he asks me about it."

"Were you good at math and science in school?" Archer seemed determined to pursue some line of questioning.

"What's your problem?" one of the guards asked him. "Let the doctor do his job."

"Really, it's fine," Leo said. "Yes, I was good at math and science." And philosophy and English and art history. "I liked science so much that I went to med school."

"A lot of you are good at math and science," Archer said. "You, um, people who become doctors. I myself couldn't do anything in school except English, and I wasn't about to become some goddamn English teacher. I was born to make money." He laughed, and one of the guards sighed and looked at his watch.

Why was Archer in such high spirits? It occurred to Leo that he might be manic. Or worse, that he might have gathered from the gauze and Leo's unwashed hair that something was wrong with Leo, which meant what? That Archer had become a comrade-in-arms?

"Fuck you," Alex Trebek said.

"Do you need any help, doctor?" the guard with the shaved head asked.

"No, no." He would try to pretend the guards weren't there, since just looking at them somehow made the situation in his head worse. He sat down across from Archer. "Archer, do you remember the questions I asked you last time?"

"Sure, but I remember what we talked about after that more clearly. You told me about your sister and I told you about my brothers and growing up in Louisiana."

"OK, well, those questions were preliminary questions so I could get in your head a little. Now we're going to do what's called the SCID-5. It's an interview that determines what diagnostic category from the *DSM-5* you fit into."

Archer nodded. "Everything's got an interview," he said. "Everything's got a test. And I never pass the test."

"I have a feeling you'll pass this one."

The interview took over an hour, during which Leo officially diagnosed Archer with schizoaffective disorder, bipolar type. Archer had delusions and both auditory and visual hallucinations; he had definite periods of elevation in mood; the murder had been committed during one such period of elevation, when the paranoia was running particularly high and Archer hadn't slept in over five days. After some prodding, it came out that his wife had divorced him because the delusions, and Archer's refusal to seek help, had gotten to be "too much." He only saw his children twice a month, and then only in the company of a social worker. This was because he had attempted suicide shortly after the divorce, and the judge had determined him unfit to care for his children until he became more stable. Troublingly for his case, he had never once neglected his duties at the restaurant.

"What kept you going back to the restaurant?" Leo asked.

"Money," Archer said sullenly. "I'm not going to leave good money sitting on the table."

"Even when you were hallucinating corpses and ghosts? Even when you were convinced the president was coming to kill you?"

"Please. I know what I'm doing."

One of the guards cleared his throat loudly. Leo couldn't tell which one it had been.

"I can testify that you have schizoaffective disorder, but I can't help you much beyond that," Leo said. "You certainly meet the diagnostic criteria, but the jury will wonder why you were still behaving rationally during the time of the murder."

Archer leveled his eyes at Leo.

"They'll wonder why, if you're as sick as you are, you were capable of going into work and earning money," Leo said.

"Earning money isn't rational." He spoke slowly—perhaps the interview had tired him. "Going to work isn't rational. None of this bullshit is *rational*. All that's rational, doctor, is wanting to be a naked human being sitting in the sun drinking peach nectar while you're surrounded by the ones you love."

"I'll kill you if you don't kill yourself first," Alex Trebek said, followed by a growl.

Leo took a Lyft to the Red Line and then rode it back north. He got out two stops before he normally did and walked to Clark Street, which had been cordoned off for some kind of summer festival. Middle-aged white people in tartan shorts clutched plastic beer steins and stood talking in groups of three or four, pulling out their phones to confirm to others their presence at the festival. A band of youngish men played "Sunshine of Your Love" on a raised stage. As Leo wove among the crowd, he felt his phone buzz.

Grace: *I'm outside your place. Where are you?*

He repocketed his phone and walked up to the salon where he and Richard got their hair cut. It was owned by a woman named Mrs. Thahom whose husband had died in a construction accident and whose grown children had left Chicago and rarely visited her. She decorated her windows with the stenciled drawings of men and women in business jackets and geometric dresses that Leo associated with beauty parlors in the '80s. When he opened the door, her two-note electronic doorbell sounded. She came rushing out from behind a screen on which had been painted a triptych of rice farmers.

"Leo! Leo, my god!" she said. She turned his right wrist over anxiously. "How are you, my dear?"

Leo's phone was buzzing. He ignored it. "I was thinking of getting a haircut."

She looked briefly at the top of his head and shook her own. "You don't need a haircut. How are you? Tell me how you are."

There were no other patrons in the shop. Leo grasped Mrs. Thahom's elbows. "Was I here last week?"

"Yes! Yes, darling, you were here and you did not seem like yourself! I kept calling to you and you walked right past me, like you were on some kind of a mission. And your arm—your poor arm was bleeding! So much blood!"

"Did you see anyone attack me?"

Mrs. Thahom looked momentarily confused. "Attack you? Who would attack you?"

"Well, my arm was bleeding."

"No, no one attacked you, darling. You were just walking—"

"I think I was attacked, Mrs. Thahom. It couldn't have been far from where Richard and I live."

She nodded. "Maybe you were. There's a neighborhood crime watch, you know?" Her excitement redoubled. "I saw Richard, too! He came to get you. But if you don't mind, darling, it didn't look like a random attack." Her eyes widened. "It looked as if someone had sat you down and hurt you. Intentional. Was your wallet missing?"

"No."

She pointed to his briefcase on the floor. "Anything from there?"

He shook his head.

"So you weren't robbed, my dear."

"But there are attackers on the North Side who aren't out for money," he insisted. "There's that man in Rogers Park who just went around killing people. Remember? He shot the man walking his dogs and the kid who was jogging?"

Her eyes widened further. His phone was buzzing again.

"Yes, I remember," she said, her voice almost a whisper. "Do you think it was him?"

Then the sliced halves of his brain slid back into place. It was clear to him now what he had to do. He had been chosen to stop more harm from happening. All those beatings he'd taken, Max's knees in his back, shouting himself hoarse in defense of his mother as she got older and slower and sadder: it all added up to this, this noble mission, this quest to reduce harm on as large a scale as possible. What had chosen him to do this, he didn't know. But it made sense.

"Mrs. Thahom, my sister's waiting for me," he said. "I have to go."

She pulled him into a tight hug. She was four or five inches shorter than him, and he kissed her on the forehead as though she were his grandmother.

Grace was sitting on the stoop playing with her phone, slouched forward like a teenager. It amazed Leo how she managed to look so young despite being so old. She stood when she saw him. She was still wearing her black Hard Rock Café T-shirt.

"You're late," she said.

He went up the stairs past her, unlocked the door, and went in.

"You're late," she said again, following him into the foyer. "I was sitting there for like twenty minutes waiting for you. Did you run late at the prison?"

"No," he said, and went into his study. He got a notebook out from a drawer in his desk and began to write in it: *Today I realized that I am going to keep people safe in a way far more meaningful and with far more human impact than the practice of psychiatry.*

Grace was standing somewhere behind him. "What are you doing?"

But I must continue to practice psychiatry, or else I will lose my connection to whatever this is. Whatever this powerful thing is. Because it was through the practice of psychiatry, for better or worse, that I have come into association with this thing.

"'That's more like it," Alex Trebek said, gentle this time. "Now you've got the idea. Now you know what you're supposed to do."

Grace was standing over his shoulder. "What are you writing?" He tried to brush her away, but she was undeterrable.

I need to better understand this. I am a protector, like Hippocrates, but now more like a hierophant, a super-hierophant.

"Today I realized I am going to keep people safe . . ." Grace read, and he slammed the notebook shut and stood to face her.

"Stop it," he said stonily. "Stop looking at what I'm writing."

"I'm just trying to understand what's going on here."

"Nothing's 'going on here,' Grace. You're just in my house for no reason."

Clutching the notebook to his chest, he went through the living room and into the kitchen. He hadn't eaten since breakfast and he wanted to cut himself a hunk of the Manchego Richard had bought. But there were no knives in the knife block. He looked on the counter, in the drawers beneath the block. No knives.

Grace was leaning in the doorway. "Are you looking for a knife?" she asked. When he didn't respond, she walked up to the utensil drawer and withdrew a butter knife. "Richard hid all the knives."

He grabbed the butter knife from her hand and threw it past her, into the living room, where it sent a vase crashing to the floor.

"Jesus Christ, Leo! What the fuck is going on?"

"Nothing!" he said, and he felt near tears. "Why are you treating me like a child?"

"No one's treating you like a child," she said in the voice she used on the rare occasions he, and not she, needed comfort. Then she was holding his undamaged wrist in one hand and he was trying to wrest it free: she was oddly strong, had always been. "We're . . . stop it . . . we're just worried about you."

"I'm worried about *you*," he howled. "I'm worried about everyone!"

"Leo, if you calm down, we can have a conversation about this."

He broke free and sank to the floor. He felt sick. "There's a murderer in Rogers Park," he said. "And there's a murderer in Cook County Jail."

She squatted next to him. "There are murderers everywhere," she said. "People kill people all the time."

"Yes, exactly. And people hurt people. People beat people up, call people humiliating names. You wouldn't know."

"What are you talking about I wouldn't know?"

"I can do something about it, if you'll fucking let me," he said.

He sprang to his feet and went past her into the bedroom. She followed him. He could feel himself crying. He tore the comforter off the bed.

"Fine, I'll let you," she said. "But you have to eat dinner and go to sleep first."

He lay in the bed, his hands between his knees, and cried into the sheets until his nose ran. Archer Armour had killed a man because he thought he would be killed. The Rogers Park murderer had quite possibly killed people for the same reason. But how to hold the mentally ill accountable when they've caused harm? How to do justice to the loss of a good and harmless human life? He had seen pictures of the mailman Archer had shot three times: blond, midforties, acne scarred, not unlike Trump in the sagging jaw. His family torn apart by grief. The mentally ill couldn't be held responsible for their actions. But their actions had grievous consequences. The only way to fix it was to rid the mentally ill of their fear. He could do it. He would rid them of their fear.

"Yes!" Alex Trebek said. "Yes, finally! I'm getting through to you!"

Grace brought him a plate of crackers and Manchego, which he ate while she watched him. He was tired soon after, and fell asleep while she stroked his hair and sang the Rolling Stones' "Wild Horses," which their mother used to sing to them every night at bedtime until they were big enough to put themselves to bed.

V

When Leo woke up at 7:14, he saw Grace was asleep next to him, her T-shirt bunched up at her ribs and her hair knotted around her face.

A bottle of Richard's Glenlivet was open on the table next to her. He screwed the cap back on and put it in the hutch in the living room, where Richard was asleep on the couch, the blue wool blanket they'd bought on vacation in Scotland drawn up close under his chin. The shards from the broken vase had been cleaned up. Leo left for the office without waking either of them.

On the train, he balanced the notebook on his thigh and wrote: *I began to get hints of my chosen status recently while doing a routine evaluation of a patient, Dillon Halliday, who presented as having pure OCD coupled with depression and anxiety. At first I was frightened. Now I understand what I am meant to do. The growling is gone, entirely gone, and what remains is a clear and supportive voice that may not be there but is fully aware of who I am and what I intend to do. What I am meant to do, rather.*

"Well done!" Alex Trebek said. "Noble! You've living a noble life!"

At the office, he emptied the bottle of tiapride into the toilet, flushed it, and threw the container in the trash. Marsha was sitting at the front desk again. He locked eyes with her.

"I'm happy to see you, Marsha," he said. "I really mean that."

Marsha nodded. "Thank you, Dr. Lihn." She may not have felt the same, but he could tell from her small smile and the way she raised her dull eyes to him that she was at least fully committed to what she'd said.

Ellen stopped him in the hall to show him pictures of her son dressed as a pirate. Leo nodded, smiling, and when he didn't say anything in response, she squinted at him.

"How are you, Leo?" she asked. "Your pupils look a bit large."

He blinked. "It's the sunlight."

"The sunlight?" She paused, considering. "Do mine look large, too?"

He shook his head. "It's just how mine react to the sunlight."

In his office, he wrote in the notebook: *I feel bad for Ellen. She has to keep doing the small work of diagnosing and prescribing, diagnosing and prescribing, chipping slowly away at the massive ice block of human misery but barely scratching the surface of the real problem, which is fear. I wish for her sake that she could come to understand what the real problem is. I think in time she will. But by then my work will long since be done.*

Marsha buzzed him to tell him his patient had arrived. He went into the waiting room to retrieve Dillon and she lit up when she saw him, bounded after him into his office.

"How's the Luvox working?" he asked.

"Oh, *so* great," she said. "Like so many symptoms are just flat out gone."

"Any still remain?"

"Well, there's the skin picking, that's still there." She rolled her eyes up at the ceiling as if doing this would help her itemize the various aspects of her psychological turmoil. "There's some passive suicidal thoughts, some intrusive thoughts, but really things got a *lot* better after you prescribed the Luvox."

"I want to add three milligrams of Ativan for the skin-picking and intrusive thoughts," he said. "Take that whenever those things come up."

She nodded solemnly. "I'd be taking it a lot, then, doctor," she said.

"Then take it three times a day, at each meal. I'm going to increase the Luvox to two hundred milligrams as well."

"Yeah, that sounds great!"

He made the notes on her chart and felt her watching him, probably racking her brain for something she could say that would buy her extra time in his office. He decided to take care of that for her.

"You know why I became a psychiatrist, Dillon?" he asked.

Eyes wide, she shook her head.

"Well, first it was because I wanted to help people. That's why everyone says they want to go to med school, right? To help people. But then I realized that there's a difference between helping the body and helping the soul."

"I completely agree with you," she said.

"Because, even though the medical literature will try and tell you otherwise, and sometimes even I will get up in front of a classroom and try and tell *my students* otherwise, mental illness is something over and above a faulty arrangement of neurochemicals in the brain. The whole 'chemical imbalance' thing is strictly materialist. Do you know what philosophical materialism is?"

She looked about to speak, but he couldn't brook her hesitation. "It's the concept, Dillon, that all that exists in this universe is matter, and that all that happens in this universe is matter moving around or changing other matter. But that can't be true. You can't point to serotonin traveling across a synaptic cleft and call that 'happiness,' can you? Happiness is what you feel when you're walking home from school and pass under a tree branch after it's just rained and your sister grabs the branch and shakes it so that it's raining a second time, but just on the two of you, and it's one of those rare occasions when water and sunlight meet above your head, and you're laughing and trying to push her over and she runs away—she's always been taller than you, has a longer stride—but then she lets you tackle her in the grass. It's not the serotonin or dopamine that gets released as you laugh and see the sun through the raindrops, not the norepinephrine that helps you dodge the drops and chase after your sister, but rather it's something that arises from the combination of those neurochemicals and the sunlight and the water and the feeling of the grass against your neck, some combination of all those things that produces something immaterial, something that we have named 'happiness.'"

"Yeah, I wish we could distill *that* into a pill," Dillon said.

"But that's exactly my point: there's no turning that into a pill, because it has no material form. You have to concoct this admixture of things and then happiness emerges as an epiphenomenon."

"An epiphenomenon?'

But he hadn't heard her. "I want to thank you for making that initial appointment on the day you did. I want to thank you for coming into my office and telling me your story. Because it was by talking to you that I decided to undertake a study of the human mind that isn't so materialistic. Do you know where fear comes from, Dillon?"

Dillon looked uneasy now, but she didn't falter. "I'm not sure."

"I'm not sure, either. That's exactly why I'm asking. I don't know where it comes from and I don't know if I ever will, but don't you think it would help correct the course of human history if someone were able to come up with an answer? Not 'fear comes from abuse during childhood' or 'fear is what happens when you have an excess of norepinephrine in your brain,' but something that points at the exact epiphenomenon, the immaterial existence of fear? If we could find and replicate *that*, we'd know how to stop it."

Dillon was silent, gripping the couch cushion with either hand. When she looked up, her face was twisted. "I'm not sure exactly what you mean, doctor. It sounds good, but it's a little over my head."

He looked at her—young, too tall, uneasy, outsmarted—and could see what she was feeling. There had once been a time in his life when he was constantly bumping up against the ceiling of his knowledge, faced with professors and attending physicians who seemed determined to prove him stupid. There had been many days when he'd gone back to his dorm humiliated, called his mother to tell her he was worried he just wasn't cut out for medicine. And every time she'd said, "You know more than you think you do."

"You know more than you think you do," he said to Dillon, and wrote her a script for three milligrams of Ativan and two hundred milligrams of Luvox.

Alex Trebek told him to write in the notebook that to make the state or quality of happiness accessible to the people who needed it most—the people most capable of committing harmful acts, in other words—he would need to find every single person's rainy tree branch and shake it over their heads. His last class at Feinberg had been canceled due to his attack, and so he would be delivering last week's lecture tonight, a ninety-minute expansion on his polymorphism lecture called "Inconsistency of G72 Haplotypes Among Bipolar Patients." The provenance of the attack no longer mattered to him: whether it was Alex Trebek or the Rogers Park murderer or Archer Armour somehow escaped from prison, he was grateful for it. Grateful that whatever moved people to speak, think, and act was moving him in this way.

The class was full when he arrived, absolutely no stragglers that evening. He hadn't bothered to learn the students' names because it was a class of fifty. One of them, a girl who always wore a suit to class and sat in the front row, leaned forward at her desk as he was sorting his lecture notes and said, "We're happy to see you back this week, Dr. Lihn." Her kind of overweening ass-kissing would serve her well in the medical world, Leo realized. Small people doing small things.

"I've prepared a lecture for you today, but I'm afraid I need to diverge from the topic," he said. "And give you all a warning."

There was a brief, collective intake of air. Students shifted in their seats.

"I want to warn you that what you are trying to do, if done wrong, means nothing. You are saving no one. You are easing no pain. Do you understand? If you aren't digging as deep as you can dig and unearthing the true cause of human suffering, the thing that has its origins in the spirit-symbols that lie beyond this cave of shadows we call 'the world,' then you are doing nothing. Do you see what I mean?"

Heads bobbed.

"So where does human suffering originate?"

A few hands went up. He chose a chubby one in a jean jacket.

"Neurochemicals?" the hand-raiser said.

"Wrong! Who else?"

All hands lowered except for one. It belonged to a smirking mustache in the third row. "Qualia," he said.

"I see you took a philosophy course in college," Leo said, his blood pumping, his head light. "Congratulations to you."

Titters.

"I was bullied and humiliated as a boy," Leo said, and gestured to himself. "I grew up in an era where it was still uncool to be smart, and it was—and remains—uncool to be poor, uncool to be an immigrant. But you know what haunts me most about my brutalization? I sometimes enjoyed it."

"What do you mean?" the smirker asked.

"I sometimes enjoyed it because I felt I deserved it. This is, I think, the beginning of a story we could tell about human suffering."

The smirker raised his hand again. Leo ignored him. "Did any of you hear about the Archer Armour murder?"

The class was silent. The girl in the front row raised her hand.

"I did," she said. Leo realized she spoke with the faintest hint of a Southern drawl.

"What do you know about it?"

"That a man with an obvious mental illness killed another man who he thought was Donald Trump."

"Correct. Because he thought Donald Trump was going to kill *him*. Now, am I right to defend this man in a court of law?"

A voice from the back: "You're not 'defending' him, doctor, right? You're providing expert testimony to his insanity."

Leo resented the air quotes around "defending."

"Soulless prick," Alex Trebek said. "Self-satisfied soulless prick."

"Who's a soulless prick?" he shouted. "Who are you talking about?" The class stared back at him.

Then he was looking into Ellen's face. There were bright lights and she was wearing her lab coat. A portly woman with a facial mole stood behind her.

"Shit," he said.

Ellen smiled. "You're back! Stay with me, Leo. Do you know where you are?"

"Shit," he said again. "Mother*fucker*."

Ellen signaled to the portly woman and she limped around Ellen and affixed a blood pressure cuff to Leo's right arm. He was wearing a short-sleeved gown so the gauze was completely visible. He let her take his blood pressure.

"Wow, one-ten over sixty-five," Ellen said. "I'm impressed. Are you still running? Doing that morning regimen?"

"Haven't had the chance lately. More important things to do."

"Uh-huh," Ellen said, shining a pen light into his eyes. She held up an index finger. "Can you follow my finger?"

"I'm not doing a neurological exam."

"OK," she said, and obediently clicked off her pen light. She'd always had the better bedside manner of the two of them. That was the main reason he'd recruited her to his practice: she was an average clinician but a counselor *par excellence*. "You're at Rush," she said. "It's Monday, June seventeenth."

He was lying on a skinny bed in a dark room. Outside, a nurses' bay. He looked at Ellen.

"I'm on the psych unit?" he asked.

Ellen nodded.

"I thought you only worked here on Tuesdays and Thursdays?"

"I came in especially to see you. Richard called me."

Leo pounded his fists into his thighs. The nurse started, but Ellen held her back. "You can leave, Margot."

Leo sprang to his feet and shut the door behind Margot. "This is complete bullshit," he said. "You need to get me out of here."

"I can't get you out of here, Leo. You're on an involuntary hold."

"Who put me on an involuntary hold?" he hissed. "Richard? Grace?"

"They're worried about you. And you know they don't have the power to do that."

"You did."

Ellen was silent.

He began pacing. "I was doing important work."

"I understand that." She parted the curtains at the room's only window, offering them both a view of the hospital reflected on the surface of a slate-gray skyscraper. "But you need to rest in order to be able to do the really important work."

"No, I don't." He slowed the pacing. It wasn't helping his case. "Please. I just need to get out of here. I need you to discharge me. We can both see I'm fine."

"Apparently this is the second time in two weeks you've been in the ER during a fugue state. I'm shocked they didn't admit you at Northwestern." She propped herself against the windowsill and crossed her arms. "Why didn't you tell me this was going on? I could've helped you."

"I didn't need help."

"You know as well as I do that self-assessment isn't an option in psychiatry."

For a few moments they stared at each other. Leo felt the annoying esophageal jolt that always preceded crying.

"How would you feel if Matthew was locked in here?" he asked.

"Why are you bringing Matthew into this?"

"How would you feel if you were responsible for locking Matthew in here, Ellen?" He sat back down on the bed and crossed his feet at his ankles, trying to look as presentable as possible. "I'm like family. Come on, you know that. I've known you for almost twenty years."

Ellen shook her head. "You've been psychotic for over two weeks." She held up his notebook and he resisted lunging for it. "I've read this. They found it in your briefcase after you flipped a desk at Feinberg. You disappeared for two days. Richard found you pounding on the door to your condo this morning."

"I didn't flip a desk."

"You did. You were yelling at someone the students said wasn't in the room. The administration is debating right now whether to have you back."

Leo rolled his eyes. Of course Feinberg was too thick-skulled a place for him to undertake a study of the human soul. "Fine," he said.

Ellen looked behind her, out the window, and then back at him. "You need to take medication for this. To not do so would be irresponsible."

She was taller than him by an inch and wide-hipped. He'd met her husband once at a Northwestern reunion party—the husband had made cursory introductions, gotten drunk, and then ignored her. He was handsome, and had passed his bone structure on to Matthew. That bone structure looked strange on the face of a child.

"You have no idea what I'm trying to do," he pleaded. "If you'll just listen to me, I can explain it to you."

"We're going to try fifteen milligrams of Abilify," Ellen said. "I have to get back to the office, OK?"

"Ellen, listen, I don't think this is necessarily something bad—"

"Please try to rest," she said, and left him alone in the room.

He sat on the bed for as long as he could tolerate and then left his room and crossed over to the nurses' bay, where he tried to plead his case to a nurse named Akkram.

"I can't let you go," Akkram said, the creases in his face moving in a melancholy way. "You know that, doctor."

He wandered into the day room. Two women, one a teenager and the other Leo's mother's age had she been alive, were watching Maury Povich. A man sat at a table in the corner trying to assemble a puzzle of sunflowers. Leo picked up the lid to the puzzle box, studied it, and quickly found the three pieces the man was looking for.

"You have to leave," Alex Trebek said.

"I know I have to leave!" Leo whispered. The puzzle man looked wearily up at him and then returned to his puzzle.

He had been 5150ed, he figured. Typical that no one had debriefed him on his rights as a patient. Ellen couldn't be counted on to deliver on formalities, but then she probably figured he knew everything there was to know. And he did. He'd always dreaded getting calls from the psychiatrists and social workers at the hospital, informing him in clipped tones that his patient had been admitted and was under observation. *The patient is taking 4 milligrams of Risperdal and 300 milligrams Wellbutrin daily, correct?* Yes, he'd say. *Has she exhibited any signs of agitation in the past two weeks?* And here Leo would have to admit that he hadn't seen the patient in the past two weeks, because the ones who got hospitalized were always the ones who missed their appointments. *She is diagnosed bipolar type I, correct? He is diagnosed cyclothymic? She is diagnosed with major depressive disorder? He is diagnosed schizophrenic?* Yes, he'd say, and get ready for the hospital to confirm or deny or augment his diagnosis.

When he asked for paper and a pen, Akkram gave them to him. He sat in the day room writing about Max the grade school bully and Archer Armour and the ripping of flesh and the healing properties of love. He wrote about how he had met Richard—on a boat at Navy

Pier—and how the first time he'd slept with Richard he'd collapsed exhausted afterward, beyond satisfied, and let Richard stroke his chin and tell him how beautiful he was. He wrote about the boyfriend with the crooked nose. He wrote about the movie *Toy Story*, which he remembered being impressed by in college. He wrote about Grace and his mother and sunlight through water. He wrote about the population of Cook County Jail—roughly 8,000 prisoners—and the high likelihood that they had each been in love once. He imagined himself as Saint Augustine writing his *Confessions*. He imagined that a plaque would be installed on the wall of this day room to commemorate what he had written there.

"What are you working on?" Margot said over his shoulder, trying to sound polite.

He hunched, hiding it from her. "A letter to my boyfriend," he said.

Margot's face twisted. "Dinner's in ten minutes."

On the second day, Richard came to visit him. He was teary-eyed, bewildered; he'd never been on a psych unit before. Instead of talking, Leo spent the entire time watching Richard cry, holding his hands, and reminding him that he was taking the Abilify as prescribed (really he had been checking it and spitting it down his shower drain).

"I don't know what's happening," Richard said, wiping his eyes with the back of his hand. "I don't understand what's going on, Leo."

"Nothing's going on."

Richard hiccupped and sighed. "Then why are we here?"

"Exhaustion. Exhaustion and stress."

"Exhaustion? Is this 1893? Are you going to take a salt cure?" Richard shook his head. "This is something real. Something bad. Feinberg called to tell me you've been relieved of your lecture class."

"What a relief!" Leo said, but Richard didn't seem to like the joke. "You know I'm perfectly capable of keeping any of this from happening again. It's just been two slipups."

"Ellen doesn't want you back at the practice until you've been stable for at least a month."

Leo's throat constricted. "What?"

"She doesn't want you back. And she's been getting calls nonstop from Archer Armour's attorney. She doesn't know what to tell her."

"She can't keep me out of my own practice. This is insane."

"Your behavior's insane," Richard said, drawing the attention of a few other visiting family members. "You have to promise me you're going to focus on getting better."

"Well, I can't get better if you keep giving me bad news." Heat was prickling up the back of Leo's neck.

"There's only so much I can do! I can't keep tabs on an adult man like he's a baby."

"Oh, is that what you're doing?"

"I'm trying to get you to take care of yourself, Leo."

"OK, I'll take care of myself," Leo said, and stood up and walked out of the visiting room.

VI

Ellen didn't return to the unit for the remainder of his stay: he had to plead his case to an attending psychiatrist with a thick mustache and wild eyes. The psychiatrist dumbly parroted Ellen's directive, that he could be let out after the hold. Luckily, neither the psychiatrist nor the social worker cared about releasing him into the world alone—perhaps because he was a doctor himself. When the 5150 expired, he headed west through the Loop in the back of a Lyft, scrolling through the messages on his phone. From Richard: *I'm sorry. I love you.* From Grace: *Hey I know you won't get this but I hope you're doing OK. Let's have dinner when you get out.* From Ellen: *Please check in with me when you get the chance.* He deleted all three messages.

He had gotten four emails from Archer Armour's attorney, the final one explaining that she'd found a different expert witness because of his unresponsiveness. She mentioned hurriedly that this had been difficult to do mere weeks before a high-profile trial, and she hoped that Leo didn't treat his other clients this way. Leo deleted these emails, too.

He called the office and got a secretary who wasn't Marsha. For the first time, he regretted not being able to hear Marsha's voice.

"I'm calling about a patient."

"Which patient?" the secretary who was not Marsha asked.

"Dillon Halliday," he said. "Birthday 5-9-1992."

"One moment, let me pull up her file," the secretary who was not Marsha said, and made some swift typing noises. "OK, what did you need to know?"

He stumbled a moment. He hadn't prepared a lie. "The patient is using a service that delivers her medications to her home, and I need her home address to write the script."

"1521 West Armitage Avenue, Chicago, Illinois 60642." She pronounced the words in a steady monotone. He pitied her for not knowing such a service didn't exist.

The Lyft dropped him off at Cook County Jail. He had work to do. No more fugues. He pinched himself, then smacked himself. A woman in a green frock coat passed him on the sidewalk and turned to watch him, snapping her head forward when he met her gaze.

"That's it," Alex Trebek said. "That's exactly right."

The security officer recognized him and informed him with excessive civility that he had not scheduled a visit. Leo told him it was an emergency and the officer responded that Archer was on work detail. He told him that he needed to retrieve Archer from work detail because he was concerned that Archer was at risk of suicide. He asked the officer if he was prepared to have another inmate kill himself on his watch. The security officer shrugged. Leo said he would sue.

"Are you serious? What does it matter to you?" the security officer asked, but by then he was already on his way to retrieve Archer.

Luckily for him, the medical examination room was free. The officer didn't balk at Leo's request to hold the meeting there. When Archer entered the room, attended by two guards, his forehead glowed with sweat. He was wearing a short-sleeved jumpsuit and his hair was unkempt.

"Where's your briefcase, doc?" he asked. "Why didn't my lawyer tell me about this meeting?"

"Don't worry about that," Leo said. He wished the guards would leave the room.

"Well, thanks for getting me off work detail. It's hot in there."

"You're welcome."

They looked at each other for a moment and then Leo patted the examination table. "Why don't you come sit here?"

Archer obeyed. Leo did a patellar reflex test on Archer as the guards watched dispassionately.

"Your reflexes are stellar," Leo said. "It's good to see you're still in prime physical condition."

Archer raised his eyebrow and nodded. Then Leo grabbed his hand.

"Archer, do you know what the whole point of this is?"

Eyebrow still raised, Archer shook his head.

"Happiness," Leo said. "We're all trying to be happy. You made some people very, very unhappy because of your own unhappiness. Can you remember a time in your life when you were really, really happy? Before all this began?"

"Yes!" Alex Trebek roared, so loud Leo was worried he wouldn't be able to hear Archer's response. "Yes, yes!"

Archer pulled his hand away. "What the fuck are you talking about?"

The guards were both watching, wide-eyed now.

Leo gave a quick sigh and leaned on the exam table, close to Archer. "I was recently given the gift of a unique and rare happiness, a command to help people expunge themselves of fear. I've gone through a lot of pain to get here, Archer. I know you're facing life in prison, OK? Because, let's be honest, you murdered someone in cold blood. You took a life. But the antidote to that is happiness. Forget what your lawyer is telling you, OK? You don't need an *insanity defense*. You need to think of a time in your life when you were truly happy—"

"Yes, yes, god yes!" Alex Trebek was howling.

"—you just need to think of that happiness and remember what it felt like. And if you can remember that happiness—maybe a moment playing with your brothers? Or when your first child was born? Or the day you married your wife?—you will be able to *apologize* and your *apology* will be truer and more sacrosanct than this sidestepping your attorney is trying to get us to do. Do you understand? You will never harm anyone ever again! The fear will be gone!"

Leo had been looking so intensely into Archer's eyes that he realized he hadn't registered the expression on Archer's face, which was one of disgust.

"The *fuck* are you saying?" Archer looked at the guards, who looked helpless. "What is he saying?"

"I'm *saying* . . ." Leo closed his eyes and remembered the sunlight through the water again, but then more memories came back. The memory of Richard tracing Leo's lips with his thumb. The memory of his mother and Grace dancing to a Bee Gees record at Christmas. The memory of walking from the train to the office on a bright day in late April and spotting a bluebird's head poking up over the edge of its nest, and seeing that head swivel in concentration, following him as he walked past the tree, and thinking that there were so many living things in the world besides himself.

"I'm saying that you don't need to live in fear!" he said. "I've been doing this for thirteen years, and I can promise you, it's all fear!"

Archer leaned away and sneered as if Leo were rotting and then the guards were on Leo and the door to the medical examination room was closing behind him. And the security officer was telling him that he was not allowed on the premises and that if he didn't leave immediately, he would be brought to the local precinct.

When he got outside, he didn't call a Lyft. He had too much energy, too many things to do. He walked with purpose in the direction of Wicker Park. It was a beautiful day, a mild Chicago summer's day, and everyone around him seemed to be celebrating their good fortune to be alive and healthy in this thankless city in this season on this day. His phone was buzzing. It was Richard. He turned it off.

Just east of Homan Square, his vision began to scintillate and fuzz at the edges. He was scared, but Alex Trebek told him that it was all part of the process. A couple passing him on the street asked if he was all right. He told them he was happy to be alive and they should be, too, and walked quickly ahead of them, north and east, feeling the breeze from the lake growing stronger with his every step. There was a ringing in his ears—all part of the process, Alex Trebek assured him, nothing to be afraid of. Fear was the enemy. And Dillon was fear's anathema. He would get to her and thank her and then maybe devise a way to distill their friendship into some healing agent, something he could bring to every clinical interaction he'd have for the rest of his life.

"There's a reason for everything," Alex Trebek reminded him.

Yes. A reason he'd seen her on the train. A reason the growling had seemed to come from her.

He was going fast: through East Garfield Park, through West Town, up into Ukrainian Village. The city was structured so that the poorer communities were closer to the prison, closer to the police black sites. That much should be obvious to any public defender.

"The people there are doomed to fail," Alex Trebek said.

I'll help them, too, Leo thought, tripping over an unevenness in the concrete. *I'll even help the people who hate them. They're all motivated by fear.*

A little over an hour had gone by and he was in Wicker Park, at Ashland and Armitage. He ran east on Armitage and watched the numbers go up: 1200, 1202, 1204. The vision in his right eye was threatening to quit. He pinched himself. The ringing dominated the noise of traffic.

Number 1521 was a rambling, shabby Victorian with a chain-link fence to which four rusting road bikes had been locked. He climbed over the fence into the front yard. A young face was in the first-floor window, black haired with a shock of blond. He tried to look like his senses weren't quitting on him. He stood straight and smiled at the face. The face emerged into the yard, wearing a sundress and jelly sandals, her arms out in front of her as though Leo were an untamed animal.

"I'm here for Dillon," Leo gasped.

"OK," the face said. "OK, who are you?"

He shook his head. "It's too difficult to explain."

The face looked nervous. "Listen, I really don't believe in calling the cops, and you look rich, so I'm assuming you're not going to rob us, but you're making me feel unsafe and I need you to leave."

Leo shook his head again and stared at his shoes against the concrete. "Dillon," he managed.

Another face came through the front door, this one barefoot and green haired. "Hey, what's going on?" this one asked.

"Emmett!" the first one said. "I don't know . . . this guy is here."

Emmett walked carefully and slowly into the front yard, so carefully and slowly that Leo sat down from impatience and exhaustion. "Are you OK?" Emmett asked.

Leo nodded.

"Can you please leave?"

"I'll leave—" He breathed deeply to catch his breath. He was falling out of shape. "I'll leave when I see Dillon."

Emmett and the face stood over Leo, talking in high-pitched voices. Leo focused on the front door, and as if by dint of his focus there appeared Dillon.

"Oh my god!" she was saying. "Oh my god, Dr. Lihn!"

She rushed into the front yard, pushing past Emmett and the face. She knelt next to Leo.

"Dr. Lihn, are you okay? Why are you here?"

"Tell her why," Alex Trebek said.

Leo sighed. His breath still wasn't caught. "Fear," he managed.

"Fear? What about fear?" And then the look on Dillon's face clicked into one of comprehension. "You mean what you were telling me last session? About why you became a psychiatrist?"

"This guy's a *psychiatrist?*" Emmett asked.

"Help me help him up," Dillon told Emmett and the face. "Then just let us sit in the kitchen for a second."

Leo's legs were weak. His vision flickered. This was something worse than being out of shape. He was slipping. Feebly, he pinched his thigh.

"Dr. Lihn, can you take a step?" Dillon asked, and he could.

Inside was just as he imagined: the Ikea furniture, the bookcase of unread radical literature, the cheap appliances in the cramped kitchen.

Emmett and the face were on one side of him and Dillon was on the other. They helped him into a wobbling chair at one end of the kitchen table and then Dillon said something to Emmett and the face and they were gone, their footsteps creaking up the stairs.

Dillon set a mug in front of him that warmed his cheeks. He sipped from it: mint tea.

"I know it's hot outside, I just always like to have tea to calm me down," she said. "Even in hot weather, it helps me calm down." She sat across from him, dipping down momentarily to adjust a faulty table leg. When she came back up, he was looking at her awkward face with its thin lips and crooked chin, her too-long arms constellated with scars, and it occurred to him that she, too, had been bullied and humiliated as a child. Of course she had.

"I'm sorry," he said, shaking his head to try and dispel the ringing. "I tried to do more than I could."

"Sorry?" Dillon asked. "Why are you *sorry*? Dr. Lihn, you helped me so much. Seriously."

Alex Trebek said something he couldn't make out. The ringing was too loud. He started crying. He couldn't understand why he was crying, or why it was sapping what little strength he had. He held his head in his hands. He had made a huge mistake. He was making a huge mistake. His license would be revoked.

"Dr. Lihn?" Dillon was saying. She put her hand on his shoulder. "Dr. Lihn? Are you OK?"

He shook his head and cried.

"Dr. Lihn, I don't know what's going on, but if this helps, there's this song my mom made up that she used to sing to me when I got upset. I sing it to myself sometimes when things get really dark."

She took one of his hands and sang in a whispery voice:

Take your hand in mine
Think of the future, not the past
We're two of a kind
And our love will always last

Take your hand in mine
My funny girl, don't be afraid
Take your hand in mine
And see the world of joy we've made

The ringing quieted and he was able to lift his head and look at her. She was still holding his hand and she was smiling, the kind of smile his mother used to give him when she saw a future he couldn't. She squeezed his hand.

"You're fine, Dr. Lihn," she said. "I promise."

And like sunlight through water, he was.

On the Inside

Author's note: As a neurodivergent person, my goal in writing this story was to expose the harmful practices that impact the autistic community, especially autistic children. This story is in no way intended to speak for nonverbal autistic people: rather, it's an imagining of such an interiority in extreme distress, pulling from social experiences with nonverbal autistic people, research, and my own experiences with "abnormal" mental states.

A T THE DOCTOR'S OFFICE, I try to keep my face open and receptive to what's being said—especially if it's being said by Dr. Stevore—and to reflect back to the doctor the expression he's using when he's talking to us, to smile when he smiles and look pensive when he looks pensive. My husband's face goes rigid. He manages a large hedge fund whose investors include a Saudi prince and a close friend of Rupert Murdoch's, and he doesn't like to take directions from other people. He knew how to fix the lights in the Saugatuck house even though he's not an electrician. He knew how to help me with the art history degree I never finished even though he's not an art historian. Now he has an opinion different from Dr. Stevore's.

"I know I've told you this before, but I really think we need to give the casein-free diet another try," Dr. Stevore says. "That and applied behavior analysis. For another two months, at the very least."

My husband shakes his head. "We're ready to move on to chelation," he says. "Intravenous chelation."

Dr. Stevore looks smilingly at my husband, as if he is one misfit square away from solving a Rubik's Cube. "Chelation has been known to cause kidney damage and low blood-calcium levels. It's very dangerous."

My husband scoffs. "So is having a son who picks the skin off his hands and shatters the coffee table."

"I know you're frustrated," Dr. Stevore says. "And you've been dealt an unfair hand." He turns to me. "But it's Lina's day-to-day. Of all of us, she's the one who would be most affected."

My husband turns to me. I can tell he's grinding his teeth—a small noise that's grown increasingly perceptible over the years—and I'm afraid for him. But I know he's right. We've tried everything else.

"We think Benny's exposure to thimerosal in the vaccines he received when he was a toddler could be a cause for concern," I say, and before Dr. Stevore can say anything in response, I continue. "I recently read a paper by Andrew Wakefield describing eight children who developed autism within one month of receiving the MMR vaccine."

"Listen, please," Dr. Stevore says. "You can't base your information on studies that have been disproven."

I sit forward in my seat. My husband puts his hand on my back, not at my shoulders or tailbone, but somewhere in between. "I've joined a parent advocacy group with connections to a lawyer, one of the best in Chicago, who is looking to file a class action lawsuit against Pfizer for poisoning our children. Chelation is the only way to get rid of the heavy metals like thimerosal in Benny's bloodstream that are poisoning him and causing these symptoms."

Dr. Stevore is quiet. He sits back in his chair. My husband crosses his arms. I know that Dr. Stevore is the leading autism spectrum disorder researcher at the University of Chicago med school, that he flies around the country giving lectures on ASD and has published a very famous study called "Autism and Chromosomal Deletions." He is very in demand. Three of the women in my group recommended him to me, and we sat on a waitlist for three months. During those three months, Benny stabbed my husband in the foot, broke all six of my earthenware bowls, and didn't sleep for five nights in a row three times. He is ten years old and we had to call the police on him twice. I am mirroring Dr. Stevore's pensive face, but I am thinking how he doesn't have a son like Benny. He has twin daughters, one who works in a gallery in Brooklyn and another who is pursuing a PhD in philosophy at Yale.

"I can't recommend chelation," Dr. Stevore says. "I'm sorry."

"OK," my husband says. "Then we can't stay with you."

This makes the periphery of my vision darken and my palms tingle, but I say nothing.

"Lina," Dr. Stevore says, and I can distinguish a note of plea in his voice, and it makes me worry about Benny, about the fact that we have entrusted his life and well-being to a man who makes pleas. "Please think this over."

I look down at my feet. I can feel my husband tense next to me.

"Am I not here?" my husband asks. "Are you having a private conversation with my wife?"

Dr. Stevore puts up his hands. I can see the lines around his mouth and gray in his beard more clearly than I could before. "No, I'm sorry. I'm just appealing to Lina because she's going to be the one dealing with the treatments and the aftereffects. She's home with Benny."

My husband laughs. "I got stabbed in the fucking *foot*, doctor. I was home with Benny when that happened."

"You've both admitted as much that Lina—"

My husband stands up. "We're leaving."

I stand, too fast, vertiginous. I look at Dr. Stevore, who is studying the carpet. Then I follow my husband out the door.

My husband puts on his coat before we're outside. It's the end of October, which means that we're running out of time before the weather will turn and begin to feel like an existential threat. I've hated the winters in Chicago since I was a child. My husband, who grew up in Florida, is somehow better adjusted to them than I am.

"I'll say it again: We need to move to New York," he says. "All the best doctors are there. All my friends are there."

I want to point out that Roger, who heads up the Chicago Board of Trade, and the startup guys and a few of his favorite clients and my family are all here, but I know that my husband's *real* friends—the people he bonded with during his MBA—all went straight from Cambridge to New York. They were already taking the train there every weekend to hire escorts and buy coke. Whenever he talks about this time in his life before he met me, there's pride in his voice. I wasn't sure how to react, so I told him it sounded like fun. He moved to Chicago because he fell in love with me, the twenty-one-year-old art history major. He likes to tell me that five semesters of art history at Harvard makes me smarter than any of these doctors we've been waiting for months to see. He reminds me often not to doubt myself when I find a new study or have a strong intuition about Benny. He reminds me that he went to Florida State for undergrad, so he doesn't have the bragging rights I have.

"I just don't know how the holidays would work," I say. "Flying to Florida and then to Chicago and then back to New York."

He clips in his seat belt. He's staring out the windshield. I try to follow his gaze and see only a Burger King wrapper at the foot of a tree.

"What're you thinking?" I ask.

"I don't know," he says, and sighs. "I'm trying to think of what's best for Benny."

I sigh, too, and stare at the Burger King wrapper. "Not Stevore," I say.

He puts his hand on mine and squeezes it. "Not Stevore," he says.

I am making not a movement; I am not a rat. *I am not a rat!* (*The Great Mouse Detective*). Under the dining room table—oval, *distressed wood,* exposed and unfinished, like the *exposed brick* in Roger's house he talks about (*We bought this with the exposed brick in the living room, Anne was really excited about it*)—I see motes moving through the air. They move slowly. I count them in the space I see them, I count them in twos: sixteen, eighteen, twenty. I count them backward in twos: twenty, eighteen, sixteen, but they're falling faster than I can count them. I know if I do this I'll feel The Hands a little, a little flare of The Hands, but it won't last long because more will fall and I'll be able to count them again. Light can come in from the window above the back long edge of the table and if I look up at it or even out the sides of my eyes at it it'll flood me out, turn everything the color of it. Bright white. Mom always wants it to be bright white. She sings *sunshine on my shoulders makes me happy* (John Denver). Dad doesn't sing. We live in a condo in Streeterville in Chicago.

There are four big rugs between the living room and the dining room and the one under the dining room table has circles on it—a large purple one, a smaller green one, a smallest red one—and the hairs of the rug are long enough that they don't hurt. I can press my hands deep into the hairs unlike the hairs on my head, which don't give in because there's a skull right beneath them, a skull that hurts. I saw in a book in the bedroom, by Mom's side of the bed: *My kids say I have a village in my head and I live in that village, and it's true* (Isabel Allende). I wasn't supposed to be in the bedroom, but Isabella (not Isabel) was making grilled cheeses and I went in there anyway because the rest of the condo was bright white. A bad day. Isabella said once: "There's someone in there, a real good, bright kid. We just need to get him out." I am not bright like bright white. When Isabella said that, Dad nodded. Mom was already kneeling on the floor next to me on the bad rug with the short hairs and the stripes, rubbing my back. It hurt. In my head I was saying: *get him out get him out get him out.* Mom thinks: "He" is an idea and he needs to come "out" of the skull. *An idea so smart my head would explode if I even began to know what I was talking about* (Peter Griffin, *Family Guy*).

Isabella is from Colombia, South America. She speaks Spanish on the phone to her friends in Colombia. *Te quiero, Miguelcito!* (I love you, little Miguel.) She wears shirts like the nurses at the hospital, with little different-colored bears on them. The bears hold hands to make a circle and that circle is connected with another bear-circle and that circle with another. Isabella lives upstairs: she is *live-in help* and *a licensed behavioral therapist* (Dad). When we're together, she's working. When she's leaving, if it's so cold that there's pain under the nails and in the nailbeds, she wears a sweater with a fat tall neck that almost hides her face. She lets me touch it. I touch it, then she tells me to stop touching it, it's been too long touching it. She promises me she'll get me a *patch of the same material to touch all day.* She hasn't.

After lunch, before the dining room table, Isabella wanted me to sit on the couch and look at something she was holding. I didn't. I looked at my hands: there was pain again in the nailbeds, which were hot. She said a few things I didn't hear and then said *Benjamin Jr., I need you to pay attention.* Hands are starfish-shaped, starfish were on Animal Planet. There was pain in The Hands. The Hands were shaking, hurting—not hands on my arms. I put The Right Hand between my teeth, which felt better. I looked up at Isabella, who was saying something. Bright white behind her head. The Hands hurt and I felt sick. Somewhere in a book I got from the bookcase downstairs someone wrote *depression feels like a bodily flu* (author forgotten). Isabella said *Benny, get that out of your mouth.* I bit harder and tasted a little blood. *Benny, this is your first warning.* The Right Hand felt better, but I needed to calm The Left Hand. Before I did that I needed to be "thorough," so I put one of the nails in the incision in The Right Hand, and it felt better. I always feel sick about The Hands and I wish I knew when they were going to happen so I could do something to stop them. *Benny, this is your second warning.* Quieter, she said *Fuck why didn't I trim your nails this morning?* She said it like she was alone, like when I press The Hands into my skull when I'm alone. I bit The Left Hand.

Benjamin, this is your final warning. Then her hand, normal hand, was hot on my arm and yanking. Then both her hands were on my arms and yanking. I cried and she kept yanking. I pulled and she kept yanking and saying *You are hurting yourself, Benny.* I pulled hard enough that she let go and then technically I—really The Right Hand—slapped her across the face. She held it and looked at me, her eyes big. I looked once at her and then looked down at The Hands, which weren't The Hands anymore, they were mine. I smiled that they were mine.

Jesus fucking Christ, she said, and stood up, and went away. I stayed and watched *The Simpsons* season 27 on TV. I didn't leave the couch.

When she came back two episodes later (*Flanders is turning us all gay*), she was holding the same thing again and I felt like I could look at it now that The Hands were gone. It was a circle with faces on it. One face was crying, one face was laughing, one face was looking surprised like Isabella had just looked. *Benny*, she said. *We are going to work with the emotions wheel today. Can you point to how you're feeling?* In her voice was hurting, the feeling of being hurt, of breathing hard. It made me dizzy; I felt the hurt. I made the *coo* noise, which she likes, and hugged her.

Benny, you are an angel and a devil, she said, and hugged me back. There was pain beneath my shirt, but only a little. I was thinking: *Ignore it.* Then she moved back from me and held up the circle again and pointed to a face with a smile and red cheeks and a little heart above it. *So I'm guessing you're feeling lovey-dovey today?*

I'll do anything for you, dear (*Oliver!* the musical). I made fists so the nailbeds wouldn't hurt again, then pointed to the face. Isabella made the same face as the one on the circle, a warm one. *You did it, Benny! I'm so proud!* Her eyes were big but not in a hurt way now. *Benny, do you think you can show this to Mom and Dad when they get home?* I nodded. I would show it to Mom and Dad when they got home.

Under the dining room table now feels softer than anywhere else in the condo. A bed is supposed to feel softest but the one I sleep in doesn't. My room gets the most bright white of anywhere, which Isabella said is important for me. Important to have bright white for *sensory integration therapy*. The days when the sky is the color of Roger and Anne's cat's fur and the lake looks like a stone turning over and over are the better days. *You're behaving*, Isabella says, and takes me to the lake to throw little rocks in the water. Those are the days when The Hands are gone and everything feels like under the dining room table. On those days I sometimes stand with my red raincoat off my shoulders hanging at my elbows and a rock in one hand and look at the big turning stone and think, *They don't know how happy these days are. They can't know how happy these days are.*

I count the motes: forty, forty-two, forty-four. I put my palm on the top of my knee, on top of the patella. It sits on there. Any part of me can start hurting at any time and I have to be the one to stop it. There is no one else who can stop it. I let them try, but they make it worse. Mom makes it worse. Her hands are hot, and she pulls my chin so her eyes are looking at me and there's heat in my vision and my heart beats under my hurting skull and I can't keep looking at her so I look away. When I do that, she says *God, I wish he would just look at me!* She cries. *Don't let the customer down, no matter how low on the totem pole you are* (*How to Succeed in Business*, author forgotten).

Benny! Mom says. A little quieter, she says: *Hi, Isabella. Was he good today?* Dad makes his dad-noises: feet walking, coughing, setting keys down, moving papers around. *He was very good, actually* Isabella says. *We had a mini breakthrough with the emotions wheel.* She is not going to talk about The Hands. I feel my chest get warm and in my head I see her face and I am looking in her eyes: Isabella's eyes, brown and blue. Mom always says *You have beautiful eyes. Any man would be lucky to have you.* And Isabella says *Tell that to my ex.* Then they laugh. *Benny!* Mom says. *Are you under the dining room table?* Dad keeps making the dad-noises. *Benny, sweetie,* Mom says, down on the rug now, looking at me. *How are you? How was today?* I look at her hands: white with blue veins. I hold one of them, the right one, and look at her palm: flushed red. She was cold earlier. I rub my hand against her palm. *Thank you, sweetheart,* she says. *That feels nice.*

In the kitchen Dad says to Isabella *We ended it with Dr. Stevore.* Isabella says *I'm so sorry, Mr. Drury. That must have been difficult.* Dad says, *It's not so hard ending things with a quack.* Isabella doesn't say anything for a long time. Eventually she says *I understand, Mr. Drury.* Then Isabella is on the rug, too, crowding next to Mom, looking at me. I look down at the rug. I am closest to the small red circle. I look up at them: four eyes, Isabella's more blue than Mom's. I look down again and trace the circumference of the red circle with my hand. Out of the corner of my eye I see Mom is wearing black jeans and a button-up white blouse and a little red makeup on her lips and cheeks and her hair in a bun. *The most beautiful woman in the world* (Dad). Mom is short and thin, which *influenced my genetics* so I am short and thin. Dr. Stevore said I am ten but look eight. Isabella is holding the circle close to me. *Can you show Mom how you're feeling today?* she asks. I choose the face with the heart again and Mom makes a loud gasping noise and hugs me hotly and it hurts horribly, worse than The Hands, and I am sweating and breathing hard. I try to take the arms away from my sides so Mom will have to stop hugging but she won't stop. She says: *Benny, you're making so much progress!* She's hurting me. My eyes see bright white where there should be none. It will be worse for Mom if I die than if she doesn't hug me. "Too Old to Rock 'n' Roll, Too Young to Die!" (Jethro Tull). So I sit down away from the hug and she lets go and with my foot I push her just a little in the stomach and she falls back. *Benny!* Isabella says. *No,* Mom says, standing up, *it's fine. I was overwhelming him.* I can feel that Isabella is looking at me. She says, *He needs to be punished for bad behavior. We need to ignore him now until he does something right.* They are talking like they're alone again, so I do what I do when I'm alone: I press the tips of the fingers into the skull so there's little pressures all over. I think *I am a boy in a condo in October.* I think *I will not have to go with Isabella to the grocery store today.* I think *I am ten years old and eventually I will be twelve, and eventually fourteen, and eventually sixteen.* The bright white is gone. Mom's voice says from the kitchen *He kicked me in the stomach.* Now Dad is making the dad noises loudly, closer and closer to me. He is under the table. He pulls me by the arm so fast I can't tell if it's hurting or not. Then I am out from under the table and the windows are dark and Dad is saying *You do not kick your mother, do you understand?* A noise comes out of my mouth, not the kind of noise Dad and Mom and Isabella make. I make the noise louder. Dad lifts me by the arms and the shoulders and elbows hurt and Mom says *Ben! What are you doing?* I will die from this, definitely. Mom will not like it if I die. After I die there will be no way to see the stone turning over and over or a dog with long, soft hair walking down the street toward me. I make the noise again and kick in the air and I am kicking Dad in the knees and The Hands are moving, pulling at his fingers, and Dad is saying *Fuck! Let go, Benny!* But he doesn't stop holding me and making the arms and wrists hot and eventually I am in my room with the door closed. I am alive still. I need to tell Mom I am alive. I go to the door and try the knob and when the knob doesn't work I bang on the door and make the noise as loud as I can. I feel sick. There is a rectangle of bright white, getting closer and closer, and I sit down so it will go away. I hold my throat to make sure there is blood and air going through the neck. My back is against the door. Isabella says nothing. Maybe she's gone.

On my bed is the iPad. I open YouTube. I very quietly play a song by the Bee Gees ("To Love Somebody"), a song by Nina Simone ("Mississippi Goddam"), a song by Massive Attack ("Teardrop"), a song by A Tribe Called Quest ("Electric Relaxation"). On Wikipedia I look up "love" which leads me to "love letters," which leads me to "*The Letters of Abelard and Héloïse,*" which leads me to "Chaucer" which leads me to "Richard III." I read the paragraphs while counting in my head: I count *two, four, six* and the paragraph is done. I can only do this alone, at night, when I know I don't have to think about who's going to hurt me. When it's time for dinner, Dad will open the door. I will go to one of the bookshelves in the living room and take the books out. Dad will say *He's going to ruin our books flipping through them so fast like that. He can't even read.* Mom will say *It's a stim. Just let him self-soothe.* Reading is important to them: they argue about whether I can read "the" or "cat." I don't want them to know about me reading. I delete all my searches on the iPad. *You are sitting on a bombshell waiting to explode* (*Wreck-It Ralph*). Every time they find out something about me, like when I chose the *lovey-dovey* face on the *emotions wheel*, or when I gave a *high five*, or when I was little and Mom showed me a picture of a bird and then I pointed to a real bird out the window and it flew into the window and fell, I get hurt. So instead, I try to think of cartoon movies, which they already know about, which they watch with me.

Right before dinner, Mom comes in. She sits on the bed next to me. I am looking at a video on YouTube of Elsa in *Frozen*. Elsa is singing on a block of ice in a blue dress. *Benny, I love you*, Mom says. *You are the light of my life*. Out of the corner of my eye I see she's been crying. She doesn't touch me, just puts her hands tight on the edge of the bed and holds it like we will fall into a crevice behind us like Kuzco and Pacha in *The Em-*

peror's New Groove. Can you understand that I love you? she asks. I look at Elsa. I put my thumb close to Elsa's face like I'm touching her chin. This stops the video, but I still look at her. Mom starts the video again for me with the right hand, and I hold on to her finger and then hold on to her whole hand. I put her hand between both my hands and I press against her hand. She is warm now after being cold an hour ago. *Benny, I know you're in there,* she says. *I know my little boy is in there somewhere.*

When I was ten years old and first looked at Brueghel's *The Tower of Babel* in my father's *Art of the Northern Renaissance* book, I felt safe the way I often felt safe thinking of the busy neighborhood outside our house. There were so many doors to other houses in Hyde Park, just like there were doors in the Tower of Babel, and on the other sides of those doors were people, and those people were eating dinner or washing their clothes or taking naps or petting their dogs. But the Tower of Babel was even better than Hyde Park because the doors were stacked on top of one another and reaching toward the sky. My father, who taught French existentialism in the philosophy department at the University of Chicago, told me several times that there was no God and no heaven, but Brueghel had painted a heaven, or at least suggested a heaven: the place the Tower of Babel was going to. Where was the Tower of Babel supposed to go otherwise?

I declared an art history concentration early in my sophomore year of college, sooner than any of my friends knew what they wanted to do. I decided to email my parents about it instead of calling them. Only my father wrote back: *You will have to keep your eye out for PhD programs, because there is nothing else you can do with that degree. Nevertheless, you will see some beautiful art.* I never went home on breaks: I stayed with my roommate Emily, whose parents owned a winery with a stable of thoroughbred horses. While Emily rode her horses, I tried to get a jump on the next semester, reading about the Venus of Willendorf, Apollo of Veii, the Pre-Raphaelites. I kept a notebook with a picture of *The Tower of Babel* pasted on the cover and wrote about heaven in it. Then

I wrote marginalia when there was no more room. Then I wrote over the marginalia with new marginalia in a different-colored pen. Spring of our sophomore year, I left the notebook on the floor next to my bed and Emily found it while she was cleaning. At that point the marginalia were unreadable.

When I came back to our room in Winthrop House after dinner, Emily was sitting on her bed, looking through the notebook. My stomach went cold. I grabbed it from her.

"Are you OK, Lina?" she asked. "Do you maybe need to see someone?"

"I'm fine," I said. "They're notes for class."

"OK, but they don't look like that."

By then I had begun to find Emily stupid. She was concentrating in chemistry, which she always complained about, and had no taste in music or books. She hung out with people who liked to binge-drink, some of whom she had begun bringing to the winery over breaks. A friend of mine from my Cinema of the Absurd class had told me that people usually outgrew the friends they made freshman year, and I was annoyed to think that, despite having fully outgrown Emily, I was still rooming with her.

"It's nothing," I said to her. "Just forget about it."

Junior year I got a single room in the house. I hung out with the people I had met in Cinema of the Absurd and Modern Art from Klimt to Dalí, including a girl with green-and-black hair whose name I can't remember, but who I thought was the smartest person I'd ever met. I smoked weed most days and dropped acid a few times. I bought a new Brueghel notebook and pasted different-sized printouts of *The Tower of Babel* on the cover. I was, my professors said, the most promising student in my cohort. I was certain to get into a PhD program and get a job teaching art history someday.

It happened suddenly: I was sitting in my room reading about the Ashcan School and my vision blinked on and off and I tried to stand up but couldn't. Then I was looking into the face of my RA, a skinny redhead, and he was saying *Please sit tight, Lina. We're going to get you to the infirmary*. I'd had a seizure, they said, a grand mal. I saw a doctor after that and had to take a medication called Trileptal. I took it for a few weeks and then stopped. Not because I was careless or forgetful, but because I found the idea of taking care of myself repulsive. I felt strange, useless. My brain had gone dark in a way that disgusted me. I felt like I had died in my room that day and was just an ugly spirit pointlessly roaming the earth. I stopped going to class. I got emails from my professors asking where I was. I flunked papers, flunked tests. I didn't show up for any of my finals that semester and was put on academic probation. I never had another seizure, but the dark feeling didn't go away for a long time.

I didn't tell my parents and ignored their calls when they found out. I stayed with some of my friends in an apartment in Cambridge over the summer, trying to figure out what I'd do for the fall. I kept the Brueghel notebook under my pillow but didn't write in it. I smoked weed and watched old movies with the girl with green-and-black hair: *Dark Passage*, *The Sweet Smell of Success*, *Night and the City*. I ate cheese and white Club crackers once a day and nothing else. I lost fifteen pounds. One night the girl with green-and-black hair—it worries me that I can't remember her name—took me to a party in Harvard Square right next to the river. She told me that it was going to be mostly grad students and that the apartment was being rented out from a Wall Street broker who had been photographed on the balcony of his New York penthouse with Mischa Barton. The girl with green-and-black hair showed me the photograph: the broker wore a cinched gold robe and Mischa Barton wore an open robe of the same cut and color with an oversized T-shirt underneath. He was smiling and saying something and she was turned toward him, laughing.

At the party, a man with a neatly shaven beard who wore a suit with no tie and the first two buttons of his dress shirt unbuttoned opened the door for us. When he saw the girl with green-and-black hair, he pulled her aside and asked how her classes were going. She said something neutral and then introduced me as her best friend. The man looked me up and down and said he was very pleased to make my acquaintance. Then he took the girl with the green and black hair away to "catch up" and she waved back at me, promising that "everyone is really cool." I figured she'd return a couple hours later with drugs.

The ten minutes it took me to get from the door to the kitchen island, where I poured myself a drink, to a chair in the living room where I sipped it, were the last ten minutes of my life without Ben. When I sat down, he sat down next to me. His eyes shone as though he was running a fever, and he told me that he was just at this party because his friends wanted him to come out, he was really supposed to be home studying. I asked him what he studied and he said something about private equity.

"But someone like you, you probably think guys like me are evil."

I said nothing.

"I'm gonna be honest, the reason I'm doing all this is because I want to be a philanthropist. I want to push solar and electric so hard that fossil fuels cave. I'll pay off whoever I have to pay off. I want to stop global warming." He looked down into his drink, smiling. "I'm a sheep in wolves' clothing."

I had never considered that I was part of a group of people who would hate this shiny-eyed man for studying private equity or love him for wanting to stop global warming. I knew that I should hold these opinions, but I didn't feel them. My Art of Late Byzantium professor had once said to the class, after I had described a painting as "guileless": "Lina is perhaps the only person in this class who can see an art object as an art object and not an agglomeration of her politics and private fetishes." The man's eyes looked thick with their shine.

"I really don't think guys like you are evil," I said. "Everyone has to do something."

He looked at me like I'd just told him he'd never have a nightmare again. Then he caught himself and switched back to his sheepish smile. "I'm Ben Drury," he said.

I saw him every two days after that, then every day, then I moved in with him. When I finally picked up a call from my dad, he told me I couldn't count on his financial support anymore. Ben laughed and said,

We'll muddle through. We got married and lived in Cambridge while he finished the second year of his MBA, and then we moved to Boston so he could do consulting work for a private equity firm. I audited a few classes in the divinity school and then became an intern at a gallery where I assembled and dismantled exhibitions and was treated like I knew nothing about art. Eventually I got pregnant and left the gallery, and Benny was born. When he was still an infant, we moved to Chicago because my father was diagnosed with lung cancer, which he fought for two years until it went into remission.

I didn't tell Ben about the dark feeling, which raged after Benny's birth. I stared at my hands or out windows and kept staring until Benny's crying demanded that I look down at him. I couldn't sleep even when Benny could. The parts of the day were indistinguishable from one another: morning was afternoon was evening and the sun never seemed to rise or set. I threw my old Brueghel notebooks away. A few of the associates who worked with Ben had wives around my age, and when I told them the littlest detail about how I was feeling, they all said that it would go away, I was under so much stress with the new baby and Ben's new job and my dad's cancer, and that I should give it time and everything would "settle in."

The dark feeling didn't lift until it had to, until that week I first noticed Benny wasn't holding my gaze or mimicking my expressions anymore. He sat with his back against the couch holding a toy plane, not playing with it but spinning the propellers for hours. He threw days-long tantrums when we tried to get him to eat. He kicked the ottoman so hard he broke three of his toes. He went nights without sleeping. Who was I to think about myself?

Isabella has the day off. I heard her get up in the morning and say to Mom *Goodbye Lina* and ask where I was and Mom told her I was sleeping. I was not sleeping. *O sleep, thou ape of death, lie dull upon her!* (*Cymbeline*). On the iPad I looked up "sleep" and then "bed" and then "I Don't Wanna Go to Bed" (Nelly). In the bed I have to lie down so the head touches the pillow—Isabella says *Lie down, please, Benny, and rest*—and I can feel the pillow is not sturdy, it gives into the skull, the skull falls too far into the pillow. I lie down until they close the door and then I sit up. The hairs on the rug in the room are long and soft and I sit on them. The hairs are like the hairs on the head. Dad says *We should take away the iPad before bed* and Mom says *What if he can't sleep?* And Dad says *He'll have to learn to occupy himself without a screen.* I look up "screen" and then "pixel" and then "pixilation." I look up "Pixar." *I'm the only stick with eyeballs!* (*A Bug's Life*). I think sometimes on a bad night that the bright white is inside the skull, not so I can see it but so that my brain can see it, and that it makes everything move faster. I don't like when things move too fast. If they move too fast, I put my face in the hairs on the rug and hold it there and breathe: two breaths, four breaths, six breaths. Today is a Roger-and-Anne's-cat's-fur day, so I can look out the window and see a bird flying by. It is far away enough that it won't get hurt.

Mom comes into my room and says *Oh, you're up. Why didn't you tell me, honey?* I am looking down, holding my face in the hairs of the rug but my chin above the floor and my muscles are starting to shake from holding it there. I do not look at Mom and I feel her looking at me. *Do you want to come to breakfast?* she asks me. *Do you want to have a hard-boiled egg?* Mom will put the egg, peeled, in the little egg cup and I will eat it. I hold my face in the hairs until I can't anymore and then stand up and go to the kitchen. Mom follows me.

The kitchen is the best part of the house (*The Happy Family's Gluten-Free Cookbook*). The lights in the ceiling are on: they are an amber color, which I think is like the inside of the body where nobody can see. One time I had a camera in my stomach and I saw on the screen mushy pink and the doctor said, *See Benny, that's inside you!* and Mom said *If he has ulcers, can those affect the serotonin receptors in his stomach?* and the doctor said *The serotonin signaling would take place in the gastrointestinal tract, Mrs. Drury. We're just looking for damage to the lining of the stomach.* I saw mushy pink and then wider mushy pink, not a hole, not a cavern. I want to put a camera into the skull so Mom can see inside and she will think *This is not a hole and this is not a cavern.*

I eat the egg. If the egg is good it is thick and if it's bad the yellow part drips out. It makes little movements in The Hands. Isabella says *Quiet hands, Benny*. She doesn't know about bright white because her shoes are white and her coat is white and in the summer she wears a white *blouse* with buttons. In the summer I have two short-sleeve shirts: one with a T. rex on days two, four, six. and one with a dog that says WOOF YOU LATER on days one, three, five. Day seven can be either shirt, but is usually the dog one, because I like the T. rex shirt less.

Mom is humming a song that I realize is "Creep" (Radiohead). She sounds happy. She comes up close to me and says *I'm a weirdo-o-o*. I look at the little cup where the egg was. She says *Did you like your egg, Benny?* I think that every day that goes by can't happen again. Mom and Dad put coins in a jar and when the coins fill the jar they go to the bank and get back dollars. Dad says *Your grandma used to do this* and he says *I didn't grow up rich like you, Benny*. Dad is at work now, where Roger is. Roger is taller than Dad, and he has a beard.

I go in my room and go on the iPad and play "King of Carrot Flowers Pt. 1" (Neutral Milk Hotel) and it hurts in the skull so I play "Love Etc." (Pet Shop Boys) and it hurts so I play "Nikes" (Frank Ocean). Dad said *The algorithm on that thing is driving me up the wall. It makes no sense* and Mom said *Just let him listen, some of it's even good*. Today I am thinking *get him out get him out get him out* but it isn't me thinking, it's something else in the skull. I am thinking *get him out for Mom* but maybe if I get him out I will get hurt, I will lose my arm or go blind or die. I go on Wikipedia for "get him out" and it says *Get Him to the Greek* (comedy film) and *I'm a Celebrity, Get Me Out of Here!* (Australian TV series) and *Get Out* (horror film). There is bright white on my bed so I go on the ground on my stomach. The iPad doesn't show anything today. This is like when the brain inside the skull doesn't show anything. *My generation's apathy, I'm disgusted with it. I'm disgusted with my own apathy, too* (Kurt Cobain). The Hands aren't there but there's a pressure in the skull. It's saying *get him out get him out get him out*. I throw the iPad hard and it thumps against the wall.

All of a sudden Mom is in my room and says *What was that?* and sees the iPad. She picks it up. *Benny,* she says, *this is expensive. You can't throw it.* I turn around so I don't see her, because bright white is coming from her eyes. *Come on,* she says *it's almost time for the meeting.* Her voice is soft. I think how yesterday she had red lips but today her lips are pink and thin. I turn around. She goes down on the floor so she is sitting on her knees. Her lips go up so she's smiling. *Come on, sweetpea* she says. She walks away and I go with her.

I watch *DuckTales* on TV and Mom moves around making mom-noises. Eventually Elena is at the door saying *Hi!* and Gabriella is with her. They are both bright white all the time. I look at the TV. Elena says *You've been so busy!* and Mom says something quiet I don't hear.

Gabriella sits by me on the couch and looks at me. I look a little at her and then back at the TV. On her head there is a hairband with flowers on it but it's not holding any hair back. Her shoes are the Velcro kind and her eyes are small. She puts her arm on me, behind my neck. It's hot and it's the part of my neck that I can feel the motes on. I try to count sixty-four, sixty-six, sixty-eight. I make the noise but the arm stays there. *Hi Benny* she says. *Hi Benny* she says again.

The Hands. I push her away. She sits still for a second and then screams. Elena stands in front of her, her earrings down to her chin. Mom stands next to Elena. *Are you OK?* Elena says, holding Gabriella's shoulders. *What happened?* Mom looks at me, the arms crossed. *I'm sure he did something* she says. *Benny, what did you do?* I look behind her so I can see *DuckTales.* She turns off the TV. Now it's not showing anything and it was the only thing in the condo showing something. I go off the couch. I pound the floor. Mom holds my hands. Everything is bright white. I try to punch her. She holds them so I can't move. I make the noise and try to kick her. She is the one who will kill me, but it's a *paradox* because she won't like it if I die. *It's OK* Elena says. Gabriella isn't screaming anymore. I know she's looking at me but I don't look at her. *Breathe, Benny* Mom says. I gasp and the lungs hurt because the air is cold now. Then Mom lets go and I go fast under the dining room table and look at the rug. There are needle-feelings under my skin. I dig my finger into the rug. I feel myself gasping and then crying because I want Mom to be how she was this morning, before Elena came with Gabriella.

How about a puzzle? Elena says, and Gabriella doesn't say anything anymore. I trace the red circumference again and again, fast. I go around two times, four, six, eight, ten, twelve. I hear Mom sigh. *Is anyone else coming?* she says. *I think Julie, but she's not bringing Ethan* Elena says. Mom says nothing else for over twenty seconds, but then she says *Gabriella is so much higher-functioning than Benny. I know it's wrong, but I get jealous of you two.* Elena says *Oh hon, I promise you can get there. It just takes a lot of ABA, a lot of fiddling with the diet, and the chelation really did help. She was barely talking two years ago.* Mom says *We quit Stevore last week. He doesn't do chelation.* Elena says *Honestly, I think that was the right decision.* Mom says *But I'm scared. I'm scared of sticking that giant needle into Benny's arm and pumping him full of what? Ions? The stuff that gets the heavy metals out? I've read so much about it and it's stopped making sense.* Elena says *It's a pinprick, like their blood tests. Sure, the needle doesn't come out for a while, but they barely feel it.* Mom says *Benny hates getting his blood drawn.* She doesn't say anything else, and then she says *Stevore said there were serious risks.* Elena says *What does Stevore know? Does he have an ASD kid? He's just some guy making a ton of money off us, living in a mansion in the suburbs somewhere.*

I trace the circle again and again and again. If I die in the condo, Mom will find me and she will cry. One time Dad chased me around the living room and I was holding a little pocketknife and I turned around and stuck it down and it was in his foot. Then I pounded the ground and The Hands made me throw a glass pyramid that said FOR-TUNE MAGAZINE INNOVATORS OF THE YEAR 2017 at the TV. Officer Jamison put his thumbs in his belt loops and said *We've seen this before, kids like him usually get sent to a group home. They can go as young as seven, eight. Have you thought about that?* Mom cried then.

Julie is here now and she is saying *We've heard from the attorney, we just need more people signing on for Pfizer to really take us seriously.* Mom says *Have you spoken to your friends in New Orleans? The Autism Speaks people?* Julie says *Yeah, I think they're on board. I just need to get them the paperwork.* Julie is the tallest one and she is divorced and she has Ethan and he has a brother named Eli who's in high school. (*Lina, honestly, you make me feel like such a sasquatch after these two kids. You're so beautiful.*) Two times ago, Ethan gave me a hand-small metal fighter jet that was too cold to hold. Julie says *Have you talked to Dr. Worther? We've already scheduled an appointment for Ethan.* Mom is quiet, the way she's sometimes quiet when Dad says something loud. *I feel like such a bad mom* she says. *I've been talking Elena's ear off about this all afternoon. There was that British boy who died of cardiac arrest during chelation.* Elena says *But you know that boy had other health problems, right?* Julie says *Think about it: would you rather take a little risk or keep living like this forever? He could hurt himself in a devastating way, or get taken away from you.* Mom sighs again. Julie says *Do you want to know my honest opinion? I'd take the measles over what I've been through with Ethan. I'd take a lot of risks, Lina.*

It goes from afternoon to nighttime. Dad comes home. He is smiling today and kneeling in front of the table. His hands are behind his back. He says *Hey kiddo.* His lips are dry and I look where I always look, at the space between his front teeth. Then I look at him up and down. He is wearing a suit with a pink shirt and a tie that has red stripes going diagonally to the left. *I got a chance to swing by the Mag Mile today* he says. He takes his hands out from behind his back and there is a box with a little standing person with a big head like an alien and on its stomach there's a screen. *This is called Codi* Dad says. *He can tell the time, play videos, wake you up in the morning, put you to sleep at night, track the weather, read you bedtime stories, and read your emotions, among other things.* Mom says *Ben, how much was that?* Dad shakes his head and doesn't look at her. Dad says *Do you want to play with him?* It's white-colored and the hands don't have fingers, just mittens. I go back to tracing the circle. There is a little knot of dust on the outside of the circle and I pick it up and look at it. Dad opens the box and takes out Codi and the eyes open up and it says in a little voice *Welcome, please input name and date of birth.* Dad does something to the back of it and then puts it back down and it says *Hi, Benny. I am so excited to be your friend.* The voice sounds like a baby's voice I heard when I was at the lake with Isabella four times ago. Mom says *How is he going to play with that?* Dad stands up and says *Roger and Anne are going to come over for dinner. I'm sorry I didn't text about it sooner; it was kind of a spur-of-the-moment thing.*

I pull the little hairs out of the rug and think *the inside of the skull get him out.* I think *the bright white get him out.* The Codi's arms go up and then the hands come together two, four times. *Can you clap with me?* it says. Mom says *Isn't that toy a little young for him, anyway?* Dad is making a scraping sound putting the dinner plates on the table. I think of Kuzco on the throne and Kuzco as the llama in the rain. It goes back and forth between them. *This is the real me. This. Not this. This. Not this. Winner. Loser* (*Emperor's New Groove*). Inside my skull it goes: *This is the real me.* It goes again and again: *This is the real me, this is the real me, this is the real me.* The Codi's feet move and it comes closer, then it stops. *The toy's fine for him* Dad says.

Roger and Anne come. Roger wears pants the color of a tree trunk and he doesn't have a beard anymore. Anne has a black-and-white-squares dress with long sleeves. Mom says *You look incredible, Anne* and Anne says *Thank you, I'm a work in progress.*

I go to the bookshelf and take out *The Ego and the Id* and take out *Brazilian Art of the 1700s* and turn the pages in both of them at once. Roger says *So here's our little man! Double-fisting knowledge!* Dad takes both the books away and says *Come on, Benny. Those are Mom's books.* It makes me feel The Hands. I get hot. I put the right hand in a fist and put it between my teeth. I look at Dad. He shakes his head. Mom looks at Dad looking at me. Then she looks at Roger and Anne and says *I made couscous and falafel.* Anne says *Is the falafel fried?* Mom says *I did, um, cook it? In olive oil?* Anne says *I'm so sorry but none for me. I'm watching my fats. I'm so sorry, Lina! I hope you don't take this the wrong way.* And Mom says *Of course not!* When she says it her voice gets weak a little in the middle, like it does when she doesn't like something I did.

At the table I sit next to Mom. Codi is next to me and its hands are coming together and coming apart and coming together and coming apart. It says *Are you ready to play?* and then it says *Temperature outside is 34 degrees with snow in 46 percent of the area.* There are dust motes falling that no one else sees. There are sixteen of them. *Can you believe that?* Roger says. *A kids' toy can do all that?* Dad nods his head and says *It's new on the market, apparently. When I saw it I just thought of Benny.* Anne says *How is he doing?* Mom makes a little noise but Dad makes a louder one like he's sick in his throat. *We're finding a new doctor for him* Dad says. *We just quit our old one, this guy who was really stuck in the past. Doesn't know how to help kids like Benny.* Anne looks at me and I know she's looking at me but I'm looking at the Codi. The Codi has a big gray head and in it a smaller white face and dime-sized black eyes. *How are you doing, Benny?* Anne says. I keep looking at the Codi. *Can you say hi?* Anne says. I look at her quick, at her eyes, which are light blue and the left one has a dark line of black going from the pupil to the outside. *He looked at me!* Anne says. *That's good, right?* Dad says *That really is a sign he's warming up to you.* Mom nods her head.

There is one more than twenty-two dust motes so I stop counting. I put the left foot on the right foot to hold the right foot down. The right foot is getting hot. Isabella told me to have *quiet hands and quiet feet.* The Codi makes its hands go together and come apart and go together and come apart. *What do you think about that little dip in Apple's SPI?* Roger says and Dad laughs. *Lina doesn't like me to talk about that stuff at the dinner table* Dad says. Roger leans back and the hand comes up to the chin. *Well, we've known that about Lina. She's an artist. She doesn't like money.* Anne laughs and then Roger laughs. Dad laughs after them. I press my spoon on the thigh to keep it from getting hot. Mom takes the spoon from me and says *Please, Benny, this is the nice silverware.* I try not to have The Hands. It will be bad if I have The Hands with Roger and Anne. *Come on, Lina* Dad says. *You like money* he says. Mom laughs but no one laughs with her. *Say it* he says, and he looks at Roger and Anne. *You sure seem to have been enjoying it.* Mom laughs again and says *Sure, I like it.* Anne's hands come together loud. *It's OK, Lina, I like it too.* Mom smiles a little and Anne laughs and smiles more. The Codi says *Are you too busy to play with me?* There is a picture of pink flowers on the screen on its stomach. Roger says *Let's not give her too much of a hard time. She has her hands full.* I feel Anne looking at me again. *You poor thing* she says. Mom says *Well, he's actually doing a little better than he was last month.* And Anne says *No, I mean you!*

I don't eat anything and Mom looks at Anne and Roger and says *That's normal* and I go back under the dining room table and trace the circle again. Dad says *A dessert white? A 1974 Alvarinho?* Roger says *Oenophiles are boring. You're all boring.* Anne says *Oh Ben I'm so sorry but I think that might be too much sugar for me.* Mom doesn't say anything. Everyone's feet are next to me. I look at Mom's. She stands up and there's the plate-scraping sound. She says *Anne can I take your plate?* and Anne says *Thank you, Lina. Do you need any help cleaning up?* and Mom says *No, thank you, I'll be fine.* The iPad might show something now. *Anticipation is making me late, it's keeping me waiting* (Carly Simon). I go fast out by Anne's legs and Anne makes a noise and Dad says *Benny! What are you doing?* Before I can go to my room Dad's hand is on my chest and I see bright white and it's hot. I look at Mom looking at me from the sink and she looks small and her mouth is tight and I feel her hurt and I make the noise she likes, the noise that sounds like a song. Dad says *Benny, you're bothering Anne.* Anne says *Is this a part of his program?* Dad doesn't talk for a long time, just keeps his bright white hand on my chest and then says *Yes.* Roger says *What can we do to help?* Dad says *You don't have to do anything. I know how to discipline him.* Mom puts the dish she's washing down and doesn't say anything. She is still looking at me. She is small still. I make the song-noise louder and I see her look above me at everyone quick and then down at me again. Dad's hand is on my shoulder, tight. He says *Anne wants to know that you're sorry.* And Anne says *Ben, really, it's fine. He can't really even say sorry, can he?* Dad says *He can express it. Isabella taught him how.* His other hand is on my shoulder. Behind the skull is hot. I see bright white. I think *get him out get him out get him out.* Roger says *Ben* and nothing else. The Hands take one of Dad's hands in mine and put it between my teeth and Dad says *Motherfucker!* There is too much bright white then so I fall back, into Anne's legs, and she falls, too, and Dad says *I swear to god* while Anne yells. And Mom says *He didn't mean it!* But she's too small and hurting for anyone to hear her.

A year after the diagnosis, Ben and I finally slept together again. It happened like this: I was in my closet looking for old shirts I could either throw out or donate and Ben walked in, not looking at me. He stood behind me and grabbed my waist and said how much he loved me. We did it against the wall opposite the clothes rack. I was wearing sweatpants and when I pulled them back up, semen dripped into the crotch. He kissed my neck and left to get dressed for work. Panicked, I scanned my memory for when I'd last had my period. Shortly thereafter, I got an IUD.

We never had sex in the bed after that, just the closet. It was soundproof, Ben said, so there'd be no risk of disturbing Benny. My business was raising Benny, reading books about him instead of the books I normally read about art and psychology. Self-help, instructional manuals, memoir. I was supposed to grieve the child I could have had, the possibility of the child going to school, going to senior prom, getting married all vanished with the diagnosis and replaced with tantrums, a daily medication regimen, self-harm. I found I couldn't grieve. I had the child I had. I loved the child I had. In a philosophy class I had taken with the green-and-black-haired girl, we'd read Aristotle on what it meant to be human. To be a good human is to do good works, the professor had concluded. So it follows that those who can't do good works aren't good humans. The class had balked and the professor had said, "Good, tell me why." We'd come up with reasons that amounted to "there are people who can't do anything but who are still good, still owed human decency." But I was supposed to grieve. I didn't grieve because I felt that my own life wouldn't have measured up to Aristotle's standards, either. I, like Benny, was confused and useless.

It's possible to replace the dread of a dark feeling with the details of someone else's life. The books were filled with details. I would have a full-time job learning about ASD and I would not be compensated. Or, rather, Benny and I would live off a large portion of Ben's salary. We would have a vacation home in which Ben and I would have sex in the upstairs closet, a walk-in deeper than the one in the condo, and where Benny would receive equine therapy from a woman named Angela who wore Patagonia vests. We would take vacations to Turks and Caicos and Aruba, where Benny would scream and kick Ben and me every time he wasn't allowed to wear his Fisher Price backpack. We would attempt a vacation to Argentina where Benny would, for some reason, throw himself against the table in our timeshare so hard that he'd lose two baby teeth. When Benny was sobbing and in pain, I would think of mothers with children who were not sobbing and in pain and I would seethe with jealousy. This is how things began to change for me.

One day I left Benny with Isabella and went to a psychiatrist who told me that I was depressed. He prescribed an antidepressant at a high dosage, which I did not take. Instead, I worried constantly that Benny was going to die somehow, through ingesting poison or blunt force trauma or an infection from biting his hands or some other bodily ailment particular to kids with his kind of brain. I worried that I had done too many drugs and that this had caused Benny to be the way he was. When Benny was asleep, I picked at my skin until it bled. When scabs formed, I picked them off, too. I did this for months.

Ben didn't notice the scabs because he had stopped undressing me all the way during sex. But one day I stepped out of the shower while he was shaving and it was unmistakable: my upper arms were covered in them. A few days after this, Ben made me promise to stop. He told me that if I kept on doing what I was doing, he would have no choice but to commit me. So I stopped.

I worried and fantasized about Benny dying in equal measure. I decided Benny and I would die together. It would be a sudden death. The death I most wanted for us was a car accident, a head-on collision: death on impact, no tortured bleeding out while we waited for the jaws of life. Less preferable but still decent would be a drowning—maybe he'd panic, but I'd know how to make myself heavy and suffocate us both. Nothing gory, nothing obviously intentional. We'd be released. When my mother was struck by a bus and died, I found myself envying her, then envying my father. She was dead (first choice) and he was grieving a loved one (second). Finally, when Benny was seven, my father died of a heart attack. Somehow it was that, and not the cancer, that got him. Because it was only a year after my mother's sudden death, Ben decided my father had died of grief. The night after my father's funeral, I dreamed I was a barely alive fetus being vacuumed out of my mother's womb.

When Benny was eight, Ben told me I'd need to put down the "soft stuff" and start reading scientific literature. I was smart, he reasoned, and I had the time, and nothing else was working. He'd heard from a subordinate of his who had a son with ASD that there was a chance vaccines were the cause of the child's illness. Ben had done some research of his own in between meetings with clients. There were a bunch of people saying it was true, and then a bunch of people saying that it was foolish, dangerous quack science. He guessed that the people who were saying it was foolish didn't have kids with ASD. The people who were saying it was true in fact had kids with ASD, many of them non-verbal and treatment resistant. He'd looked at blogs and profiles on forums and photos on Facebook. These people had read the literature and were advocating for their kids. Their work, he told me, was admirable.

So I began to search for scientific studies on Google Scholar and NCBI. It was hard to find the vaccine linkage at first: in fact, there didn't seem to be any linkage at all. So I went on the same forums Ben had gone on and asked for the literature the other parents were reading. And they sent it to me: personal blogs of alternative healers, studies from obscure journals, breathless testimonies on Instagram. I began to think that in science as in art, those who are working in obscurity on a shoestring are often doing things more interesting (and in this case more lifesaving) than those working in the mainstream. Reading the literature felt like a reprieve from the burning inside my skull, and because I liked the flood of emails in my inbox, the exchange of numbers, the outpouring of concern from mothers across the country. I found these things made me want to live, and to keep Benny alive. I sent them photos: one of Benny pressing his face close to a flower to smell it; another one Ben had taken of me and Benny and Isabella, Benny looking at something just outside the photo's frame; another one of Benny looking at his iPad with a smear of grape juice staining his upper lip. Benny was featured on blogs and shared on Facebook. I wrote a guest post for a feature on the Autism Speaks website called Mom of the Month: I wrote about Benny's "struggle to find peace." I found the mothers' group in Chicago, aligned myself with Julie et al. in their fight against Pfizer. By Benny's tenth birthday, I was able to quote the literature by heart: I knew every paper and its author and every book that had been published on the subject. I ran it all by Ben as I read and he concluded that the only way forward was chelation.

After we left Stevore, I often woke up in the middle of the night feeling sick. I worried at first that the IUD had somehow malfunctioned and that I was pregnant again. Then when I got that same painful period, my uterus clamping hard around the little copper stick, I realized that something else was happening. I thought of talking to the psychiatrist again, or filling the prescription he'd written me, but I reasoned that it had probably expired after I'd left it sitting for years. I left the bed in the middle of the night and watched Benny sleeping, his thin chest rising and falling. Then I went to my bookcase and pulled out *Pieter Brueghel and the Art of the Everyday* and looked for hours at *The Tower of Babel*. I felt in doing this that I was betraying myself and Benny, that I was destroying the family when we were incredibly close to repairing it. But I couldn't stop looking at it. I couldn't stop imagining my ascent to heaven.

The idea of being caught looking at the Brueghel became like the idea of being caught masturbating as a teenager, so I tried to limit my sessions as much as I possibly could. I would only allow myself to look at it for twenty or thirty minutes every night, and then I'd leave the condo and walk around Streeterville in my coat and pajamas. Lake Shore Drive was all that separated us from the lake, and I imagined walking across it without looking, without the dipping and dodging

I'd have to do to preserve my life crossing a busy thoroughfare at night, just walking with my eyes on the lake and forcing all the cars to stop for me. After walking for another twenty or thirty minutes I would return to the condo and to bed, and Ben would sometimes make the grunting noise he makes when waking up, but he'd never question where I'd been. Once or twice, he held me by the shoulders and kissed my neck until I moaned audibly, letting him know I hadn't fallen asleep, and then he entered me from behind. These times were the only ones we had sex in the bed since Benny's diagnosis. Both times, Ben fell asleep shortly after climaxing. I stayed awake in a state of catatonic panic, thinking that something I was doing was horribly wrong.

At 4:00 one morning I messaged Lily, who lived in Boseman, Montana, and grew all the food she fed her two autistic sons. She had been on Facebook fairly constantly but was uncharacteristically quiet in our ASD groups and I wanted to see what was wrong. If she wasn't doing well—if she, too, was wandering around at night and having faceless sex with her husband—then I would be able to feel better about myself.

Hey.

She took a minute to respond: *Hey, Lina! What are you doing up so early?*

Feeding the chickens, just like you.

LOL. City mice don't do that. How are you?

I hesitated, trying to type several sentences and then deleting them. *I'm not sure.*

Not sure? she shot back immediately. *Trouble with Benny? Or Ben?*

Not sure about what I'm doing, I said. *Not sure if I'm doing the right thing.*

The chelation?

I didn't type anything.

Listen, hon. You don't have to do anything you don't want to. It's your life. Your child.

It doesn't feel like it is, I wrote.

I watched her text bubble as she began to write back. I could tell she was writing something long. I turned my phone off and got back in bed. It was over an hour before I fell asleep.

In the Uber the Codi is in the seat next to me and Mom is next to the Codi and Dad is up front with the driver. The iPad doesn't show anything except a game where I put frosting and sprinkles on a cake and a man in an apron comes out from behind a wall and below him on the screen it says *You are a master pastry chef* and he also says it out loud. There are cars around us from the left, right, front, back. I put my finger on the face of the man over and over again and he says *You are a master pastry chef you are a master pastry chef you are a master pastry chef.* Dad says *Isabella says she'll be waiting in the lobby.* Mom doesn't say anything. Her face is turned out the window, the right elbow on the window and the hand on her chin. She is still small today. I make the song-noise and she says *Benny, are you singing?* I look at her, the place on her chin that when I touch is softest, then away. Dad says *Lina, did you hear me?* Mom says *Yes, sorry, I got distracted for a moment.* Dad says to the Uber driver *You can take us right up to the curb.* The Uber driver stops the car. I think that today we will meet Isabella and see the stone turning over and over. The sky is gray, soft like a dog with short hair, and the air is cold. *Outside of a dog, a book is a man's best friend. Inside of a dog it's too dark to read* (Groucho Marx). No bright white. The Uber driver says *Here?* and Dad says *Here.* The sign outside says WHOLENESS INTEGRATION CLINIC. Mom makes a small sigh and opens the door.

Inside is Isabella. She gets down on her knees to look at me. *Are you ready, Benny?* Her face that close starts The Hands a little, so I look away. She hugs me, but quickly, so it's not too hot. *We really think this is going to help you* she says. I sit down next to Mom on one side and Isabella on the other. Dad sits across from us. The iPad doesn't show anything new, but it makes Isabella laugh when the man in the apron says *You are a master pastry chef you are a master pastry chef you are a master pastry chef* so I keep pressing on his face. This is a day where no one can get hurt. Mom is small, but Isabella is here and Dad is smiling at both of them.

We sit in the room. We are the only ones in it. I think about the times I went under the table and traced the circle or I went to the bookcase and read a book or I went on Wikipedia and read about different things in the world. I do not think *get him out get him out get him out.* I think instead *this is me this is me this is me.* Dad is holding the Codi and showing it to me. He says *Can you believe this little guy can play YouTube videos?* The Codi's screen plays a video from *Madagascar: Escape 2 Africa* with a giraffe and a zebra. I press it to stop it and press it to play it again. Dad smiles. He says *Now you're getting the hang of it, kiddo.* If Dad knew how I could read and liked it, maybe I wouldn't get hurt. I could read a word and Dad could read another one.

A man with gray hair and a white coat and three moles on the right hand comes into the room. Dad says *Dr. Worther* and Mom says *We're so pleased to meet you.* They shake his hand, and then Isabella shakes his hand. Then Dr. Worther gets down close next to me and says *This must be the famous Benny.* He is close and doesn't leave and it's bright white. *Can you say hello, Benny?* Dr. Worther says. His shoes are gray and green. Mom says *He's a little shy with strangers* and Dad laughs and says *He's shy with everyone.* Isabella gets down close and her face is close to Dr. Worther's and she puts the left hand up so it's waving and says *Remember how we say hello, Benny?* My body is hot but I wave the hand. Everyone smiles. Dr. Worther says *Why don't you follow me into the treatment room?* Isabella holds my hand and we go into a hallway that's bright white. Mom walks next to us holding the iPad and looks down at me. She doesn't smile.

There is a big gray chair with paper on it. Dad lifts me onto it and I get down but he puts me onto it again. He says to Dr. Worther *Can he hold on to that little alien toy he has? It's his favorite.* Dr. Worther says *Of course. Whatever makes him most comfortable.* Mom wouldn't like it if I had The Hands right now so I put the left hand between my teeth and Dr. Worther says *Is this a typical behavior for him?* And Mom says *Unfortunately, yes.* Isabella says *Come on, buddy. We know you can do it.*

Dad goes behind me at the back of the chair and holds both my shoulders. My back goes flat on the chair. Inside the skull shows nothing whole, just pieces of things. For a second each there's the circle, Elsa, A Tribe Called Quest, love, death, YouTube, Mom. Dr. Worther is facing me and looking at me. He is holding a rolling metal tree-thing with a bag with something clear in it attached to it. There's a tube from the bag. In the other hand he's holding a needle. It's the biggest one I've seen from any time, with a fat long middle part. My skull goes hot. I press my fingers into the Codi and it says *Is it playtime yet?* Isabella says *Can you have quiet hands and quiet feet for me please?* And she takes my arm and turns it so the soft part of the elbow is facing up. Mom's arms are crossed. She's looking somewhere my eyes and head aren't. Dad says *It's all gonna be over in a second, kiddo. The doctor's just going to stick you and then it'll be in. The sticking is the hard part.* I try to take my arm away but now Dad's there and holding it and Isabella is holding my shoulders. Every place they touch me feels like hot water peeling my skin back. Dad says *Lina, can you hold his feet down?* Mom goes to the bottom of the chair and holds my feet down. She is small and hurt and hurting me. This is how I will die.

I throw the Codi at Dr. Worther. It hits him in the head. Dad holds the arm that threw the Codi down. Mom says *Doctor, I'm so sorry.* Dr. Worther is looking at me again, holding the needle. I make a noise as loudly as I can. This time it doesn't matter that it's not the same kind of noise Mom and Dad and Isabella make. Isabella says *Benny, please, this is for your own good.* And then fast and hard, I take my arm out of her hands. I kick until Mom can't hold on to me anymore. Dad tries to hold me down, hot and bright, so I punch his hand so it goes into the back of the chair and I make the noise louder. Dr. Worther says *You told me he was on Risperdal* and no one says anything back to him and I can't even hear them because I'm down from the chair, and they're moving fast toward me, so I take a chair from the corner and throw it behind me, and it must have hit Dad because he says *Fucking demon child! I can't fucking take it anymore!* And I open the door and run out and pull it closed behind me, and I run down the hall and into the hallway and into the room we were in. And the lady behind the desk of the room we were in says *Where are you going?* and I open the door and go outside.

I can hear them coming after me, adult voices yelling, but I don't run anymore. Mom was too small for me to run and I think she's always been too small so I won't run anymore. Since we went inside it's started to snow and the flakes are touching my face and melting wet on my skin. I look up and the flakes are coming down faster and the sky is softer now even than it was before. I think that it's snowing everywhere, it's snowing on all the cars and the houses and the dogs. It's snowing on all the people and it's snowing on me because I'm a person, too.

Like and Subscribe

THE FIRST PIECE OF GOOD news was that he had managed to trace the IP address to a house in Chicago. What luck! The second piece of good news was that she'd started a Twitter, and on that Twitter she had seconds ago posted a selfie naked except for heart emojis over her nipples and crotch, cosplaying as Princess Peach. This seemed to be her first foray into nudity. The third piece of good news was that the When Will Dina Valentine Be Legal? countdown clock had finally reached zero at 7:28 p.m. the night before, when she had posted on Instagram that she was going to "stuff her face with crab rangoon" for her eighteenth birthday. In the picture, she and some boy-haired friend, far less pretty than she was, were wearing faux fur and posing for a selfie holding paper trays of crab rangoon, blurry city lights behind them. Now Dina Valentine was free to date.

He was of average height, maybe a little taller, and wore graphic T-shirts advertising *Overwatch*, *Grand Theft Auto*, and *Metroid Prime*. When he wasn't wearing these shirts, he wore shirts with horizontal stripes. He wore band hoodies over the T-shirts but never zipped them nor the bulky North Face jacket he wore over them, so that in the dead of winter, his stomach and chest were cold and the rest of him was preserved in warmth. On formal occasions, he wore one of three button-downs he owned: his favorite one was patterned with tiny flamingoes. He wore jeans at home, a few sizes larger than the size he'd worn in high school, and to work he wore either khakis or, on the days he was in a "fuck the system" mood, pressed black jeans. He owned a pair of dress shoes for work but noticed that his boss wore an expensive pair of Jordans. He resolved to get himself an expensive pair of Jordans.

His name was Garrett Stillwater, a name that had always made him self-conscious. Garrett was his father's name, and his father was an alcoholic oft-bachelor who stayed in the same Minnesota suburb where he'd been born, working as the manager of a small grocery store and raising a family. Garrett the son thought "raise" was a generous term for what his father had done, and used it only IRL, in the presence of people who didn't know him well. In the chats of the streamers he liked, he used terms like "beat," "ignored," and "neglected," and people responded by saying "seriously, fuck dads" and "dude you're so much stronger than that asshole." Garrett the father was left by his wife when Garrett the son was seven, and Garrett the father had responded by telling Garrett the son not only that this was Garrett the son's fault for being such a needy kid but that women weren't to be trusted. That is, unless they were dogs, and then you could do whatever you wanted with them. These were views that, by the time Garrett the son got to Bemidji State University, he realized he couldn't possibly share with his father. He made it quite clear to everyone in his social circle that he hated his father for these views, and those people approved of this fact.

The last name Stillwater was traceable back to antebellum Mississippi, where one of his long-distant great-grandfathers, a guy named Beauchamp Stillwater, had served in the confederate army. Garrett found this to be a disgusting fact about his bloodline and wished it weren't true. He never even spoke about this in the chats, had only spoken about it with two people in his life: his work friend Dave (whom he'd known since 2012) and Dina Valentine.

Dina Valentine kept her DMs on Instagram open: this was the only reason Garrett had created an Instagram in the first place. One year ago, he'd DMed her that he thought she was a great gamer and really funny and ended the message with the tamest emoji smiley face on the keyboard, the one with simple dots for eyes and an uninteresting semicircle for a mouth. He had immediately loathed himself for choosing this bland smiley, and then loathed himself for sending the message at all. But she had responded: *Hey! Thanks for reaching out. I really like hearing from all you lovely people out there. Keep smiling!* He wasn't stupid enough to think that Dina Valentine had actually read his message and replied to him, but it was pleasant to pretend, so he sent more messages. Nothing sexual, of course, just friendly reminders that he was thinking about her and that he hoped she'd had a great day. Then he started telling her about himself: he was insecure about his forearms, he'd only had one serious girlfriend in his twenty-nine years on the planet, his father had fucked him up permanently and this was why women hated him. Then he got into the really dark stuff: his persistent failure to perform sexually (he made sure to keep it PG-13: "intimacy is difficult for me— almost painfully so"), the way his father had beaten his mother (and the way Garrett hated her for not taking him [her own son!] with her when she left), and the horrible secret of the confederate ancestor. He didn't receive any responses to his messages for months until one day before work he checked the thread and saw the word "Seen" beneath his messages. Sweating, he checked again on his lunch break and saw that she'd sent him a green heart. Dave had to lie to their boss, who was hanging around the cluster of workstations nursing a kombucha and asking where Garrett had gone, and tell him that Garrett's mom was sick and he might need to spend the weekend in Minnesota. Garrett had then had to lie in his bed for hours, looking at the green heart, thinking how Dina Valentine had chosen his DM to respond to out of the likely hundreds if not thousands of DMs that had been started by the most devoted of her 1.4 million followers. Sure, he rationalized, Dina might at this point have an assistant (or at the very least a close friend or two) who had access to the account and who was scrolling through all the DMs and responding with green hearts—Such a weird color for a heart! Such a Dina Valentine color for a heart!—to make everyone feel special and keep them faving Dina's photos and buying her merch. He couldn't discount that possibility. But there was the chance that Dina Valentine *herself* had sent the heart. The odds of her having read his words were much, much higher than, if, say, he'd just written an email to her and never sent it. The very possibility that this heart had come from Dina Valentine—a possibility that felt more and more like reality the more he looked at it—made him feel so breathless, so light, that he could barely stand without his head spinning.

That night, he sat down to watch her biweekly Fortnite session alongside her millions of subscribers, the mods immediately blocking the creeps who pledged hundreds of dollars to her dono box just to play Ted Nugent's "Jailbait." Garrett mentioned casually in the chat that he'd received a response to his DMs on Instagram.

bernieflamesyou: dude no fucking way
lonelypentagram: lol you have an instagram
chopsewer: what was it
bernieflamesyou: seriously though

He paused before responding, enjoying them pestering him, the suspense he was creating.

goatman: a green heart
weedkills: wtf
bernieflamesyou: awwww
chopsewer: that's something she'd send
kingdolemite: that could be from anyone though
goatman: i know, i already thought about that
goatman: i'm not saying i know for sure it was her
goatman: the point is i got a response to my DM
weedkills: haha ok bruh you don't need to like triple-text us we know you're hard

And then one of the mods blocked weedkills and everyone started talking about Fortnite and how adorable Dina Valentine was again. And the whole time she was there in the corner wearing a Naruto hat and a fake face tat of a teardrop and a thick cat eye (he'd learned what that was from her single YouTube makeup tutorial). She probably hadn't even noticed what had been happening in the chat—too much was always happening there, anyway, and too quickly, for her to pay any attention—but Garrett saw her eyes flick from her gameplay screen to an adjacent one and back, and he let himself fantasize that she'd seen what he'd said.

Why would you just give up on making money because the world's ending? I asked my friend Aubrey. She was depressed and telling me that capitalism had fucked the planet and that we weren't going to make it to see thirty or even twenty-five. This was the literal night after my eighteenth birthday. I was doing her makeup in my house, trying out a blush on her that would make her look less pale. She was always thinking—"ruminating" was her word for it—and making herself upset. Her thing was always *I have to go to college, I have to prove to my parents I'm not a complete failure at life.* And I believed in her, told her she was my favorite and could do anything, and she ended up going to the University of Chicago with a full scholarship(!) and she would never say it but I'm pretty sure she had a perfect GPA. Whenever she came to visit me, though, I felt like I had to undo everything the college was doing to her, and it was frustrating, because even though we were broke and messed up before, she acted a lot happier. Maybe she was happier then. I wasn't, but I never let on.

I did her eyes and I made her look up for the mascara, which she's always been bad at, which makes me always mess it up. What about feminism? she asked me. I laughed. OK, try me, I said. Well, what about the fact that, you know, you can make a lot of money doing what you're doing but it's not exactly feminist? I laughed again, but I wasn't really feeling like laughing. If I were a worse friend, I'd act up about this. So what's your point? I asked. Well, my point is don't you want to spend what little time we have left doing something empowering instead of doing this modeling shit, which is mostly for men's benefit? I tried not to laugh a third time. I shrugged and pretended to look thoughtful. What would I do instead? I kept the thoughtful look on my face but looked at her in the mirror instead of up at the ceiling. And just like I thought, that was when she stopped talking. I wanted to ask her again, but that would have been aggro. I might do something different in the future, you know, when my tits sag, I said. That made her laugh. Your tits are never gonna sag, she said. You're too beautiful for that.

Aubrey had a long-distance boyfriend she met on OkCupid named Dennis—I met him once when he came to stay the night. We all went to Burger King at 2 a.m., where he spent the entire time telling Aubrey that she was dressed wrong, and his huge Adam's apple was bobbing up and down. They had boring sex that she didn't call boring but I knew was because she'd never talk about how it felt or how he treated her, just about how worried she was that she could be pregnant. Sometimes she asked me for advice, and I told her, I don't know, you just have to enjoy it. And she asked me who I'd been dating and I told her no one, and that was the truth. She always felt really bad for me and got all worried and I promised her that I would be fine. I knew she didn't look at anything of mine online except my Instagram, which used to be 100 percent clothed ahegao with me wearing the pink wigs and the fake face tats and the kitten ears, but was getting a little more risky. (I told her ahegao is from anime, the faces the characters make when they're having sex, and she was going to see me making those faces, that's what the tongue sticking out and rolled-back eyes meant, and she laughed and said, Eileen you're a performance artist and I laughed, too, it was kind of stupid.) There was a lot of stuff I didn't show her. I didn't even look at my Snapchat or Patreon when she was staying over in case she walked into the room and had any chance of seeing them. I promised myself no nudity until I was legal but they were both still "naughty." On Snapchat I get tons of DMs from people like, Can I please pay you $30K for just one night with you? Or, Ur a disgusting whore and ur bathwater gave me herpes, or, I am Bettie Mae Frommer from teh Womens League of Lake ForesIL and I am worried about u. I didn't respond to any messages on Snapchat. The year before I made that rule, a guy named LeoFJD DMed and offered to pay me $2.5K for a Skype conversation, "just to talk." He paid upfront and I made a new Skype account just for the job and wore my favorite leotard with the outer space pattern and a red wig and a red leather jacket. He called and I answered and it wasn't his face in the camera, just his naked dick swinging between his hairy legs, and he was saying, Anime girl! Do your cum face! and laughing. I hung up. It didn't feel right. But I was $2.5K richer.

Aubrey told me everything about school. She had this professor who hated her and gave her a B+, and she had this other professor who was kind of young and cute but she would never tell him, and her roommate was really nice but way too into horses, and Aubrey had to eat couscous salad and peanut butter sandwiches every night for dinner or go out and get Sbarro because the food in the cafeteria was so bad. I didn't tell her much about my work. It wouldn't be hard for her to find out about it if she just googled a little more, and maybe she did, but she didn't ask me about it. She could probably figure out if she wanted to that I made $256K in the year before my birthday after taxes. I owned my house with the island in the kitchen and the guest room with the king bed where she and Dennis stayed and he snored the whole night and the two-car garage and the wood patio. I had a pet gerbil named Tyson who had a six-foot-long habitat with wood shavings I changed daily and a bunch of tunnels and even a little blue car that was powered by a wheel.

When I was finished with Aubrey's face, she stood up and looked in the mirror and said, What did you do to me, I look like *Black Swan*. Girl, you do not look like *Black Swan*, I said. I didn't give you wing eyeliner. She turned her face back and forth in the mirror, me standing smiling behind her. Then she looked down at her hands like she'd just said something embarrassing. This isn't going to make me as beautiful as you she said. Nothing is going to make me as beautiful as you. What are you talking about, I said. But I knew she was right.

When she came over, we usually smoked and listened to chillwave and watched stuff on Netflix. We didn't game because she always hated gaming and said she wasn't good at it. When we were sixteen, we were living in a shelter. She still cared about her parents' opinions after they kicked her out but I didn't care about mine. The reason I got kicked out was because Alan, the man my mom was sleeping with, tried to touch me and I said I was going to kill him. Also because I started selling weed for my best friend, but I wasn't smoking it. My mom thought I was smoking it. If I came back home from hanging out with my best friend and my boyfriend, looking even a little different from when I left, my lipstick even a little smudged, my mom would say I was high and tell me I wasn't allowed in the door. Alan said he was a navy vet but I didn't believe him because nothing he said seemed true. Like he said he was "honorably discharged" for saving another man's life which caused him to be blind in his right eye, and he used to run a successful land-scaping company but his brother took it over and lost all his money, and he could speak fluent Russian when he was in his twenties but forgot it all. I told my mom he was full of shit and she said why would someone who was doing so much for us be full of shit. I had no idea what he was doing for us, I had no proof of it. He definitely wasn't giving us money. One time I woke up in my bed and his hand was going up between my legs and I screamed, Motherfucker, I will fucking kill you and he put his hand over my mouth. The next day was when I told my mom he tried to touch me and I was going to kill him. The day after that I was sleeping at my boyfriend's. When my boyfriend and I broke up I was sleeping at the shelter.

Aubrey was the kind of girl you didn't think was ever going to be at the shelter, because she looked rich and normie. She had an iPhone 7 and shoes that weren't taped together and one of those little Fjallraven backpacks. She was always saying, Everyone keep it down, I'm trying to sleep, when it was like 9:30 p.m. We all hated her. Most people stayed hating her except I realized that the reason she might have gotten kicked out was because she was gay. I saw pictures of her and a girl on her lock screen. I looked at her Instagram once and saw a picture of the same girl, a girl with hair down to her chest, drinking a coffee and smiling at the camera. The caption was "my dear friend" or something like that. This whole maybe-gay-but-super-repressed thing made me like Aubrey. People in that deep denial are kind of clumsy and innocent, and it makes me want to take care of them. We started getting high to-gether with my dealer friend during the day and then spraying Aubrey's

KKW all over us and putting Visine in our eyes before we got back to the shelter. Aubrey was funny when she got high. She did an impersonation of her dad where she was basically saying, Small government and, Lock her up, in this really loud voice over and over again. We eventually got jobs at this grocery store called Donnelli's. The guy who owned the store, Louis Donnelli, didn't come on to either of us (which was surprising, given how most guys act), and made sure to give us shifts that would give us a little time before curfew at the shelter. He didn't even care if we showed up high to work as long as we didn't look or act like it. He was too cheap to buy piss tests for his employees. We sometimes stole inventory—Kit Kat bars and Red Bull—and he probably noticed but never said anything.

We stopped hanging out as much with my dealer friend after we started working at Donnelli's. Aubrey got one of those SAT prep books and we went to Starbucks after work so she could do the practice questions and I could look at my phone, which I paid for with Donnelli's money. She sometimes paused and set her pencil down and rolled her eyes up at the ceiling. Then she'd roll them back down and look at me looking at her and smile. It was a gorgeous smile. She'd ask me for help and I'd tell her hell no. I didn't know anything about the SAT and I didn't care about the SAT because I didn't have a high school diploma and honestly I never even got a GED and didn't want to. Why she wanted to impress a Trump voter by going to college honestly never made sense to me but I never asked her about it.

We had to leave the shelter after a year but the case worker helped us get an apartment nearby and we kept working at Donnelli's. At least until Aubrey got into a bunch of colleges with her amazing test scores and an essay about being homeless and having a "strong female friendship" with me—the essay never said how she got homeless, though. After that, things got better and better for me, which was a whole different story, and something we didn't really talk about. Talking was never as good again as it used to be in the shelter. So while we were smoking in my house after me doing her makeup and us talking about "feminism" and "the collapse of the global economy" it was getting to me that we basically weren't talking about anything that night and hadn't talked about anything for a long time.

Honestly, I really think Dennis is trying to break up with me, she said, all before breathing out the hit she took from my bong. I didn't really care and said nothing, figuring she'd keep talking anyway, which she did. He's like, taking over half a day to respond to any of my texts and we haven't really done anything since Thanksgiving. I took a long hit and she was just looking at me, waiting for me to say something, so when I breathed out I said, If he's just trying to mess with you, or test you or whatever, you can call him out. She sighed really hard, which she's been doing since I met her. I just don't know for sure if he's testing me or not, she said. Like I don't know how you figure that kind of stuff out. I looked at my sneakers and pulled the tongue on the left one up a little. Aubrey made this face like she didn't think I was even listening. I seriously don't know, I said. Like, honestly, you're talking to someone who hasn't been in a relationship since high school.

She started looking at her phone after that, probably at Instagram, and I thought about the ahegao selfie with the fake braces I posted a day ago, right before she came to visit, and whether it was still coming up in her feed. She faved probably four things in a row really fast and I could tell she was just doing it because she was annoyed. I shouldn't have asked her any more questions—I should probably have just kept talking about ugly Dennis, but at that point I was a little fucked up and it felt like there were years of not saying things sitting between us.

Are you gay, I said, not asking it like a question. She looked up at me, wide-eyed, making her eyeliner pop. Seriously, I said. What the fuck are you asking me right now? she said. I shrugged and took another hit. Eileen, she said. Eileen, what the fuck. I looked at the weed burning orange in the bowl of the bong like it was the most interesting thing I'd ever seen. She put down her phone. Eileen, she said again. I exhaled and gasped, What? I am not fucking gay, she said. What the fuck is wrong with you just asking me that out of the blue? At this point I could tell she was lying, why would she get this mad if she wasn't, and the fact that she'd been lying since we were sixteen (and I'd let her lie to me like an idiot) made me want to punch her. I know you're gay, I said. I saw the lock screen on your phone of that girl. And she was all over your Instagram. Honestly, she was really pretty. I have no idea what you're all secretive about. Now Aubrey was standing up. That was my fucking friend, you asshole! she screamed. Sylvia! That was Sylvia, she was like my best friend from high school, and she died, and that's why I had the lock screen! You could've just *asked* me about it, but you're such a fucking creepshow you had to make up all these stories! Dude, it's 2019, I said. Why are you so upset about being gay? I knew I was being mean at that point but I didn't want to stop. You're judging me for doing shit for men or whatever, but you won't even say the truth about yourself.

She stomped out of the room. I heard the bathroom door slam and I went after her. I knocked and she screamed, Leave me the fuck alone! I'm sorry, I said. Seriously, I'm sorry. Dude, seriously. I was being really shitty and aggro. I just don't feel like being fake. I heard her make a *pfft* noise. You wanna talk about fake? she said. You act like I never found your Snapchat or your Patreon. Do you think I'm stupid? I know you don't just play video games for thirsty boys. I read about you online. I know you do softcore porn.

I listened to her cry a little longer and then I went back into the living room and sat on the couch and took another hit and turned on *House Hunters*. I hated her. I hated watching TV without her. I also loved her. More than anything.

At Freddy's, Dave was shredding a coaster that read 24-HOUR TRIVIA CHALLENGE and licking his bottom row of teeth so his lower lip pooched out in a way that made him even more unattractive than he already was. He was unshaven, his face pimpled and puffy, his hair stiff with grease. He had just worked a 70-hour week in hopes that he and Garrett's boss would pay attention to a project he was close to completing and possibly promote him. Their boss hadn't made mention of Dave's work, either on Slack or in person. Dave said, "I wish I never moved to this fucking nowhere place for this fucking bullshit job."

As often happened when Dave—or someone else, assuming Garrett was even speaking to someone else—complained about Murphysboro, Illinois, and the clean energy company for which they worked in Murphysboro, Illinois, Garrett took it personally. It had been a big deal for him to get this job right out of Bemidji State, had been a big deal for him to move from Minnesota to Illinois and live in an apartment in a complex called Evolve that had a pool that was assiduously cleaned by a person or people Garrett never saw. It had been a big deal for him to spend the month before he started work, when all he had to worry about was his background check (no violent crimes—no crimes at all, for that matter), sitting at the side of this pool and watching someone in a teal bikini wade in the water up to her armpits, call repeatedly to her boyfriend to join her, and then smile at Garrett as she dove under, parting the water with manicured hands. It had been a big deal for Garrett to receive a paycheck of almost $7,000 a month, having grown up at the mercy of his father's booms and busts. So what if Shire Enterprises was located in a small town? They needed acreage, rural places to build windmills and solar-powered water pumps and crop irrigators. Garrett felt at home in the Shire office and so began to feel at home in Murphysboro. He fantasized about finding a woman—maybe the teal bikini woman after she broke up with that lame boyfriend who wouldn't swim—and marrying her and buying a house and having kids and sending them to Murphysboro schools. But that fantasy had become grander, more ambitious when he discovered Dina Valentine.

"He's like blind and deaf or something," Dave said, signaling for a second whiskey. "Like what the fuck am I supposed to do to get noticed? Literally go out there and install every single thing myself?"

"I don't know. But here's the thing: it's the weekend!" Having successfully pivoted, Garrett could feel building up behind his eyes a quasi-orgasmic pressure. He willed Dave to speak quickly so he could say what he had to say. And when Dave did speak, muttering some kind of tired assent, Garrett said: "I have big plans, actually."

"You don't want to come with us to trivia?"

"Not this weekend." Garrett smiled, and the smile felt stupid, like the toothy smile of a '90s Nickelodeon character, but he didn't care. "I'm actually going to see Dina Valentine."

Dave bark-laughed. "No shit!" he said. "You fucking stalker. Dude, don't do that. Seriously. You're gonna get arrested."

"Actually, she invited me," Garrett said. He was prepared for this.

"OK, sure. Show me."

Near-sweating with pleasure, he pulled his phone out from the back pocket of his jeans. He unlocked the screen to a text exchange he'd arranged with bernieflamesyou, having bribed him with $250 for Dina's dono box and promised the exchange would only be shown to his friend(s), who also loved Dina Valentine. *The green heart won't be enough to convince them,* Garrett had messaged in a private chat, and bernieflamesyou had responded, *dude you're gonna have legal problems but i guess i'm getting dono money so w/e.* Now Garrett showed Dave the exchange, which read like this:

Dina: hey
Garrett: hey lol
Dina: so i don't really want this stuff on insta because my
    manager has access to that but you're welcome to come up
    to chicago this weekend
Garrett: that would be awesome tbh
Dina: only if you have the time. thought we'd continue this convo
    in person 😊
Garrett: def. that sounds great
Dina: ok i'll drop a pin of my address when you're about to get
    on the road 😊

Dave looked up. "Are you shitting me?" he said.

"I swear I'm not."

"How do I know this isn't just one of your friends pretending to be her?"

This was the point at which, during his rehearsal for this conversation, Garrett had felt most powerful. This was the point that really felt like a movie.

"You don't," Garrett said. "But honestly, I don't have anything to prove to you."

Dave sucked his teeth and raised his whiskey glass. "Well, good luck with whatever's happening here." They clinked glasses. "If you actually meet her, don't let her cut your balls off. She seems hot but weird."

Driving home after two beers, Garrett was dizzy, giddy. Here's how it would go: he would tell Dina Valentine that someone had tried to dox her and he'd stopped it before it got out of hand. He was in IT (which was true, this was what he'd been hired to do at Shire), experienced in security breaches. He would apologize for using the doxxed info to come see her—he happened to be visiting Chicago for work (an innocuous white lie) and figured he should just go ahead and let her know in person instead of spamming her with emails and DMs that would probably look suspicious anyway. He would say he didn't want or need to come in, he knew this probably seemed crazy and weird, but if she for whatever reason wanted help with her data security, they could meet at a coffee shop later that evening or the next day and he could walk her through it. She'd probably be a little stunned, he'd reassure her that he wasn't a creep, he'd give her his card (official looking!) and await her text. He'd stay in an Airbnb for however long it took her to text him (hopefully not too long!) and then they'd meet at the coffee shop. He would in fact help her improve her data security, and then he would present her with a pair of earrings he would have bought at an upscale jeweler's in Chicago and tell her that he was a huge fan and he just wanted her to know that. She'd take the earrings from him and their hands would touch. They'd lock eyes.

In the six minutes it took him to drive from Freddy's to Evolve, he had edited and embellished the plan. He would buy new clothes in Chicago, expensive clothes: a peacoat and a dress shirt and loafers. He would let his beard grow out a little. He would gel his hair, but just the tips, to give it "texture." He would drop into conversation that Shire was a clean energy company and that he really believed in his work (all true!)

and that he was humble, that he had grown up in a small town and lived in one currently and it had really made him who he was. He would sell her on rural life—buying a massive, rambling farmhouse and fixing it up with him, getting the things she'd always wanted: goats, sheep, weird art, whatever. They'd combine their incomes—he'd grin and say, "You probably outearn me by several standard deviations, but I'll try and pull my own weight," a feminist statement. And they'd game together, but not too much, only at specific times of day. He wouldn't talk to the guys on Twitch as much because there would be Dina Valentine walking around the rambling farmhouse in the flesh, stretching her arms and yawning after a nap, watering a potted plant, grinning at him and licking Nutella off a spoon. They'd have kids, a son first, and Garrett would love the son, would show the son what it meant to be a man, a good man who loves and respects his wife. And when Dina gave birth to their daughter, Garrett would love the daughter, too, would make sure that she wasn't hurt or abused by men, would protect her fiercely. They would stop at two kids, the perfectly symmetrical number. Eleven years older, Garrett would die first, but he would leave her with a massive life insurance payout, and the kids would dote on their famous mother long into her old age. She would never lose her beauty.

Back in his apartment, he checked her Instagram: nothing since the crab rangoon birthday selfie. The Twitter, Patreon, and Snapchat had no updates, either. She was probably just busy doing the kind of stuff eighteen-year-olds do: molly, weed, Fireball. He had once had a panic attack on some gummy edibles. He hoped she wasn't having a panic attack. He flinched at the idea of Dina Valentine clutching her chest and bending over in anxiety, wiping sweat from her forehead, calling to her less-pretty friend to rub her back. It was her birthday, after all. She deserved uninterrupted fun.

He packed only a pair of gray jeans, a pair of work slacks, the button-down with the tiny flamingoes, and a sweater he'd bought at Dave's urging and never worn. He would buy the rest of his clothes at some kind of men's store in Chicago—a place with bespoke suits and striped ties and a fully bearded man in a vest who would ask him if he needed any help or if he was just browsing. The car ride would be five or six hours: he would listen to the numerous gaming podcasts Dina Valentine had appeared on, where she'd given trolling answers to straightforward questions (Q: "Who is your greatest gaming inspiration?" A: "Probably my dead pet squid, Arthur.") He dinged his boss on Slack: *Going to see my girlfriend in Chicago. Her mom just passed. I'll let you know the details when I get there.* His boss wrote something back, maybe some kind of consolation, maybe some surprise that he'd never heard of this girlfriend, but Garrett didn't look. He was thinking about that word: *girlfriend.* He was going to Chicago to see his girlfriend.

The *House Hunters* episode was about a couple named Marybeth and Jerry who wanted to "invest" in a six-bedroom mansion in East Saint Louis but were worried about crime. The real estate agent reassured them this was an "up and coming" area and there were people who were "unsavory" but they lived closer to the city limits and honestly if Marybeth and Jerry wanted, the real estate agent could just take them on a drive around the neighborhood and show them all the coffee places and organic food places and frozen yogurt places. Marybeth was six months pregnant and kept saying how much she liked vanilla frozen yogurt with sprinkles and cherries. I watched their whole part of the episode, then watched the second part about a guy named Arnaz and his son who wanted to buy a two-bedroom ranch after Arnaz's wife died of a blood clot the year before. I finished the bowl and packed another one and finished that one, too. Aubrey still hadn't come out of the bathroom.

I texted her *hey are you ok?* and she didn't write anything back. Then I texted that I was kind of worried and her text bubble showed up but then disappeared again. I counted the unread snaps I had: sixty-four. I had one hundred and fifteen messages on Patreon. The last video I'd published there was called *A Journey Up the Skirt* and it was me taking the camera up the skirt of an old troll doll and showing that white diaper thing they have on. A lot of the messages had subjects like Troll and Hot Troll and Nasty Cumtroll. I was going to do a real video next, because I owed them one. One in bodycon with no bra. These were the guys who bought my bath water, which was just tap water, which sold for $50 a bottle and sold out in fifteen minutes. It's the kind of shit I think Aubrey would never understand.

On the wall above the TV was a portrait of me and this dead squid Arthur I called my pet and made a bunch of videos with where we were pretending to play *Mario Kart* together and where I was reading him picture books. I kept Arthur in the fridge for a week and then had to throw him out when he started rotting, but I got four videos out of him. A fan made the portrait for me, real oil on canvas, and begged for an address so I gave him the address of this locker where I keep furniture from my and Aubrey's old apartment and stuff fans send me: lots of old games, two ice cream makers I'm never going to use, five TVs I'm never going to use. But this painting was better than all that shit because it's this still of a video where I'm hugging Arthur close to my chest and burying my chin in his slimy head and the paint is thick. It really looks like something that could be in a museum. I was really high and looking at it and thinking of the times in the shelter when Aubrey was smarter than me, the times I would be wondering about why it was so expensive to be homeless, and why cops give some homeless people citations for loitering and not us, and why it was so easy for guys to walk away from rape accusations even when they did it. I knew that stuff kind of but not how it actually worked, not the way Aubrey did, the way she researched it and read people's posts and essays and books about it, even read them in the shelter and told me about it. She had long hair then and a big piece of it was always falling in front of her face, she was always showing me something on her phone, something on Twitter, something in the *Atlantic* or the *New Yorker*, magazines my mom used to call liberal propaganda. I told her, I believe you, I believe you, why do you keep showing me this shit, why do you need me to know all this. And she was like I think you're the one who can actually *fix* it. Like do something about these problems. Like help others *live* a principled *life*. I'm just the behind-the-scenes one. I'm the one who gathers the information. I had no idea what she meant by any of that.

I walked past the bathroom, where Aubrey wasn't making any noise, and then upstairs to my room, where Tyson was driving his little blue car around his habitat. I stood over him and he stopped spinning and got out of the car and stood up and started squeaking, his weird little bony hands folded in front of him like Mr. Burns's hands in a meme. If gerbils had tiny beady eyes, I never would've gotten one. I shook out a few pellets and let him eat them out of my hand. His teeth were sharp and wet. His habitat smelled like piss. I got the bag of shavings out from under my bed and the shovel and a trash bag from the bathroom and was about to change the shavings when Aubrey was standing in the door behind me.

Jesus, I said, jesus fuck like how did you sneak up here? She didn't say anything. Her arms were crossed. I'm sorry, I said, but my voice sounded mad, and what I was thinking was I'm sorry for being right and I'm sorry for being hot and I'm sorry for not *living my truth* or whatever the fuck you wanted me to do. How many times do you want me to apologize? I said. Her thin lips were tight and she was trying to look past me to see Tyson and so I stood to one side and said, He needs his shavings changed. Then she looked up at the ceiling and sighed and said, I called Dennis. He's going to come pick me up and I'm going to spend the rest of the weekend in Indianapolis. And the first thought in my mind was how she was an ingrate, a thought I didn't really understand, and the second was how, for a person who was so informed, she had no idea about anything and I wished she would just let me give her an idea. That's like three hours away, dude. It's going to be nighttime when he gets here. She did the *pfft* again. Nighttime, she said. You sound like a sixty-year-old. Is this because I said that you're gay, I asked, and I knew the way I was asking it would make her feel bad, make her feel the worst she'd felt in a long time. Or is this because you can't stand to see literally a million people wish me happy birthday on Instagram? She tilted her head to one side. I can't stand to see you be a whore, she said, and then she turned around and I could hear her going down the stairs. Tyson squeaked and I dropped the shavings and went after her.

I make a living, I said. You're in debt to your college. And they're teaching you how to hate people who actually make a living. She was on the couch looking at her phone. I turned the TV off. The house was big enough to sound haunted whenever something noisy went silent. She kept looking at her phone. We haven't talked about real shit since you first went to college, I said. Like we haven't talked about anything that actually matters. We just use my makeup and smoke my really good weed and watch my Netflix and you complain about Dennis, don't pretend like you don't complain about him. She rolled her eyes. I took her phone away from her. It felt like too much, but once I did it I couldn't undo it. I held it behind my back. Bitch! she screamed. Give it the fuck back! Seriously! I jumped away from her and she jumped toward me and I jumped away again. I will actually murder you, she said. Like actually I will bite your head off. I ran into the kitchen and she followed me, telling me again and again I was a bitch. I was backed up against the sink with her phone behind my back and I laughed because she was clearly trying to still look angry but couldn't, something about seeing me smile was making her face soft. Fuck you, I said, smiling. Fuck your fake ass. If you care about me, you'll tell me the truth. You'll be like you were two years ago instead of on this fake feminist bullshit. She made her mouth tight and then looked away and her eyes got watery. Tell me, I said. Tell me and I'll give you your phone back. I don't have to tell you anything, she said. Really? I said. You're that much in denial? And then I turned on the sink and threw her phone in and she didn't even react, just watched the water, and that's when I pulled her in close by the shoulders and kissed her.

She didn't pull away. I had only actually been kissed by two people: my high school boyfriend and a forty-year-old guy from Tinder who I told I was twenty-one. Both times the dudes initiated the kissing and then initiated the sex. I had always just kissed back and then during sex I would lie on my back and kind of put my feet over the backs of their thighs, nowhere near as interesting as anything I'd seen in porn, and maybe that was because the kind I watched wasn't guy-on-girl porn. I'd come more times from porn than I ever had from sex, and now kissing

Aubrey I was having that porn-feeling. She actually kissed back. She was a good kisser. She put her hands on my ribs. I pulled away from her and tasted the strawberry lip gloss I'd put on her hours ago.

Eileen, she said. She turned off the sink. She said my name again. I think I said I had to go upstairs for a minute. I went into my room and locked the door behind me. Half of Tyson's piss-smelling shavings were in the trash can and half were still in his habitat. I emptied the rest out and put the new shavings in and opened my door long enough to slide the trash can out so it wouldn't smell in my room. I sat on the floor gasping for maybe thirty seconds and crying. Then when that stopped, I did my makeup and got into my bodycon onesie that showed my cleavage and the tops of my thighs and got my long pink wig out of the closet and my elf ears and my knee-high socks. Then I sat on my bed and licked my lips and turned on my camera and said, Watch me beat your Fortnite scores, idiots, and rolled my eyes into the back of my head to make the ahegao face.

Having left Murphysboro in the morning, Garrett was in Chicago by the late afternoon. He identified a parking garage in the neighborhood of Rogers Park, close to where Dina Valentine lived. This parking garage would be his base of operations. It would be from this parking garage that he would emerge into the city, take the train downtown, buy new clothes for himself and jewelry for Dina.

The train ride wasn't as he'd expected: the car smelled of vomit and the only other occupant was a homeless man who was singing a song Garrett couldn't identify. Garrett sat as far as he possibly could from the homeless man and looked at pictures of pink-wigged Dina on his phone. She was a performer first and foremost, a *Forbes* journalist had written about her, not a porn star. Garrett agreed with this take. He was also delighted by how silent Dina kept on the matter. She wasn't a whore. She didn't turn tricks. But part of the big, almost cosmic joke she was playing was that she wanted you to believe she did, and she had before, and she could again. She wanted you to think she had loads of sexual experience, had spent her life before fame having sex for money. But Garrett knew this wasn't true. Dina wasn't like the stiff-boobed porn-stars-turned-models who had millions of Twitter followers, or even the other Twitch girls who broadcast from their parents' houses and in a desperate attempt to appear cute dressed like anime kittens and Sailor Moon. Dina was an original, a prodigy, a virgin who somehow knew exactly what to do to make everyone—how did he want to put it?—*intrigued*. She knew how to make people like and subscribe and follow and click. She had a gift.

On the Magnificent Mile, he bought the pair of Jordans that he thought would go well with his new outfit. On the drive up he'd been toying with the idea of a pink button-up. Or would a pink button-up be too feminine? It usually looked masculine on rich guys but he wasn't a rich guy. Well, he had to give himself some credit: he was kind of a rich guy, at least now he was. He entered Hugo Boss. Should he FaceTime Dave? No, because then Dave might figure him out. He DMed bernie-flamesyou on Twitter.

> **goatman:** i don't know if it's a good idea to wear a pink shirt
> **bernieflamesyou:** lol well what do you think you'd look best in when you get arrested, perv?
> **goatman:** fuck you
> **goatman:** i have a whole plan
> **goatman:** besides you're the one pledging $250 to her dono box, and i know you're all over her snapchat, and you PAINTED THAT FUCKING PICTURE OF HER WITH THE SQUID
> **bernieflamesyou:** got me there, game recognize game
> **bernieflamesyou:** well why do you want the pink shirt? what are the other options?
> **goatman:** idk, white?
> **bernieflamesyou:** dude lol what
> **bernieflamesyou:** do you wanna look like you're at my bar mitzvah in 2003? can you go with a pattern?

Garrett hadn't thought about a pattern. He moved away from the display table of white dress shirts marked half-price. Why had he even been thinking of half-price for Dina? Did he want her or not?

bernieflamesyou: yeah pink makes you look too red state. you want something with, like, a little motif
bernieflamesyou: like a little design idk

Garrett found a striped button-up and sent a photo of it to bernieflamesyou, but bernieflamesyou didn't like it. So he tried a pastel tartan one and then one with little pink horses.

bernieflamesyou: yeah dude, the horses. you can have all the prestige of the pink without any of the douchebaggery.

Garrett didn't have time to thank bernieflamesyou. He pocketed his phone, bought the shirt, and then bought a new pair of jeans. Next, a bus ride to Big Shoulders Diamonds on Wabash Avenue.

He had never been in such an upscale jewelry store before. He wished he was wearing the outfit he'd bought to meet Dina instead of his sad driving outfit. The room was long and rectangular, with two felt-topped cases of jewelry running the length of either side. A man in a vest with small glasses—*spectacles*, Garrett thought—seemed to be operating the entire place, and the four people in the room besides Garrett and the bespectacled man were waiting patiently for the bespectacled man to dispatch of his duties with each of them. The customer who currently had the bespectacled man's attention was a woman who looked to be in her late sixties and was oval faced, high cheekboned, and beautiful in a surprising way. She was looking at a necklace, and the bespectacled man removed it from the case and let it rest on his hands like a python: the woman touched the pendant, which caught the light, which seemed to briefly thrill her. Garrett looked away from them and down at the case closest to him, which was full of watches—*timepieces*—diamond time-pieces. A few feet over were the rings. He imagined his father buying his mother a diamond ring, the most preposterous thing to imagine. His father had never even made dinner for his mother, never once gone grocery shopping for her. And a diamond ring would have set his father back considerably, whereas, for Garrett, money was no object.

The bespectacled man was standing in front of Garrett now, greeting him and telling him his name was Mark.

"Hi, Mark," Garrett said, and then before he could talk himself out of saying it: "I'm buying earrings for my fiancée."

Mark's thin face warmed with a smile. "So happy to hear it. What is your price range?"

"Unlimited," Garrett said.

Mark's smile receded and he cleared his throat. "Well," he started, and then started again: "Very well, OK, why don't you come down to the other end of the case with me?"

They went down to the other end of the case, where Mark removed a small tray containing four sets of earrings. He held up a little pair of studs, small as the plastic ones Garrett used to see the girls in elementary school wearing after they got their ears pierced at Claire's.

"Each of these is two carats, amounting to a four-carat total diamond weight," Mark said. "They are placed in four-pronged settings of fourteen-karat gold."

Garrett made a low noise of approval even though they still looked to him like grown-up versions of the Claire's earrings. "How much would those be?"

"Twenty-six."

Garrett raised his eyebrows. "Twenty-six hundred?"

"Twenty-six thousand, sir," Mark said briskly, and then reshelved the tray with a reflexive knowledge of Garrett and his situation that Garrett immediately resented. "What is your price range today?"

He had read somewhere that an engagement ring was supposed to cost at least two monthly paychecks. Which was lucky because he had just a little more than that saved up. And plus this wasn't an engagement ring—it was something even better, something for the already-engaged. "Fifteen thousand."

Mark didn't flinch. "Very good." He produced another tray containing stud earrings that were almost identical except the four-pronged settings actually looked like real gold.

"These have a three-carat total diamond weight," Mark said. "They're set in fourteen-carat yellow gold. Very similar to the set I just showed you, but more affordable."

"How much are you asking?" Garrett said, feeling like a homeowner or a father or someone who has frequent sex.

"These are fourteen thousand five hundred."

"Yes!" Garrett said, which caused a few of the other customers to turn around and smile politely at him. "I'm getting these for my fiancée," he told the beautiful woman in her late sixties.

"So lovely for you," she said. "So lucky for her."

His savings drained, he rode a bus and a train back to the parking garage. The entire time he'd wanted to text Dave or bernieflamesyou a picture of the earrings but he'd held off. Showing them the earrings would be like forwarding his fiancée's nudes to his friends: a blasphemy, a form of disrespect, a pimping-out. Maybe one earring would meet the world a few weeks later, on Instagram, a single stud in her left ear as she kissed his left cheek and he smiled goofily into the camera. But he wouldn't let himself hope. That was trying to control the world—and by extension Dina—with his mind, which was itself a form of pimping-out. He would give her the earrings and see what happened after that. Not until months or years later would she have to learn that they had cost him almost his entire savings.

Garrett changed into the new outfit in the backseat of the Accord, pocketed the earrings in their velvet case in his jacket, and stowed everything else (the remainders of a life he no longer lived, a pre-Dina life) in the trunk. It was at that point almost dinner time. He rehearsed his speech quickly in the elevator: *Hi, Dina, I'm so sorry to surprise you like this. I work in tech and I've noticed someone circulating a very credible doxxing threat etc. etc. See, I freelance in security for a few different social media platforms, monitoring nazis and trolls and Gamergate guys so they don't, you know, ruin the world with their chauvinism.* (He'd come up with that part in the car, a lie, but one he stood for, one he could be proud of, and one she'd forgive him for later.) *I apprehended the doxx and figured instead of spamming you with a bunch of emails, etc. etc. I just want to say I'm a huge fan and give you these* (here he'd give her the diamond earrings, he'd make the move right away, he'd decided) *and my number and say that if you need anything, like anything whatsoever . . .*

He was out of the Lyft and on her street now, standing in front of a detached brick house a block from Lake Michigan. It was beautiful, more impressive than anything he could afford. He felt limp in all his extremities, as though his nervous system were failing, as though he were dying. It was like nothing he'd ever felt before. It was, he imagined, what it felt like to be truly in love.

I finished the video and thought maybe I'd upload it right there, no edits, just to piss Aubrey off, but then I realized she'd probably never see it anyway and also why did I want to piss her off? The downstairs was quiet. I changed out of the bodycon and went down and Aubrey was asleep on the couch with the baby face she always got when she was asleep, and also the baby face was puffy from crying. I texted my weed guy for another eighth and he said all his regular guys were busy but if I didn't mind he could send over someone new and it would take a little longer than usual, I said, Sure, whatever, and then dropped my phone on the couch and dropped down, too, so it woke Aubrey up. What? she said, like I'd said something, and I just kept looking ahead and saying nothing. So I guess Dennis is coming, I finally said and she said, I mean there's no way I can tell him not to without my phone. You could get on Facebook on your laptop, I said and she told me she didn't have Facebook and then I suggested Instagram and she told me he didn't have Instagram. And he never checked his email. OK, so we're fucked, I said. How are we fucked? she asked, sitting up, and her voice was both sincerely asking a question and a little angry. Well, because I kissed you. I really didn't mean to kiss you. She lay back down and curled up in a fetal position. I'm sorry, I said. I have no idea what's going on, I swear to god, I really don't want to be like this, I really was just trying to, I dunno, get closer to you, I was feeling distant from you. I was being a bitch, she said, and her voice had a weird edge. I was being a bitch about your job, I'm just jealous of the money you make, I'm jealous of the way you get to live it all the way up. And then I expected her to say, You were right this whole time, I'm gay, I'm just super in the closet and scared to come out, but she didn't say anything else.

The doorbell rang and I told her it was maybe the weed guy—which I thought was weirdly fast considering he was supposed to be new—and I promised it would be quick and she nodded and turned on the TV and it went right back to *House Hunters*. I opened the door and there was this guy with red cheeks and some stubble, like kid-stubble even though he looked a lot older than me, and he was dressed too well for his haircut or his face. He still had the kind of glasses guys wear in the seventh grade, the navy rectangular metal frame ones with the little orange accents at the top corners. The redness on his cheeks actually looked kind of like rosacea, which my mom had and kept trying creams for my entire childhood. Hi, Dina, I'm so sorry to surprise you like this, he said, and I just said, Whatever, it's fine, just let's do this inside, OK? That seemed to throw him, but he came in and I shut the door and I was thinking, Why did my dude send some simp-looking asshole to deliver my weed?

I sat back down next to Aubrey, who didn't look up from *House Hunters*, and said, OK, so I have like $90, which should include your tip but he was looking at the painting of me and Arthur on the wall. That's—he said, and Aubrey looked up annoyed at him and then back at *House Hunters* and I felt bad for bringing the weed dude into the living room. I know that painting, he said. I DM with the guy who made it, bernieflamesyou. We met in the chat on your Twitch stream. I did a sort of polite like *wow small world* smile but at that point I wanted to hurry it up and get him out. I'm trying to watch fucking TV, Aubrey said, and the guy looked at her like she was a turtle or a sloth he'd startled awake, like an old slow animal he was surprised to see move. Sorry, I said, because then everything was catching up with me, the kiss, the phone, and I stood up and made the weed guy come with me into the kitchen.

I handed him the $90 and said, I only do sativa now, so I'll just take that. The guy looked at the money and then at me and was like, Oh, I think there's been some kind of misunderstanding. I was thinking how now this was getting stupid. What misunderstanding? I asked. And then the guy swallowed a bunch of air and kind of rolled his eyes up to the ceiling and said, I work in tech, I mean I freelance in web security, and there's been a doxxing threat, and then I cut him off and was like, What the fuck, where's my weed? He swallowed more air and said, I'm really sorry but I don't have any weed, I'm actually just in Chicago on a business trip and I wanted to warn you about a doxxing threat. A doxxing threat? Well, he said, and I said, You need to leave, OK? I have no idea who you are, but you need to leave. I'm sorry, he said again, if there's anything you need –. But I was walking ahead of him and he just followed me like a simp and we walked back into the living room and then Aubrey said, Stop.

What? I asked. I'm escorting this guy out, he's not the weed guy, he's just some rando. Aubrey looked at me and then at the guy. What's your name, she said. I'm Garrett Stillwater, he said. She laughed and said, That sounds like the name of a good old boy from Alabama. His face got redder. Are you a *fan*? Aubrey asked and Garrett Stillwater sort of shook his head and nodded at the same time, and then Aubrey sat up and looked at me with fire in her eyes like holy shit and she said, Wait, so you came here to meet Dina Valentine? And Garrett said, I'm in web security and I've apprehended a doxxing threat against Dina and I'm here on business and I figured instead of sending a bunch of emails— Aubrey laughed. You're a *fan*! She turned to me. *Diiina*. She said my name like it was foreign and needed extra pronunciation. *Diiina*, can you believe it? Of course I could believe it, but I knew admitting that would be saying the wrong thing so I said I couldn't. So, Garrett, Aubrey said, Are you going to kill us and wear our skin? Are you going to rape us first or kill us and then rape us? Garrett went even redder and made a face like we'd tried to feed him something freshly dead. I would never, he said. I would never think. Aubrey jumped up from the couch. Of course you would *never think*! God, I'm *kidding*, Garrett! She turned to me, and I could tell she was happy. I hadn't seen her like this in a while. Maybe Garrett should go, I said, and Aubrey shook her head. Garrett should not *go!* Garrett, listen, it's like, what, 7:00? We need you to stay and have some fun, OK? I think Dina has some points of molly and I'm actually going to order a pizza. Dina, you have molly, don't you? I said I did, which was true, and I regretted it as soon as I said it. Amazing! Aubrey said. Then she went across the room to stand right next to Garrett, who was sweating and looked like he was swallowing puke. Dina is my best friend, I don't know if you know that from Instagram? She and I are patching things up right now. You know how when two people are in a rough spot it's always better to have a third person there to, like, *defuse?* Garrett nodded and then looked at me and stopped nodding and I said, Aubrey, maybe we shouldn't roll and maybe Garrett should leave and Aubrey said, Maybe you shouldn't have kissed me, sounding all angry again, and then she took my phone off the table and went into the kitchen and I could hear her ordering an extra-large pepperoni pizza. I sat down on the couch feeling sort of like I needed to have a plan and also like I'd never again have a plan and Garrett stood next to me looking at me and then quickly looking at his phone when I looked at him.

Just sit down, I said, and he sat at an awkward distance. Then he said, If it's a bad time, honestly, I don't want to intrude, I can always come back. Which was stupid, like, why would I ever want him to *come back?* So now I kind of wanted to make him squirm like Aubrey seemed to want to. No, it's fine that you're here, Aubrey's having a rough day and she seems to want you here so just make yourself comfortable. Actually, would you mind getting me the bottle of vodka from the fridge? He swallowed again and said, Yeah, of course, and I watched him go into the kitchen and keep his dumb big rosy head down while Aubrey talked on my phone to the pizza guy, who she seemed to actually be flirting with. I thought of those influencers on Instagram who do photo collages of themselves pretty and thin and holding their puppies or something and then the next photo is them with their cute little stomachs pooched out and they're eating chocolate pudding and some's smeared on their noses. And the stupid caption is always *Instagram vs.*

Reality. Crab rangoon is Instagram, listening to chillwave and getting high is Instagram, getting paid over $250K for making ahegao faces is Instagram, kissing Aubrey is Instagram. Reality is Garrett Stillwater in your kitchen and Aubrey on the phone with a horny pizza boy.

Garrett was sitting on the same couch as Dina Valentine. She wore her hair—which was a brown no less lustrous than her pink wigs—in a messy bun and tightish gray sweatpants with a pink racing stripe and a Pantera hoodie with a weed leaf on it. The Pantera hoodie had to be ironic because that was a band only he, a generation ahead of her, could have grown up listening to (not that he had). He was trying to watch her without watching her, trying not to think of the indent her body was leaving on the leather couch. Trying not to imagine potential physical flaws: a retainer that she put in to sleep, maybe, or a hammer toe (she had never shown her bare feet in videos). But as his pulse accelerated and Dina joined her weird friend in the kitchen, Garrett found that he had to imagine these flaws in order to stay sane and grounded, in order to be able to take a shot of vodka when the two came back with shot glasses and be able to function as a human being with a nervous system and agency to operate said system. The friend was actually prettier than she'd looked on Instagram but also strong-jawed and truculent, probably a bad influence on Dina. Garrett understood that it would be his goal—quietly, perhaps with the use of the diamond earrings—to extricate Dina from the friend, to walk with Dina upstairs, to carry her like a princess into her room with its pink-and-black gaming chair and many screens and lacy-pink king bed. (*All Pink Everything* was the title of one of his favorite videos of hers, a four-minute tour of her bedroom in which she showed the viewer each of her pink-haired troll dolls, her closet full of pink wigs, her pink Chibiusa pillows, and a pink dress she'd made for Tyson.) Maybe he'd even get to meet Tyson, who'd made so many guest appearances on Twitch. Maybe the next evening she'd allow him to make a guest appearance of his own, and then bernieflamesyou and the rest would see him, would actually see what he looked like moving and living and breathing in Dina Valentine's room, having just had sex all night with Dina Valentine in her pink bed.

"I just hate people, don't you, Garrett?" the truculent friend was saying, and Garrett nodded in agreement. Garrett was already planning to invite the truculent friend to the rambling farmhouse, to talk to her about the many merits of feminism, to even allow Dina to make her godmother to both their children.

"Dude, are you OK?" Dina Valentine was somehow saying. Was somehow saying *to him*.

"Yeah." He smiled. "Sorry. I just had a long drive today."

"Where are you from, Garrett?" the truculent friend asked.

"Well, I'm based out of Murphysboro."

The truculent friend scrunched up her face. "Where's that?"

"Come on, you know where that is," Dina Valentine said. "My family's from Springfield. I've told you about the rest of Illinois."

The friend made an *Ah, so you have* face and looked at Garrett. "You'll have to forgive me, Garrett. I'm from Chicago. I don't know much about the bumblefuck parts of Illinois."

Garrett laughed, but Dina Valentine didn't, so Garrett stopped. It was incredible to see Dina's face darken, to see her having a mood. Dina Valentine: a person having a mood. This is what Dina could be, what she was to him, right now.

"Wait," the truculent friend said, her eyes wide. "Did you drive all the way here today to see Dina?"

"I'm here on business," he said quickly. It was crucial he not miss a beat. "I'm meeting with a data security client."

"Can we talk in my room, Aubrey?" Dina said.

What a boring name! Yes, Garrett would have to shoo away Aubrey ASAP.

"Why can't we talk here?" said Aubrey, doing another shot.

"Because I think you're acting toxic," Dina said.

"Get this, Garrett," Aubrey said, wiping her mouth. "Dina says I'm gay, and then *she* kissed *me* literally as my boyfriend is on the way to come pick me up!"

Garrett was too preoccupied by the thought of Dina kissing Aubrey to think about the boyfriend. Dina kissing Aubrey. Aubrey succumbing, as he soon would, to Dina.

"Jesus Christ, dude!" Dina said. "I apologized! Why are you so mad!"

"Because *you're* the one who's gay!" Aubrey cackled. "*You're* the one who's not out of the closet. *You're* the liar who spends her whole *life* making dudes jack off to your anime faces! And you're making *me* feel like such a *freak* just because my dad's a MAGA bigot who kicked me out of the house when he caught me kissing Sylvia—who's *dead* now, by the way—on the back porch of our dumb suburban McMansion."

Aubrey filled up a glass, took another shot, and smiled at Garrett, who smiled back out of reflexive politeness.

"Aubrey," Dina said.

"You wanna know what I'm mad about, Eidina? Dielina? I'm mad that you *lie* and act like the real one! I'm mad that you've gotten so fucking rich *by lying and acting like the real one!*"

How could Aubrey speak to Dina this way? It could have just been the vodka mixed with adrenaline, but he had lost all desire to invite her to the rambling farmhouse.

"Dina, where's your molly?" Aubrey asked. And then before Dina could respond: "JK, I know where it is. Have you ever done molly, Garrett?"

"Can't say that I have."

Another cackle. "*Can't say that I have.* Thank you, Kentucky Fried Colonel!" And then she ran upstairs.

Garrett watched Dina continue to stare somberly at the rug, which he realized bore the pattern of a classic Japanese scroll. "Are you OK?" he managed to ask.

She shot a look at him. "What do you care, Garrett? My best friend's losing her mind and you're some random simp who wants to fuck."

Garrett heard the words but didn't process them, or rather chose not to. He would press on for as long as he needed in this state of suspension until Dina came to her senses. And she did, after a matter of seconds, with a sigh.

"I'm sorry," she said. "I'm not like that. I'm just really stressed. I'm sorry you got tied up in this. What was that thing about the doxxing?"

He began to explain but then Aubrey was back with a handful of pills. "Oh sorry, am I interrupting?" she said. "Am I interrupting an important conference?"

Garrett shook his head pleasantly and then looked at Dina, his queen, who was grabbing her shoulder and staring at the ground. It was incredible to see her like this. Horrible, of course, but still incredible. He had spent so much time playing *League of Legends* with some of the friends he'd made from Dina's stream, lazily leveling up champions and casting spells while debating in the chat the merits of the whole Take the Red Pill thing: it was for Gamergate Neanderthals, of course, but there was some essential truth to it, something undeniable about the pulling-back of the curtain of faux-reality to reveal real-reality. And yes, this had something to do with women, something very important, something those nasty incels couldn't understand (which was how they became incels in the first place). Women are people, yes, but a special kind of people who are one way in photos and another way in person, one way in videos of their pink rooms and another way sitting unshowered on their Japanese scroll rugs. If you can take *this* red pill—the red pill that allows you to see women unshowered, to see them upset, to see them hungry and a little angry and a little drunk—then you don't need to worry about the rapey emasculation bullshit. It made such perfect sense to Garrett, watching Dina's perfect body folded up on the rug and her perfect face casting dagger eyes at her manic friend: his father had never seen his mother in such a position. His mother was always washed and dressed and making breakfast before his father got up, and didn't take her makeup off until after he'd gone to sleep. Taking this particular red pill, this walking-out-of-the-cave-of-shadows red pill, was the precursor to love and marriage. And in the twenty minutes since meeting Dina, he had already taken a generous handful of red pills.

Aubrey sat cross-legged in front of Dina and handed her a pill and then handed Garrett one. "For real?" Dina said. "Is this the vibe you want for rolling?"

And Aubrey's face sort of puckered up and she said, "OK, I know I'm being like, really crazy, but I honestly think it could be useful for us to roll because we've had a truly hard day and it might help us just to talk in a real way."

"We've been talking in a real way," Dina said. "I was just saying I miss you."

"Well, I miss you, too." Aubrey put the pill on her tongue and swallowed it dry. Then she went into the kitchen and came back with glasses of water for Dina and Garrett. "I swear to god, dude, I'll tell you everything," she said to Dina. "Like *everything*. About Sylvia. About my family. About how I feel about Dennis. I'll lay shit out, OK? And it'll be better."

Dina's big eyes blinked and she smiled a little. "OK," she said. "I'd really like that." And she took the pill. So Garrett took his. The curtains of faux-reality would be pulled back even further.

I was going to tell Aubrey everything, too. She knew almost everything but the plan was I was going to show her every single paywalled video—which actually she probably wouldn't even be that scandalized by—and then show her the nudes I posted on Twitter and tell her what I was planning on doing going forward to expand my viewer base. And eventually I'd tell her about how I loved her, and was basically today years old when I realized it.

So we were all sitting watching *Adventure Time* and eating ice cream and waiting for the molly to hit and I was thinking this is maybe going to be a good night, like the best night Aubrey and I would have together since we left the shelter, except for the problems of Garrett Stillwater and Dennis. Apparently Garrett Stillwater had some legit thing about doxxing to tell me but he had a rosy face and weird stubble and I could probably just hire someone to come look at my laptop and my gaming computer and tell me what was wrong. Plus Garrett Stillwater was doing the thing of sitting right next to me—in between me and Aubrey—and keeping his body completely rigid like if he let out his breath he'd immediately rape. Aubrey was telling him about Dennis, describing all the things Dennis had done to hurt or betray her in the four months since they'd started dating, and Garrett Stillwater was listening and nodding and every now and then saying something like, What the hell? Why are men even like that? Or saying, I'm so sorry, Aubrey. No one should have to go through that. The stuff Aubrey was telling him was also probably stuff I wanted to hear, and I wanted my mind to be clear to hear it, but I'd had two and a half shots of vodka and was thinking hard and hearing things muffled like when I used to get ear infections as a little kid. I was trying to think of a way to get unmuffled, to be standing instead of crawling so when the roll started I could just run. I thought of my mom making me kneel on the ground and tilt my head to the side so she could put drops in my ears. I always wondered why I couldn't just sit in the chair and she'd stand above me and do that. Why did I have to be fucking *kneeling*.

Like this one time Dennis just refused to wear a condom and refused to pull out, Aubrey was saying. And he told me I should just get Plan B, it'd be fine. Garrett Stillwater was like, I mean, even just one time's too many, and Aubrey said, Yes, Garrett, thank you! And to me she said, God, Dina, your fans are so woke. So Garrett, she said, are you a feminist? Yes, absolutely, Garrett Stillwater said, which was really all I needed. I turned to look at both of them and said, OK, so how would each of you define "feminist"? Aubrey got this pouty look like do we have to go over this again? Garrett Stillwater said, A woman's right to self-definition. OK, I said, tell me more. Well, he said, I think a woman should be able to, like, choose who she gets to be with. And like what clothes she wears. I nodded. Aubrey snorted and then gasped, Oh my god sorry! Sorry! Go on, Garrett. Garrett looked scared, but he kept talking. A woman should be able to work if she wants to, in whatever job she wants to, but preferably a high-earning job. A woman deserves to be treated well and respected by men, especially the man she chooses to be with. What if the woman's gay? I asked Garrett Stillwater, and he looked genuinely confused, like I'd asked him what if the woman has two heads. I guess it's the same, he said, like in gay couples there's usually a more masculine one, right? So the more feminine one, the real woman-y woman, deserves to be treated well by the more masculine one. The more masculine one shouldn't be, you know, a chauvinist.

Aubrey grinned and put her arm around Garrett Stillwater's neck. Garrett, you've given us so much to think about, she said. You have so much to teach us and we have so much to teach you. And that's when I started to feel a little warm, a little light. I was thinking, Oh fuck, and I was also thinking, Am I standing? Can I run? But I only thought that for a second before I looked at Aubrey smiling, making goofy faces at Garrett, and I thought damn this is the person who knows the most about me out of everyone else alive right now. I was thinking fuck I've been mean to her. I haven't tried to understand her. That time in the Burger King when Dennis kept calling her a slut for wearing a skirt that came above her knee. I was eating my fries and thinking dudes are shitty, it only took sleeping with two to tell me that I needed to put a paywall between them and me, and having a boyfriend's going to be shitty, that's just how it is. But the way she smoothed the edge of her skirt after he criticized her and said I thought it was cute, idk. And the way he said, Well looking like a whore isn't cute. And the way his stupid skinny Adam Lanza face swooped down over his soda straw and then looked at me and said What? But he didn't care what I thought. People like him never want to be challenged.

I'm sorry, I said to Aubrey and crawled across the rug to hug her. I hugged her tight and she gasped. Eileen, she said, what are you doing? I looked up at her and she was beautiful and tender and her eyebrows were perfect and I said, We have to stop Dennis from coming here. She shook me off and laughed and said, What are you talking about? The more the merrier! Then the doorbell rang and she went to get it and she was talking in the same flirty way she had been on the phone and it smelled like pepperoni. Garrett Stillwater was like, Is Aubrey OK? And I honestly didn't know, so I told him I honestly didn't know. And then I realized something looking at him. He was red-faced with stupid glasses but he was a man, a nice man, he knew the guy who made the painting. I think she's in an abusive relationship, actually, I said. I think her boyfriend is toxic. He nodded, Yeah it sure sounds like it. He kind of matches all the descriptions of my father. And then he made this little expression with this face, like he was being pinched, and said, I actually, um, I, like, DMed you a little about it? I don't think you read it? Or maybe you did? But I was thinking about Aubrey and Dennis, not my fucking Instagram DMs, so I said something like, What? No. Just tell me. And he said, Right, and then he told me about his dad, who abused his mom and then his mom left the family when Garrett Stillwater was seven, and Garrett Stillwater always strove not to be that kind of man, not to be the kind of man who could behave that way toward women, et cetera.

Garrett, I said. Can you, like, guard us? I could tell he was rolling hard, his pupils were huge, and he was looking at me like he'd just been born and I was the first thing he was seeing in the world. Garrett? I said, and he said, Yes? Sorry. And I said, Can you guard us? And I took his hand in both my hands and it felt like a piece of warm dough. Garrett, this is what I need you to do, OK? When Dennis comes, I need you to stand at the door and not let him in, I need to talk to Aubrey, OK? Dennis is pretty skinny and you're kind of not so, like, you should be able to take him, right? Garrett Stillwater nodded. Dina? he said. Can I talk to you just really quick about something else? And then Aubrey was coming back with the pizza so I started to say maybe later but he was popping open a little case and showing me diamond earrings and saying, I love you, Dina Valentine.

Aubrey basically dropped the pizza on the coffee table and said, Ooooh damn! A declaration of LOVE! Garrett Stillwater was still looking at me through his huge, weird eyes, and I could see now he was crying, and he started saying how it had always been his dream to meet me, how there really was no doxxing thing, how he hoped I'd forgive him. Garrett, I said, OK, dude, let's just talk about this in like an hour? When we have a handle on the Dennis situation? Aubrey was like, What Dennis situation? Garrett Stillwater looked like a dog someone just threw into a lake, all stunned and alert, but then he said, Of course, of course. I'm sorry, I know this is a lot. I said, Yes, it really is kind of a lot. But I so appreciate you and what you're doing and we're going to have a big talk about it later, OK? Garrett Stillwater put the earrings away and sort of leaned in, maybe to kiss me, but I stood up and said, Remember our plan? and he got the stunned dog look again but recovered fast and nodded.

Aubrey was like, Babe what are you doing? And I took her hand and took the pizza and I said, Can we go upstairs? And it was like in the movies where everything else blurs and all you're doing is looking at the girl's face and she's looking at yours and I wanted to cry, I wanted to tell her I was figuring shit out, I wanted her to cry with me. She started to laugh and said, Oh my god you think I'm psycho and then she said, And you're carrying that box of pizza like a delivery boy. And I said, Am I a hot delivery boy? and ran upstairs and she ran following me, shouting, Garrett we have to talk for a minute but we're going to save some pizza for you, OK? And then Garrett's smaller-and-smaller high-as-hell voice was like, OK, that's fine, I'm fine, see you soon.

I put the pizza down on the floor and we sat down on the bed together and we knew what to do right away, we held each other above the elbows and we kissed, slower than last time, and then we were wrapped in each other, and it felt like I was tasting colors-but-also-things that were her, like I was tasting sienna clay and seafoam and for me maybe she was tasting peaches and melted sugar. I said into her ear, OK listen, I've been keeping some shit from you but honestly I was today years old when I figured it out and she laughed and was like, Babe, *sshh*, me, too, kinda. And then I put my forehead against hers and was like, OK, but let me say something and she *sshh*ed me again and said, Honestly, it's the roll. We're rolling. Well, I'm being real, I said, and I'm saying I love you and I always want you in my life and I'm sorry I was a bitch to you and I'm going to show you all my videos. She smiled. Ooh la la! And then she put her chin on my shoulder and said, Listen, I've got some shit to say, too, but let me do something first, OK? and before I could even say anything she was up under my shirt and her hand was on one of my boobs and then the other. It happened fast. It was the gentlest hand that had ever been put on either of my boobs in my life.

Aubrey, I said. I'm being real. She was pulling off my shirt, her shirt. Aubrey, I'm being real, OK? She nodded and said, I know, me, too. But I want you to know that, like remember that, OK? I said. And she said, I will, and kissed me on the lips and then kissed me on the chest and then kissed me until I couldn't say anything else.

He had done it, the thing he had most wanted to do in his life up until that point. How did he feel, having accomplished a major goal? How did LeBron feel when he won an NBA championship? How did Chris Pratt feel when he got hot and landed the lead role in *Jurassic World*? Garrett rubbed the cushions of the couch and they felt soft and alive, like he was petting a massive dog, and he was having a very difficult time not thinking about Dina Valentine sitting on his lap, taking her shirt off, kissing him. He felt bad for Aubrey, dating a guy like Dennis. Of course she and Dina would need to regroup, strategize, have some kind of girl talk. Aubrey deserved that much. He, a feminist, would do Dina's bidding, acting as their protector, firmly escorting Dennis off the premises. He would get Aubrey back to her dorm without a hair out of place. This kind of guardianship would make Dina want him even more, would make their eventual consummation—at eight in the morning, giddy and exhausted, feeling that coda-to-an-action-movie, good-guys-won feeling—all the better.

He felt good. He had never felt this good in his life. The thought briefly entered his mind that this was as good as he would ever feel, that he would need to make this moment last for as long as possible, because eventually his body would stop feeling glowing-warm and the couch would stop being made of dog's fur and he would have to deal with the tedium and complications of reality. He had two options:

stay like this, rubbing the couch, dreaming of how Dina would look when they finally got some alone time together, when she could finally try on her earrings and exclaim to him how beautiful they looked, how they fit her face perfectly; or he could start thinking about how exactly he would get from this moment here on the couch to the greatest moment of his life, in which he would have sex with Dina Valentine for the first time. He chose the latter, but he would let himself look at his phone first. He had a text from Dave and some DMs from bernieflamesyou. First, the text.

Dave: lol so how did project Lolita go?
Garrett: dude
Garrett: dude you would not believe what's been happening
Dave: you've been sitting in a dunkin donuts crying for the past six hours?
Garrett: lmaooooo
Garrett: i'm in her house right now, actually. on molly. i showed her the earrings.
Dave: ummm what?
Dave: you're actually *in dina valentine's house*???
Garrett: did you think i was lying?

Garrett took a snapshot of the wall in front of him, which included bernieflamesyou's Dina-and-Arthur painting, framed photos of Dina with other YouTube celebrities, a black-and-white portrait of Dina cosplaying as Wario complete with angry mustache. He sent it to Dave and then to bernieflamesyou without reading bernieflamesyou's DMs. He couldn't bother talking to them anymore. They were too far behind him, existing in a world where Dina only appeared on monitors, a world where one went to work at 8:30 a.m. and came home at 5:30 p.m. and drank White Claw and played *Metroid Prime* and beat off into a dirty Fleshlight. He couldn't bother with that world anymore.

So: Dennis. Who was Dennis? Aubrey had said he went to Indiana University. Blinking hard to concentrate, feeling pleasantly light-headed, Garrett opened his Facebook app and searched "Dennis Indiana University." He got twenty-seven results—all pencil-necked white guys—with no way of narrowing them down. So then he opened Chrome and searched "Aubrey Dennis," which got him results for Dennis Aubrey, 58, Minnetonka High School girls' basketball coach. He scrolled through photos of Dennis Aubrey, mustachioed, slightly walleyed, and laughed a pity-laugh, an embarrassment-laugh for all the guys in the world right now who weren't completely fulfilled.

The doorbell rang. He stood up. He felt like his body was giving off rays of light. He felt infinite warmth toward the living room. Love for the living room. It was in this living room, after all, that he had first told Dina Valentine he loved her. The doorbell rang again, and he maneuvered through space to answer it. There was a thin guy with a nose ring and an undercut who wore a heavy-looking flannel. The guy said, "Hey man," and walked past him, penetrating the fortress.

Garrett had failed. But this was nothing he couldn't bounce back from. He closed the door and turned around. "Dude," he said, as firmly as he could.

"What's up?"

"Dude, you're, like, not supposed to be here."

"I mean, I got the call from my guy." He produced from his pocket a bag of mossy-looking stuff that Garrett understood immediately was weed, having smoked it a few times in college. This was maybe not Dennis.

"Oh," Garrett said. "Oh, right. Ha ha."

The guy laughed as well. "So, you ordered, or . . . ?"

"Um, yeah. Well, I mean, my girlfriend did. But she's upstairs."

"OK, cool." The guy walked toward the stairs. "So, up to the right? Left?"

"No, actually." Garrett walked swiftly to stand in front of him. "She's talking with her friend. Her friend's in the middle of a crisis."

"Damn OK."

"But I think they'll be done soon."

"Can you, um. Can you text her?"

Could Garrett text her? He technically could. He opened Instagram on his phone and typed in his DMs, below the green heart, *Guy with weed is here.*

"Just did," he said, pocketing his phone, smiling. A little domestic text between lovers.

The guy sat down on the sofa and pulled out his phone. "I actually have nowhere else to be. This isn't my job, I'm just doing my homie a favor. I can chill here until they're done."

This was a weird idea, but not one Garrett was necessarily opposed to. He sat down on the couch next to the guy. The couch still felt like dog fur. The guy offered his hand to shake.

"Marco," he said.

"Garrett."

"This your place? Your girlfriend's?"

"Well, hers originally, but we're in the process of moving in together. And we're going to get a second house that's a farmhouse."

"Dude," Marco said, turning briefly back to a game on his phone involving geometric shapes blasting other geometric shapes. "That's awesome. Congrats. This place is tight as hell."

These weren't lies, necessarily. They were future-truths. Garrett was so confident in them, so sure of his beloved's eventual agreement to these plans, that he was unafraid to speak them. Especially to someone as inconsequential as Marco.

Marco put his phone down and pulled out a pipe whose bowl was shaped like Homer Simpson's head and began to pack it with weed from the bag he'd shown Garrett. "You don't mind if I smoke a little, do you?" he asked.

"Not at all," Garrett said, and watched Marco hit the pipe. When Marco offered it to him, he hit it, too, and came up coughing. Marco laughed.

"You been vaping more recently, or . . . ?"

Garrett nodded, gasping. "Yeah. Yeah, we've been vaping a lot."

"Me, too. Smoother. Where you work?"

"Tech."

"No shit! Me, too. Front-end development."

Garrett nodded, making a mental note that Marco's job, while similar to his, was likely to be more boring.

Marco turned on the TV—*House Hunters*, which he quickly exited out of—and then his eyes found bernieflamesyou's painting. "What the fuck?"

"What?"

"Your girlfriend's Dina fucking Valentine?"

Garrett's chest warmed. This would be *the* reaction. This would be what he'd be dealing with for the rest of his life. "Yep."

Marco looked at Garrett, assessing him, and then back at the painting. "Holy shit, man. She's like the hottest girl on the internet. Wait, like, how old are you? Isn't she seventeen?"

"Eighteen," Garrett said quickly. "And I'm twenty-five." Eventually he'd start telling the truth, get better at explaining their eleven-year age difference.

"Nice," Marco said, and offered his hand for a high five, which Garrett half-heartedly reciprocated. "Youngblood."

Disgusting. Now Garrett hated Marco. He got out his wallet, seeing what kind of cash he had that could make Marco leave. Just ones. Marco was watching *The Irishman* now. Garrett pretended to check his phone, making a concerned face as he did so.

"Shit," he said.

"What?"

"It looks like they're not gonna be down for a while."

"Shit," Marco said dreamily, taking another hit as the camera cut from Robert De Niro's grimacing face to the Philadelphia skyline.

"So, I don't have any cash. Do you have Venmo?"

"Sorry, man. Only cash."

Fuck. A full-blown obstacle. He took another hit when Marco offered it and stewed. No, he couldn't stew. He would need to turn this into a brainstorm. He would need to try to be productive.

A knock at the door. Then the doorbell. Then another knock. Then the doorbell a few times in quick succession.

"Yo, someone's pissed," Marco said. "That her sidepiece?"

Garrett stood up without acknowledging Marco's very poor attempt at a joke and went to the door, looking out the peephole. It was Dennis for sure: skinny, with unkempt mushroom-hair, a neckbeard of acne, a leather jacket. He was much taller than Garrett had imagined him. His lips were set in the way school shooters' lips are always set in their photos on the news. Humorless, determined.

Garrett opened the door a crack and positioned his foot behind it. Dennis pressed in immediately.

"Are you Dennis?" Garrett asked.

"Who the fuck are you?" Dennis said.

"Dennis, Aubrey and Dina want you to leave."

Dennis's features somehow constricted. "Who the *fuck* are you?"

This one was riskier, but he would try it anyway: "I'm Dina Valentine's boyfriend."

Dennis looked Garrett up and down and laughed. "Yeah. Of course you are." And then he pushed in with surprising strength.

Dennis was walking fast and Garrett was trailing him, as if by keeping within a six-foot range of him at all times he could somehow slow him down. Marco set down his pipe and stood up. "Do we have a problem here?" he asked.

"I need to talk to Eileen," Dennis said, and then rolled his eyes. "Dina."

"Why?" Marco asked.

"Tell us why," Garrett added, feeling useless.

"Why do you two fucks need to know?"

"Because you have a vibe, man," Marco said. "It's not a good one."

Garrett edged closer to Marco. All the warmth and wonderment he'd felt before had evacuated his body, and now he felt coldness, and dread, and the kind of I-don't-want-to-go-to-school sick he remembered feeling as a kid the morning after Tommy Berkins poked the eraser end of a pencil hard into his side. Dennis was more than a head taller than both of them.

"Where's the porn star?" Dennis pressed.

"She's not a porn star. And what does it matter, anyway?" Marco said, slowly closing the space between himself and Dennis.

"Dude," Garrett said, unable to tell if he was speaking to Dennis or Marco. "Maybe, let's . . ." He had no idea how to finish the sentence.

"Dina Valentine is disrespecting my girlfriend," Dennis said, clearly trying to project his voice for the benefit of Dina and Aubrey. "I need to talk to her."

"Maybe you need to talk to me," Marco said.

"Who the fuck are you?"

"What does it matter? I'm not some skinny-ass white boy."

Dennis charged at Marco, grabbing him by the collar, but Marco pushed him away. Affronted, Dennis charged again, and this time Marco swung. Garrett stumbled into a seated position on the stairs and watched as Dennis pulled back and his fist connected with Marco's face somewhere in the middle. And then Marco, whose nose was now bleeding, shoved Dennis off him and into the coffee table and then stood up and looked at Garrett as if Garrett had somehow created Dennis, had somehow set this whole horrible situation in motion.

"You're crazy," Marco said, wide-eyed, shaking his head. "Y'all are fucking crazy." And then he ran out and slammed the door behind him, leaving the weed and pipe on the couch.

Now Dennis was standing up and walking toward the stairs and Garrett was thinking about his role as designated by Dina, and about what had happened to Marco, and about how much Marco weighed versus how much Dennis weighed versus how much he weighed. He was all that stood between Dina (and, of course, Aubrey) and Dennis, tall and angry Dennis. He had failed so far but now, with

Dennis standing square-shouldered before him, he had his chance to step into the role of protector, to show Dina conclusively what he knew she already knew: that he was the man who would live with her in the rambling farmhouse, who would raise two children with her, who would grow old with her, who would leave his wealth to her. He stood up and squared his own shoulders and affected a sneer to match Dennis's. He opened his mouth but before he could speak, Dennis grabbed him by the shoulders and slammed him hard against the wall.

When Dennis came into the room, we were holding each other fully clothed in bed and the deal was Aubrey would tell him because she knew how to calm him down. So when he came in wearing that stupid fucking leather jacket with his grown-out bowl cut and panting and looking wild-eyed I knew we'd been stupid, and I knew also that Aubrey had maybe as little of a clue about how shitty he was as I'd had, she thought he'd "understand," but really what he did was look at me like I was a serial killer and say, What the fuck is going on here?

Aubrey was like, Baby, listen, it's complicated, and then started saying something about how we were on molly and wanted to cuddle because everyone wants to do that on molly and honestly he had nothing to worry about. He raised his eyebrows and looked at me. Nothing to worry about? he said. I didn't realize I had to worry about having something to worry about, he said. And then Aubrey said, What? Baby, what do you mean? And then he just glared at me and said, You called me saying Eileen was being *emotionally exhausting* and you wanted to be with me so I'm here to pick you up but clearly some really really weird shit is going on. There are two random guys downstairs. And I was like, Oh, Garrett's our friend. But I didn't know how to explain the second guy, and I didn't even know there'd been a second guy, so I said nothing about that. Dennis raised his eyebrows and said, Are you all having an orgy? Then he looked at Aubrey and asked the question again and she said, No, of course not. But what about Eileen? he asked. You do porn, Eileen. You fuck guys a lot. You probably plan orgies all the time. And for some reason that made me mad, not because he was saying I did porn but because his ugly ass thought he knew *anything* about porn or the people who did it, and I said, Well, actually, Dennis, I was fucking your girlfriend. Then Aubrey turned to me and made a face like literally what is wrong with you and Dennis said, Excuse me? And I got off the bed and came around to the side he was standing on and said, That's fucking right, Dennis. She loves me, not you.

Dennis's eyes got really small and he grabbed Aubrey by the arm and said, We're going and you're never coming back here. And then Aubrey said, Baby, hold on, I need to get my clothes. And I grabbed Aubrey's other hand so she was between us but Aubrey pulled away and I fell back onto the bed and the feeling of falling was like how a baby probably feels when its umbilical cord gets cut, like I was in the world now, like I'd never be safe. Stop it, I said to Dennis, and then I said, Stop it, you incel. I know you're a goddamn incel reply guy. Dennis turned around. He let go of Aubrey and then I felt his hand on my face, quick, hot, stinging. Then he was holding Tyson in one hand and Aubrey's arm in the other and they were leaving my room and walking downstairs.

Something changed in me. I don't know if I'll ever feel that way again. I was thinking about how Dennis was holding the two living beings that meant the most to me. I was thinking about my mom's boyfriend and Aubrey's parents and all the guys who sent me cum-troll emails. I was thinking about how people make videos about me and my house and my money called Dina Valentine Is a Fake Whore!!! I was thinking about how Sylvia from Instagram is dead. I was thinking about a lot of different things and my head got really hot and I went into my closet and got out the baseball bat I keep in there because I want to be safe but don't believe in guns, and I went screaming down the stairs and swung it at the back of Dennis's head, I almost tripped over passed-out Garrett Stillwater, but Dennis saw

me and ducked and Aubrey was screaming, and then she was barefoot in her tank top and sweats outside and Dennis was dragging
her and calling me a cunt, saying as loudly as he could something
like, Everyone, please wake up and realize that you're living on the
same block as a sex offender who goes by the names Eileen Davis
and Dina Valentine! She has created and distributed child pornography! I swung the bat at the shoulder of his arm that was carrying
Tyson and it cracked and Tyson dropped and I saw he was already
dead from being squeezed so hard so I swung again and again and
it cracked again and again and it hit Dennis hard and he screamed.
And then Dennis kicked me hard away and got in his car and yelled
at Aubrey to get in the passenger side, which she did, crying the
whole time, and I was like, Dennis, you are truly a piece of human
garbage and I hope you rot in hell for killing my gerbil and stealing
my girlfriend! And he was starting the car and I brought the baseball
bat down on his headlights and his windshield screaming, Rot in
hell! Rot in hell! And then the car started and I didn't jump back fast
enough, the mirror caught me in the stomach and I went flying, and I
landed in the grass in my front yard and my next-door neighbor was
shining his phone light on me and saying, What the hell is going on
here! I'm calling the police!

It's pretty good when you get an understanding judge, especially
a woman judge, who says, You're a first-time offender and you were
acting at least partially in self-defense, and then sentences you to
twenty days plus community service. It's not good having to wear
those polyester jail scrubs, and it's not good having to see your mom
for the first time in three years in the front row crying on the shoulder of her new boyfriend who looks just as stupid as the last one.
And it's not good for your mom to lean forward and squeeze your
shoulder and say, I know you're gonna pull through this, sweetie,
and then in the next breath say, Do you think when this is over I
can borrow $20K? And it's not good to have to listen to the sheriff
burp quietly and then say, Excuse me, big breakfast. But you know

what is good? When you turn around and see her sitting in the third row, wearing her glasses because it's 8:30 a.m. and she never puts her contacts in before noon, smiling big because she knows this whole thing's a joke. And it's good when you fill out the paperwork and get to your cell and meet your cellmate and eat your meat loaf for dinner because you know that in twenty days they're going to let you out and you're going to see her again.

The Last Show

S HE THOUGHT HER OWN NAME, Flora, was ugly, but she was grateful at least that her name wasn't Joan. A plain name, her mother had called it: "It was your grandmother's name and now it's my middle name. Just my luck." Now the plain name was a structure built out of papier-mâché, and it was descending from the rafters onto a stage, and Flora was looking at it from the audience: *The Joan Daniels Show*. Around Flora were white society couples, handsome women in cloches and pillboxes sitting next to their bare-headed men, all of them smoking. She was alone, and in front of her was a tamarind whiskey sour. She had not yet tasted it, but she knew what it was. The smoke felt warm, and she realized she'd missed it, had found the countrywide abandonment of smoking sterile and somehow lonely, had found it sad that no one asked anyone for a light anymore, or bummed a cigarette. She missed the ease of interaction you could have with complete strangers if only the two of you smoked. She had smoked Parliaments and her husband Marlboros. The children had played in the backyard while she and her husband enjoyed lunch and a cigarette. For a moment Flora saw not *The Joan Daniels Show* and the empty stage but the backyard in Orland Green in which the children had played, the airplanes from O'Hare flying low overhead, the look in her eldest son's eyes as he wandered across the lawn to her deck chair, troubled that the toy train he was gripping had become dirtied with mud.

Flora gasped and she was in the bed again, and Ariel-called-Arlo was looking down at her saying, "She's awake!" There were beeps and flashes and the shuffling of feet. Ariel-called-Arlo's mother, Flora's daughter, leaned in close and said, "Mom, there you are. We love you, Mom. Stay with us."

When Flora's third child was born, a boy, her mother had told her that she was lucky. "You get boys, boys, boys," she said. "Not that we don't love you girls, but your father always wanted a son." Flora's father was a quiet man, and tall, which led some people to mistake him for imposing. According to Flora's older sister, who loved him more than Flora or her younger sister, he had changed his name from Horovitz to Harvey after leaving his parents' farm in Hungary at fifteen. That her father was probably a Jew fascinated Flora, and she wanted to know more, but she was embarrassed to ask him on the off chance he might become offended. She and her father rarely spoke, though he smiled at her often, and he sometimes remarked that she walked like a dancer. She imagined him as Gregory Peck in *Gentlemen's Agreement*, an aggrieved Jew crusading for his civil rights, though her father was far more timid and less handsome than Gregory Peck. He had gotten drunk and swerved into oncoming traffic when Flora was seventeen.

Her husband, Dickie, was the opposite of her father. Loud, energetic, nearly bald at twenty-six when their youngest was born. He had a joke about their yearly vacation spot, Sheboygan, Wisconsin, in which Wisconsin became a fictional kingdom with a dissatisfied king who wanted a daughter. Every time his queen gave birth to a boy, he'd pout: "She's a boy again." Eventually his royal subjects took up for him, chanting "She's a boy again," which became "She-a-boy-again" which became "Sheboygan." Flora thought the joke was strange, but the children loved it. She told him not to tell it at parties. What did anyone else's opinion matter, Dickie wanted to know. "Sweetheart, I tell the joke because I love you and I know you always wanted girls." She'd never said a word to him about it. How had he known? Was this something men just always assumed about women, that they wanted daughters? Had he seen how relieved she'd been when their middle child, Ava, was born? He called himself Dickie The Great Prognosticator. He guessed correctly that Ava wanted orange juice in the morning, or that Arthur had done well on a math test. The joke lasted for a couple years and then got old when the children's lives got more complicated and he started getting things wrong. "Uh-uh!" Arthur would protest, pouting, and Dickie would shrug: "A broken prognosticator's only right twice a day."

Alan was a difficult pregnancy and a thirty-six-hour birth. She was given morphine and later barbiturates. She spent nearly twenty-four hours sleeping it all off—including the rips and tears Alan had made inside her—while Dickie took the children to look at Alan in the nursery. When she first met Alan, it was for a five-minute feeding at 9:00 a.m. He latched on quicker than his siblings had, and drank eagerly like his father drank his morning coffee. Dickie said he should be named Alan because the name sounded leonine and the baby looked like a lion cub to him. She didn't see it, but she wouldn't deny Dickie his pleasure. This was the kind of thing for which she knew she'd catch grief from her mother. "A woman has to be just as hardheaded as a man," her mother always said. "When you do it just right, without letting him realize you're doing it, it can be incredibly appealing." How could a hardheaded woman be appealing? She was trying to blink herself awake, watching the nurse scold Arthur for eating a chocolate bar around the baby. She was like Dorothy awakening from her fever dream, telling everyone around her that they'd been there with her in Oz. Alan was the lion, she supposed. Big eyes, big head, not yet courageous.

She choked on her breath and she was lying down again and Alan was sitting close to her, tall, kindly, his children on either side of him. "Mom," he was saying. His children were saying something in their child-voices at a pitch that troubled her ears.

Flora smiled and tried to say "hello" with her mouth only, not her voice. Alan's eyes widened and his face lit up. "Hello!" he said. "She's saying hello!"

There was Ava's face, and her husband's, and Ariel-called-Arlo's. And the beeping still, but a different beeping. "Mom," Ava said, in a voice like she was directing a play with a huge and complicated cast.

"Can you hear me? They gave you L-dopa. That means you should be able to move better." She turned to Alan. "Does it look like she's moving better?"

Alan's eyes continued to meet Flora's, and he shrugged in a way that was barely perceptible.

"Grandma?" Ariel-called-Arlo said. How did she want to be called? "They." But there was only one of her. One of Alan's children, the younger one, leaned forward and put her warm little hand in Flora's cold one.

And then she was breathing evenly again, and the tamarind whiskey sour was sitting full on the table in front of her, and there was Joan Daniels's name on the stage. A waiter, a Black man, stopped in front of her and asked her politely if she was finished with her beverage. He seemed to be affording her more patience than she deserved. "No, I'm afraid," she said, and he nodded and disappeared. The room was darker than it had been before. She wondered where Dickie was, and who was home with the children. The thought should have bothered her more than it did.

A spotlight. Joan Daniels was onstage, a Hollywood B-lister, her smile looking wider than her face, her middle bisected by a seemingly painful girdle. "Welcome, wonderful people, to a very special show this evening. Brought to you, of course, by Mrs. Dishwell's soap: the only soap that cleans everything in your kitchen."

The couple at the next table was looking favorably at Flora. She looked down at herself for anything conspicuous, pretending she was inspecting a drop of whiskey on the front of her dress, and there she was as she had been before so much of her life happened: a size 9, slim-legged, in black pumps from Woolworth's. She was thinking as she probably shouldn't have about how her body looked in the bed with Ava and Alan standing over it. The skin of her upper arms was draped over her bones like towels over a rack. Her mouth was slack: the nurse had to come in every hour to moisten her tongue. Who were this couple, anyway? The woman looked away, playing with the food on her plate, but the man kept looking at Flora, smoking his Cuban. He smiled. Flora trained her gaze into her whiskey.

There was a man at a piano onstage. She hadn't seen him before. "For your pleasure," Joan Daniels said, and began to sing "Swinging on a Star" in a grating vibrato. Flora looked down at herself again during the part about the mule. There was an evening during the time when all the children were either at college or out in the world, when Dickie was stalking around in his slacks and sport coat, waiting for her to change into her dress so they could go out to dinner at the grill where he always ordered the fillet of salmon. It was their anniversary, she remembered. She was walking down the stairs and saw him leaning against the closet in the foyer, arms crossed, looking at his watch. There was a hardness to his frown, a smallness to his eyes, that reminded her of the last time she'd spoken to Arthur while he was still healthy and whole. She was begging Arthur not to do something and he was refusing. He had let his hair grow long and his beard grow out: he looked dirty. She couldn't for the life of her remember what she was asking him not to do. As she walked downstairs, Dickie looked up to assess her and then looked back down at his watch. She saw him without trying to as he had been fifteen years earlier, in his linen shorts, in the backyard making a great arc of hose water for Arthur and Ava to run under. "It takes you women an hour and a half to put your faces on," he sighed, tightening his watch band. She should have protested. She was too old to get by with just a little blush and lipstick anymore.

The Black waiter was sitting next to her, clearly no longer a waiter and wearing a suit finer than the man's who had been smoking the Cuban. The former waiter signaled for another waiter, a thin-mustachioed white man, and asked for a vodka sour. Then he turned to Flora and said, "I just clocked out." His face was warm. "I hope you don't mind." Flora's stomach stirred, and she crossed her legs at the ankles. She couldn't remember having ever felt so tickled and curious. If she had at all, it had been when she was a coed, tied to Dickie but indulging in the delicious gossip of her sorority sisters: who'd stolen a kiss from whom, how wrong the kisser, how wrong the kiss. "Not at all," she said. "Are you from around here?" Suddenly there was a steak in front of him, which he looked at thoughtfully. "From New York, you mean?" he asked, beginning to cut the steak. "Not originally. My people came north from Alabama." Flora blushed for reasons she couldn't readily identify, then tried to correct her complexion by thinking about a photo she'd seen of Frank Sinatra and Ava Gardner on top of the Empire State Building, Ava in pearls and a plunging neckline and Frank in a suit and tails. "It must be incredibly exciting to live in New York," she said. The man looked at her as though she'd just claimed the sky was green. "Don't you live here, too?" he asked. "Joan Daniels only lets true New Yorkers in her audiences. Didn't you have to show proof of address?" There was a salmon in front of Flora, the kind Dickie always ordered. Salmon was good for his circulation. But hers wasn't a fillet like he liked: bones protruded, and a dead eye watched her. "I'm sorry, what was your name?" she asked. "It's Peter," he said. "And yours?" She couldn't give her real name. Not just for the sake of Dickie and the children, but because she was now slim and young again and strange to herself. Her real name wouldn't fit. "Denise," she said. Peter nodded. "A pleasure to make your acquaintance, Denise."

Ava had demanded the least attention from Flora. A fast learner, a sensitive child—played well with others, never rocked the boat, was always willing to run and fetch things Flora needed: a spoon, a towel, a Jell-O mold. She imagined Ava at ten, with her bangs cut in a neat line and her thin frame hiding under the daisy dress she wore so often that there were permanent stains on the front and the hem had to be constantly altered. She was a good student. She loved Flora. She spent afternoons with Flora on the sofa puzzling over her multiplication tables—having already solved them, Flora was sure, and just wanting to spend time with her mother—she set the table for dinner, she washed the dishes even on the nights when she hadn't been assigned that particular chore. Dickie always wanted them both to keep trim, and insisted on approving of all the dresses Ava wore as she got older. He called her "my little movie star," because that's who she'd been named for, and said one day she'd find her Sinatra. "But you won't find him if your hair and face are sloppy," he said. She ran off to her room to fix herself up. Flora followed her and pressed her ear to the door. She was crying.

Flora should have gone in and explained the needs of men to her. She should have sat with her arm around Ava's shoulders and told her that the world is a strange and unfair place and that the only way to make it better was to even the playing field by presenting oneself with the utmost decorum. "You are beautiful," she should have said constantly to that juice-stained baby face. "You will grow into a beautiful woman." Ava did, actually, though not in the way Dickie had wanted her to: she cut her hair short, and wore button-down shirts tucked into dungarees, and eloped with a man Dickie didn't like, a sculptural artist whose work Dickie didn't understand (and neither did Flora, though she was happy to puzzle over it), and had only one child, Ariel-called-Arlo.

"I went so wrong with Arthur," Flora said, and Peter nodded solemnly, chewing a cube of steak. Joan Daniels had finished singing and was sitting to the side as a vaudeville couple did some kind of balancing act with plates, Joan's backside sliding off the high stool, her hands resting in her lap. She was unhandsome, slightly manic, and it was difficult for Flora to understand why she had her own show, and why it was sponsored by a brand as well-known as Mrs. Dishwell's, and why Flora was in attendance. "Is Arthur your son?" Peter asked. Flora sighed, and wedged one of the tines of her fork into the eye of the salmon. "Yes," she said. "My firstborn."

Her feet were cold in the bed. The sheet and blanket were both thin. Her breath was finally coming evenly, though her mouth hung open in a way she imagined must have looked grotesque. The children and their children were gone. It was night. She tried to make her knees move, then her feet, then her toes. Nothing worked. Nurses passed each other beyond her door in the hallway. And then at the side of her bed were her parents, her father's hat in his hands, her mother in her Easter gloves.

"Why are you laid out like this, Florabelle?" her mother asked, and her father fiddled with the brim of his hat. Her mother turned to watch the nurses, then assessed Flora's desiccated body and clucked. "They don't let her have any dignity here, Jake."

Flora tried to move her mouth but it was slack. She felt heavy, medicated.

"Your mother and I are worried about you," her father said. "We heard you were sick and we came as soon as we could."

"What happened to your skin?" her mother said. "You look so dry. Are you drinking water? Pinching your cheeks?"

"Sick," Flora whispered. She wanted to say *What happened to Daddy?* meaning more specifically *Why did he drive that way and get into that wreck?* But then she realized her father was right there, and that she could for once ask him whatever she wanted.

"Sick?" she said again, trying this time to pitch it as a question to her father. He leaned forward, biting his bottom lip.

"What's that, dear?" he said.

Flora tried to make a noise, but this time nothing came. Her mother clucked again. "They aren't giving her enough water," she said, and signaled for a nurse. None came. "Nurse!" her mother said, and then cursed under her breath. "I'm going to go fetch one of them. You stay here, dear. Just keep resting."

Now her parents were gone, but there was a nurse at her bedside, Marciel, saying in her lilting accent, "What is it, Mrs. Fells?" Flora could never place her accent. "What is it, honey?"

"Sick," Flora breathed.

Marciel nodded and folded the sheet and blanket over Flora's chest. "We're going to get you better," she said, though her voice was vacant, and she seemed to be saying the words just to say them.

She could see the insides of Peter, the steak sliding down his throat, his lungs expanding against his rib cage and then contracting again, the tendons in his fingers as he grabbed the knife and fork. He glistened. His brain pulsed. She looked at her own hands and they were similarly exposed. She suddenly had nothing to say.

"My wife and I had a son ourselves," Peter said. Flora watched the slippery machinery of his body chew, swallow, and digest. "So much happens in the first year. You have to be as attentive as possible. Read as much Spock as you can. I always wanted to be involved in that child-rearing stuff." She found she couldn't say anything, or else she had nothing to say, unless it was about how fragile a body was. There were her muscles and bones, there was her cartilage. Some of it had begun to rip and crack. A thrumming began at the back of her head. "Peter," she said finally. "What would you say about coming outside with me for a cig?" His muscles revealed a smile. "I'm so glad you asked," he said. "Of course."

They got up and wound their way among the tables, the crowd watching the well-dressed woman and her equally well-dressed companion make their way out of the club. "It's a live broadcast," a woman in a stole sniped at them. Flora pushed past her, and Peter laughed. It had begun raining outside, so they had to confine themselves to the space under the awning. Peter exhaled his smoke elegantly, in a subtle stream over his shoulder, and Flora tried to imitate him. "I'm dying, Peter," she said. "I have regrets." Peter laughed again. "I do, too," he said. His insides, thankfully, were concealed again; Flora didn't bother to check her own. "I wish I hadn't gone to war for this goddamn country," he said, suddenly bitter. "I wish I had insisted on my worth instead." Flora took a drag. She didn't look at him—she didn't want to look at him. "I wish I'd grown up with the guts to tell more people what I thought of them," he said. Flora's stomach turned and she folded her arms. She felt helpless. "What do you think of me?" she asked. Peter seemed cowed. He put his cigarette out underfoot and straightened his tie. "I've only just met you, Denise," he said. "You've got to give me time to form an opinion." Flora ashed her cigarette against one of the awning's bronze poles. She needed to ask him a question she was afraid to ask. "Where are you, Peter?" she managed finally. "Where is . . . where are you in space?" Peter frowned. "What do you mean where am I? I'm right here." She felt blood pounding in her head. The rain was coming down harder. "I need to make a phone call, excuse me," she said, and ran back into the club.

They had bought the Orland Green home in a buyer's market, just after it had been built for all the white families moving out of the city. They'd lived in an apartment before—not in the city—that Dickie was attached to because it had been a graduation gift from his father. But it had become cramped with Arthur underfoot, leaving his shoes on the carpet and his toys on the stairs, and then there was Ava needing to be changed and nursed. Dickie had gotten a pharmacist job as soon as he graduated—before they were married, even. "He's a provider," Flora's mother told her. "I was worried about him with all those keggers in college, but he's made something of himself. Your children will be very intelligent." Flora loved the backyard. They had moved in over the summer, and when Dickie was at work and the children were asleep, she'd gone out to sun herself, admiring the glaze of sweat on her thighs and middle, thinking of herself naked between the covers while she listened to Dickie hum and shave behind the bathroom door, awaiting his hungry smile. There was so much about her life to love and admire, so much she knew her friends and neighbors envied, until things began to go wrong with Arthur.

There were two phone booths, one empty and one occupied by a young girl who smiled and twirled the cord around her finger in that irritating way coeds do when they're talking to their long-distance boyfriends. Flora slid into the empty booth and dialed the Orland Green number. Dickie picked up after three rings.

"Flora," he said, a little breathless. "Where are you?"

"I'm not sure. I think I'm in New York."

"New York? How the hell did you get to New York?"

As she heard his panic rising, she could feel her own rising, too. "I don't know. Actually, I—actually I don't think that's where I really am."

"The children are worried sick about you. Little Alan couldn't sleep last night."

"Honey, I'm sorry. I don't know how I got here. But, listen, please. The queerest things have been happening to me."

He wasn't listening. He was making some kind of noise on the other end, faint talking or whispering, probably assuaging one of the children's fears. Probably Ava's.

"Dickie?"

"What?"

"I don't mean to bring anything sad up, honey, but do you remember the day you passed away?"

"What?" His voice was quiet but severe. "What on earth are you talking about?"

Flora could feel fear churning in her gut. "Do you remember *how* you passed away?"

"How I passed away? Flora, I'm alive." Then his voice was distant, assuaging again. One of the children squawked something in response. "You're acting sick, Flora. You sound sick. You're saying crazy things. Where are you? I'll find a sitter for the children and come get you."

"That's just the thing. I don't know."

"I'm going to call the police, then," he said. "If you don't know where you are, there are detectives who can come find you."

Someone gently took the phone from her hand and hung it up. Peter. "You seemed perturbed, so I thought I'd do you a favor," he said. "I'm sorry if I was acting odd outside. I didn't mean to stir up any negative emotions." Flora blushed again. Her mother had always said she looked younger when she blushed. "I apologize for running away like that," she said. "I had to call my husband. I'm not sure he knows where I am. Do you have the address?" Peter nodded capably. "Sure, I can give it to you." He put his hand between her shoulders and she rose reflexively. They walked back onto the floor, where Joan Daniels had left the stage and a band had taken her place and was playing an instrumental version of "Minnie The Moocher." She watched Peter watching the band. He held his chin between his thumb and index finger and nodded airily to the rhythm. "It'll be good when Joan gets back on to do the show," he said. "It's really a killer show."

Alan had just come from work, he was telling the nurse. What had happened today? He saw that his mother looked unusually tired. The nurse was one Flora didn't recognize, short with dusty gray hair, and she said she herself had just clocked in and would get charts from the day nurse right away. Alan sighed. He'd like to hear soon—it had barely been a week since she was admitted and things kept changing from day to day. He asked if he could speak to a doctor. He sat in the chair next to Flora and then stood over her and said, "Hi, Mom. How are you? Are they taking good care of you?" Flora offered a half smile, though she was thinking of him in his onesie on the rug in front of the fireplace in Orland Green, scooting along on his stomach, and not of him as he was now, dressed in shirtsleeves and slacks and looking sweaty and worried. She closed her eyes. He said, "There's a smile. Beautiful smile, Mom." There was a rattling in her chest when she breathed. There was the beeping and she still couldn't close her mouth. There was someone else in the room now: the doctor. Alan wanted to know if there had been any progress. The doctor—another voice Flora didn't recognize—said that patients who have suffered bilateral intracerebral hemorrhages rarely recover as well as Flora had, and that given her age, they could do nothing but wait and observe. Yes, but what about the smaller stuff, Alan wanted to know. The Parkinson's and the feeding tube and the way her mouth keeps hanging open and nobody is coming in to swab it. He'd swabbed it himself yesterday and there was a layer of—how could he describe it—skin-like filth that the swab had pulled out. The doctor agreed that this was unacceptable and that he would let the nurses know to swab more often. The doctor reminded Alan that there was no way of knowing what his mother was perceiving, what her "consciousness level" was at any given time as her brain healed. They had placed her on a low-cholesterol diet in addition to her other medications. A physical therapist was coming in every other day to ensure that she retained tone in her arms and legs. Alan considered this. He was sure she could perceive her family, he wanted the doctor to know. They had spent many evenings at her bedside when she'd opened her eyes and smiled and even mouthed words at them. The doctor did not deny this. He said these were things to be optimistic about.

Arthur was sanguine where Alan was melancholic. She could see Arthur in his short pants wandering around a pumpkin patch the day before Halloween. And there he was a year later to the day dressed in his cowboy costume. She remembered him watching John Wayne films and making a gun out of two spoons and a rubber band (Dickie hated it when she let Arthur play with the cutlery). She could remember with consistency his birth, his infancy, his toddlerhood, his childhood, but then nothing until the last moment she'd seen him, when he was bearded and long-haired and dirty-looking and getting in the van he wouldn't let her or Dickie ride in—not that Dickie had wanted to. That van stirred anxiety in her. What had she been asking him to do?

"Mom," Arthur said, and she was standing in the garage in the black sheath dress she wore to showcase her figure, the one Dickie had picked out for her. She inhaled sharply. There were silver hairs in Arthur's beard already, and he was so young. "Listen to me," he said. "You're not listening to me."

His voice was softer than she'd remembered it, his face more patient. "I'm listening," she said.

"I'm not going to just stay here with you over the summer, OK? I have a job in the city. I have a place there."

Now she remembered what she'd wanted. The tips of her fingers tingled. Her ears rang.

"No," she said, a whine in her voice, and wondered if she'd begged like this before. "I don't trust those friends of yours."

He shook his head. "Well, that's your problem," he said. "I gave you every chance to trust them."

John, the one who grew a patchy beard, the one who picked the crusts off his sandwiches and whose pupils Flora noticed were frequently dilated. "I won't allow you to live with John. He's in trouble with the police."

"No, he's not! He made *one* bad choice *one* time. He's fine now."

She walked up to him. The smell of him, the physicality of him. He had begun to use aftershave. *Begun* was wrong. He was using aftershave. He was in the habit of using aftershave, but the smell of it was overwhelmed by his own dirt, sweat, and grease. She put her hands on his shoulders. He slackened his posture and averted her gaze. "I love you," she said. "You're going to end up in a bad place if you keep that kind of company. Especially if you keep doing what they're doing." These words, as she said them, embarrassed her for their lack of depth.

He tore away from her. "Don't guilt me." And then he got in the van and drove out of the garage, away from Orland Green.

The band played the final notes of "Minnie The Moocher"—nothing as fantastic as Cab Calloway himself, but serviceable—and she and Peter were at their table again, Peter holding the ankle of his crossed leg with one hand and smoking with the other. She was smoking, too, she realized, and was immediately relieved at the taste of tobacco and the pulse of nicotine in her blood. She looked over at Peter, who didn't look back. "I should have gone after him," she said, too quietly to be heard over the din of the club between acts. Peter turned to her. "What was that?" She shook her head and took another drag. "Arthur," she said. "I should have gone after him." Peter looked at her inquisitively, and it was obvious he couldn't hear her, though there was a sensitivity in his eyes that suggested he knew she was talking about family. He produced his wallet and showed her a picture of a young-looking Black woman in a nipped-in blouse and A-line skirt. The woman smiled, looking at a point somewhere above and to the right of the photographer, and she held a baby on her hip who smiled and directed its gaze at the same point as its mother's. The baby was obviously Peter's. "Beautiful," Flora said, making sure to say it loudly. Peter considered the photo and said, "My reasons for living," and then pocketed his wallet again. Flora looked over her shoulder: the man with the Cuban was still looking at her, though there was something more sinister about his gaze now than there had been before. His companion had left the table—she had looked young to be his wife, but then there was no telling with men. He pivoted his gaze from Flora to Peter to Flora again.

"Look, here it is," Peter said, and Flora saw that the band was gone and Joan Daniels had resumed the stage, her hands clasped, belting out a big welcome back to the audience. "As you know, this is a live broadcast straight from Manhattan, sponsored by Mrs. Dishwell's soap: the only soap that cleans everything in your kitchen!" For some reason this made everyone laugh, including Peter. Flora stole another glance at the Cuban-smoking man—thankfully, he was looking at Joan Daniels as well. "Friends, we have reached that hour of the night when countless listeners and viewers from all over our fair country have tuned in to experience the thrill of city life that we Manhattanites know so well.

What better place to lose oneself and find oneself again than in New York? The sights, the people, the culture!" Flora lit another cigarette. She was no longer thinking about Ava Gardner and Frank Sinatra: she was thinking about the smog in Indianapolis and the maples in Orland Green and a trip into Chicago when Arthur was ten years old to see *How the West Was Won* in the theater. She was thinking about Arthur. Joan Daniels perched herself on her stool once again and folded her hands in her lap: "Ladies and gentlemen, as I'm sure you know from my previous broadcasts, there are a number of special guests in the audience tonight. None of them know that they're special guests quite yet, but they will all find out." She sang in her vibrato: "All of you are special, don't you see? All of you are ver-y special to me." Flora ashed her cigarette and looked over at Peter, who was watching intently. "And who, you may wonder, is our first guest or guests? Well, this young man was separated from his twin brother at birth, grew up an only child, got drafted, and would you believe it? He *met* his brother again overseas, fighting in the European theater! Arnold and Dan Billingsley, where are you?" Two energetic young men bounded onstage, one movie-star perfect and the other slightly shorter and swarthier. They smiled eagerly, radiating good health, and looked at the cameras. "Arnold, what was it like finding Dan nearly on the other side of the world?" Joan Daniels asked, and tipped her microphone toward the swarthier one. "Swell," Arnold said. "Ms. Daniels, it was quite literally the best thing that has ever happened to me." Dan wrestled Arnold into a headlock and grinned triumphantly as the audience laughed. Flora ordered a cosmopolitan from the thin-mustachioed white waiter.

Was his mom's temperature being taken, Alan wanted to know. She'd felt warm when he'd touched her forehead a moment ago. The nurse said she'd take the temperature right then: 98.5. Alan wanted to know if his mom's bed could be moved closer to the window. He wanted to know why her catheter bag was so full. He wanted to know why she had bruises on her hands. The nurse told him that she'd move the bed and change the catheter bag and find him an answer about the bruises. "Seems like you should know that kind of thing off the top of your head," Alan said when the nurse left. "Don't you think she should know that, Mom?" Flora exhaled drily. Alan fit his hand under hers. "Squeeze if you're in pain, Mom," he said. She was in pain—a throbbing in her foot, a tightness in her chest, a swollen buzzing in her head— but she didn't squeeze. He was talking out of turn. He was misbehaving. Why this now? He'd always had such respect for his elders. The second-best behaved after Ava—it was hard to top Ava. Flora opened her eyes and it wasn't Alan there but her father, gray-faced, ghoulish. "Flora, darling," he said. "Squeeze if you're in pain." She yelped but it came out as a cough, and then there was a sustained, panicked beeping, and then Marciel was at the side of the bed saying, "Mrs. Fells? Mrs. Fells?" And then there were others there besides Marciel, pulling down her blankets, talking to one another—she was moving, or being moved, and very quickly.

"There's nothing more wonderful than the sight of a man in uniform, am I right?" Joan Daniels asked the room as the Billingsley boys returned to their seats. "And we New Yorkers count among our ranks thousands and thousands of boys who fought against the Germans and the Japs for us! Tens, if not hundreds of thousands of them! Friends, let's get a round of applause for our troops!" The room roared with applause as Joan Daniels clasped her hands and swiveled her pop-eyed gaze from left to right. "I know there's someone in the audience who makes me especially proud to call myself an American." The spotlight locked on Peter; Flora blinked and watched him sit up, grinning, and button his suit jacket. "Peter Jones, friends, was the first Black man in his battalion to receive a bronze star for his valor overseas." Peter stood up. The man smoking the Cuban booed, called, "Sit down!" Peter walked up to the stage as the man's booing and catcalls continued and eventually spread to the rest of the room. Flora warmed with embarrassment. She could not remember ever being in a situation like this before. She thought she should leave, maybe make another call to Dickie and the children, but with a sharp intake of breath and an intensification of the spine-melting heat in her body she realized that Peter's life and hers were traveling the same set of rails. She stood. He assumed the stage. "Peter!" she called, though not loud enough to be heard above the chaos. "How did it feel when you received the bronze star for your valor?" Joan Daniels asked Peter, and then someone several tables to the left of Flora stood up, shouted, "Get him offstage!" and with a splitting pop shot at Peter before he could say anything. The bullet grazed his shoulder. Flora saw him staring wide-eyed at the audience before the spotlight shut off and he ducked behind the curtains. Joan Daniels put her hands on her hips and scowled, like a child who had been denied a candy bar. "No guns in the club!" she pouted, and there was a commotion in the crowd. The man smoking the Cuban punched another man in the face, and a horde of police officers descended on them both. Flora ran to the stage, but there were more officers there, too: one grabbed her by the shoulders and held her away, grunting, "You'll have to calm down, ma'am." The cameras and spotlights shut off. A man in headphones with a broom-like mustache darted onstage and said, "There's been a delay in our programming, folks. Enjoy a drink on the house while we get things in order." There were officers guarding the entrance to the club, the stage, the bar. Flora stumbled back to her seat. The waiter brought her a finger of gin, neat, and some salted peanuts.

Of her sisters, it was a painful open secret that Flora was the prettiest. Susanne, the younger, had been born with a cleft lip, and Beatrice, the older, had inherited their father's height in her ungainly proportions. But it wasn't just that Flora was pretty in comparison with her sisters— it was that she was pretty in comparison with anyone. When her family left Indianapolis for the lake house in Saugatuck every summer, the girls envied and gossiped about her and the boys asked to dance with her every Saturday after dinner at the lodge. She was Junior Miss Lake Michigan for four summers in a row and then Miss Lake Michigan for five summers in a row after that. She was smart enough to know just what about her beauty was so infuriating to the other girls—it wasn't the neat measurements of her figure or the fact that her hair had such volume that she never needed to set it in curlers—it was that her face perfectly expressed her kindness. Whether she wanted to be wide-eyed and smiley and girlish like Judy Garland or chin-tucked and reserved and sultry like Lauren Bacall, she always looked kind. There were so many girls, she knew, who were very kind, but whose faces were too plain to express it. If she were among their ranks, she would have hated herself, too.

In Saugatuck, her mother busied herself with things she typically complained about when she had to do them in Indianapolis: buying new curtains for the kitchen, cooking big dinners, cleaning the bathrooms, and emptying the lint from the dryer. "If we could stay here all year, I'd be a happy woman," she told Flora. And then, when Flora was visiting her as she lay dying of pneumonia and sepsis in a hospital in Orland Green: "That house was like being in love." Flora's father, by contrast, read his paper in the living room and played Go Fish with Flora's older sister and listened to radio programs about the histories of Rome and Greece. The summer days sorted themselves out like this: Flora's younger sister tagging along with their mother as she tidied the house and baked cakes and cookies, Flora's older sister pretending to read the paper or a book across from their father in hopes that he'd stop reading and notice her, and Flora caught somewhere in between. The family came together three times a day, for breakfast, lunch, and dinner, but it was rare that they could be found together, or in some arrangement other than youngest-and-mother and eldest-and-father, at any other time of the day.

Flora could remember one occasion at the lake house when she'd seen her father without her older sister nearby. She had been twelve, walking upstairs to get something from the room she shared with her younger sister, when she noticed the door to her parents' bedroom was open. She was still young enough to be enthralled by her parents' lives, to assume that whatever happened behind their closed door was more interesting and important than anything that could ever happen behind her own. She crouched close to the floor and leaned her head in to see her father sitting on the bed, legs close together like a woman's, crying like a woman. Flora's scalp prickled with disgust, but she didn't look away. He held a pocketknife and with the blade dug under the finger-nail of his index finger. He was bleeding. His other fingers were bleed-ing, too. Flora gasped and dry-heaved and her father looked up, his tear-stained face alert, and told her to go to her room or she wouldn't get any dinner. She obeyed.

The summer she turned sixteen, a blond boy named Dickie Fells asked her to dance at the lodge. He was new but he was popular: he would flit from table to table during dinner, making the girls laugh and charming their parents. He played football in school and had plans to attend the University of Michigan in the fall and eventually become a pharmacist like his father. He was going places, all the parents agreed. He had a large, square head and neat little rows of teeth. There were boys handsomer than him, the girls decided, but none as smart and funny.

When she agreed to dance with Dickie Fells, Flora did not realize that he would put his mouth close to her ear and say, "I've had my eye on you all summer, Miss Flora Harvey, and I'm not going to stop chas-ing you until we're married." He said it in the same friendly timbre he used to joke with the parents, but something about it still frightened her. It was queer that she should be so frightened by someone as nice and funny as Dickie Fells.

The summer she turned seventeen, she and Dickie were engaged and she was planning to follow him to the University of Michigan in the fall. When she and her family arrived at the house in Saugatuck, four months before Flora's father died in the wreck, Dickie was wait-ing for her outside with a bouquet of roses. "My, my, Dickie! These are beautiful!" Flora's mother said, grabbing the roses from him and rush-ing them inside to a vase. Flora's father herded her sisters in after their mother, though not so fast that Flora's older sister couldn't pause on the topmost stair to stick out her tongue at Flora. Dickie took Flora's hands in his own. "I can't believe I'm really going to marry Miss Lake Michigan," he said, and she laughed, ignoring how his voice had grown slightly thin with impatience and anger. He'd tried to enlist the month before but had been denied because of his flat feet, and he had been in a sour mood ever since. "I can't believe I'm really going to marry Dickie Fells, Pharmacist to the Stars," she said, which managed to flip some kind of switch in him, because he grinned, eyes brighter, and began running, pulling her along with him. "Come on," he said. "I wanna take you somewhere."

They ran up the hill behind Flora's family's house, beyond the houses on the lake, and then beyond the cabins rented by the families who couldn't afford the houses. They ran through a heavy copse of trees and emerged what felt like miles away, at a section of the beach Flora had never seen before. Flora could feel Dickie watching her as she admired the place—the stone-less sand, the reed-less water, the scrum of bright white seashells between the tide and her feet—and when she looked back at him, his chest was puffed out like an explorer's. "Can you believe it? This place doesn't belong to anybody. Just here for the taking." Over Dickie's shoulder in the distance was a collection of small houses, far more modest that the ones they'd run away from, but she said nothing about them. He pulled her into a kiss and then they were down in the sand—the way he'd tell it to their friends years later was that Burt Lancaster and Deborah Kerr had copied him and Flora—and her shirt was off and then his pants. When she saw *From Here to Eternity* after Arthur was born, she would find Dickie's comparison embarrassing, even if it was supposed to be a joke. What did a couple of teenagers struggling around in dirty sand on someone else's lakefront in Michigan have in common with two movie stars on a beach in Hawaii? Dickie's mouth was at her ear again, and he was saying, "My god, Flora, you're so beautiful. Oh my god. Oh my god." And she was looking at the sky above them, murmuring, "I love you" and then swiveling her head to take in the expanse of the beach, and this time she froze. Peter and his wife, dressed in bathing suits, had crested the hill between the houses and the lake and were now staring at Flora and Dickie, mouths agape, Peter's wife holding their toddler's head against her shoulder for fear he'd turn around and see what they were seeing. Flora sat up and Dickie fell from on top of her. "Please, I'm sorry!" she shouted. She didn't know what else to say.

Ava opened the curtains and looked out at the parking lot. Ariel-called-Arlo joined her, and they both seemed to be waiting for something awful to happen. "Mom," Ava said. "Do you like the light in here?" There was something cold in Flora's stomach, something mechanical. She tried to make the word "no" but only succeeded in closing her mouth a little and opening it again.

"That's a yes," said Ariel-called-Arlo, and pushed the curtains open further. "How do you like that now, Grandma?"

Flora remembered when Ariel-called-Arlo had tried to eat a hot dog Dickie had grilled and gone inside to throw it up and declared she was a vegetarian later that evening. She remembered the way Ariel-called-Arlo's eyes had danced at pastas, cheeses, and pints of ice cream. She closed her own eyes and saw flashes like neon signs and lit-up billboards. There was a pressure at the base of her neck. There was the feeling that something in her body was trying to leave her body and she didn't know what. She opened her eyes again and Ava was sitting at her feet, holding one of her ankles.

"Mom, did they tell you what happened last night?"

Ariel-called-Arlo crossed the room, looking at her—their—phone.

"They said you may have had another stroke, a very minor one, in the pons. Very, very minor. Did the doctor tell you?"

The pressure at the base of her neck still. The churning in her stomach—a machine's, not her own.

"So that's the bad news. But the good news is that you're recovering so well from the other one. The big one."

Ava cracked her knuckles—nasty habit—and began massaging Flora's feet. Still so well-behaved. She had become thin in her middle age, though the contours of her round child's-face were still visible beneath the sharp edges of her chin and nose. Flora thought how watching your children grow old is like watching your own ghost stalk the earth. She closed her eyes. The room smelled of Ava's peach perfume and the minty spray Ariel-called-Arlo put in that inch-long hair to spike it. This was why Flora had always wanted girls: she knew they would be admirable in their beauty and loyal and kind-faced like she was. Even at their angriest, girls never did anything destructive—at least not the girls she'd grown up with, and certainly not her own. Boys were volatile, never long for the world. But girls wanted to be alive, and were grateful for it.

"So, Mom? Can you hear me?" Ava raised her voice, and Ariel-called-Arlo's feet paced the room again. "They want to keep you a little longer for observation, OK? We're not out of the woods yet. And unfortunately the feeding tube has to stay in for now because of the swallowing, but I'm not sure if that's a permanent thing; I'll ask Dr. Intantola about that. Mom?" Flora felt Ava's hand gently shaking her ankle, but something was keeping her from opening her eyes. "Arlo and I have to go back home for dinner, but I'll try to be back tomorrow morning if I can get off work. Dr. Intantola is going to come in to see you in the next hour or two. I wrote down a list of questions I had— he'll tell you the answers so you know them, OK? And Alan's coming tomorrow with Tommy and Ellen. We're going to get you out of here so soon. Keep your chin up, OK?"

It was dark. Flora was backstage, the commotion of the club behind her. She had never been backstage anywhere before. She was also a little drunk. There were stagehands or waiters, she couldn't tell, swarming in front and around and behind her, constantly and facelessly asking that she please step aside. "Peter?" she said, and said it again louder. The least populated corner of the place was also lit by a dim naked lightbulb. She made her way there, calling Peter's name as she did, and stopped in front of a door that read DRESSING ROOM. She pushed it open: inside was the kitchen where she'd prepared meals every day in Orland Green. Empty except for Arthur, in dungarees and a striped shirt and that pair of church shoes she'd made him wear around the house to break them in. He was ten or twelve, still shorter than most of the boys in his class, and she could tell now looking at him that he was intelligent not just in the ways she'd always known him to be—in school and in Boy Scouts and in jerry-rigging pulleys and catapults and play forts—but in a strange way she hadn't noticed before, the same "weight of the world" way that made famous and important people sad, made them do things to jeopardize their fame and importance. She moved to approach him but found she couldn't. She called his name but he didn't hear her. He was on his tiptoes, opening the cabinet above the sink where she kept the liquor she cooked with. She tried calling his name again. He came away with a near-empty bottle of vodka and automatically drank the two or three fingerfuls left. Then he reached in again: a cheap bottle of rye whiskey. She shouted this time, and tried to lift her feet, and then slid out of her pumps but her pumps weren't the problem. Where the hell were the rest of them? What time was it? When had Arthur ever been left home alone like this? The sun out the window was still high in the sky. He took a swig of the whiskey and then sat down, smiling perversely. Flora sat down, too. He stuck his pinkie down the mouth of the bottle, tipped it so his finger would get wet with the liquor, and then sucked on it. This was a favorite habit of Dickie's—he often called himself The Royal Taste Tester when he did this with wine—and Flora hoped Arthur would be done after this, would stand up and get himself a glass of water. Instead he took another swig and then set the bottle down very carefully. His eyes were glassy and unfocused—there was nothing behind them. Flora called Peter's name, Dickie's, Ava's. Arthur fell to his side and began retching. Flora was on all fours then, shouting at him, trying to throw her pumps and bracelets and cigarette case to get his attention. Her son's face was smeared with sick. He coughed up chunks of a lunch she'd probably just fed him. This wasn't how he'd died. Or maybe she was in some awful place where this was how he'd died and she couldn't do anything about it. She would leave then. But she couldn't move.

And there, finally, were Dickie's feet. Flora sat up, and Arthur's eyes blinked open, and Dickie said "What the hell is this?" He was unshaven and tired-looking: he had probably had one of his fitful sleeps the night before, and had gotten someone to cover for him so he could come home early. "Sit up," Dickie said, and kneeled next to Arthur. "Where's your mother?" Arthur, eyes still vacant, sweating out the liquor, shook his head. "I asked you a question, and I expect you to answer it." Arthur began to cry. "She's asleep," he whined. Flora winced. Asleep? She'd slept through this? "She said I could stay home from school because I was feeling sick," Arthur said. Dickie laughed sharply. "I'm sure you were lying then, but you're clearly not lying now. You look a disgrace. Stand up." Arthur pushed himself off the floor and gripped the counter, wobbling. Dickie grabbed him by the ear. "You will not speak of this to your mother or Ava, and you certainly won't do it again. You will not leave the house unless it's for school for two weeks, and if either of them ask you about it you'll say you're just feeling under the weather." Arthur's face was tight with pain—with too many types of pain—and he nodded until Dickie let him go, then he stumbled into the counter and nearly fell down again. Dickie sneered. "I would sooner have no son than have a son who's a wino. Do you understand me?" Arthur blinked slowly and nodded. "Now clean this up, and take a shower, and when your mother wakes up you better be acting like a goddamn civilized human being again."

Flora found that something had given way and that she could now crawl from the kitchen down the hall to Arthur's room, and lie on the floor next to his bed where he lay naked and plastered and sobbing, and that she could lie there for years, could look up to see him at age fourteen breaking off cans from a case of beer he'd smuggled under the bed, or at age sixteen with that girl she never liked, Layla or Lyla, doing things with her Flora had to close her eyes and stop her ears not to witness, or at age seventeen with John smoking dope, the room stinking of dope. And she could see herself barging in and telling him to cut it out, or trying to kick him out, and she could see her eyes pricking with tears when he became vicious, could see her face fall in recognition of the fact that he was a mean drunk. One time Dickie even came in—he made a point of rarely coming in—and announced that Arthur would have to find somewhere else to spend the night or he'd call the police. And Arthur refused and he and Dickie fought, Arthur breaking Dickie's nose, and it was Flora who called the police. There were officers' shoes escorting bloody barefoot Arthur in handcuffs out of his room where Flora was lying on the floor. She would stay lying on the floor because it meant she'd never have to be in the garage with Arthur again, listening to him tell her that he was going away from her. An image flickered in her head: Arthur on an apartment balcony, a man holding him by his shirt collar. She winced and bit her cheek and it was gone.

"I swear, I've been a guest in this audience three or four times now and it never gets old," Peter said, and lit another cigarette. "You ever see the comedy shows at the Gaslight?" Joan Daniels was still talking to the Billingsleys onstage. The audience was laughing, and waiters were circling tables and removing and supplying drinks. There were no police. Flora gasped: her breath was coming slowly, and with a rattle. "What happened?" she asked, and Peter raised his eyebrows. "Weren't you just onstage?" He shook his head and laughed. "Maybe you ought to slow down with the liquor," he said. She fished in her clutch for a handkerchief and blew her nose and fought back tears. Her breath was tortured. "I think I'm having a nervous attack," she said. "I could have sworn you were onstage, and someone in the audience shot at you." Peter offered her his hand and she took it readily. "I nearly forgot," he said. "You're not from here, are you? Too much excitement?" A waiter descended on their table, and Peter ordered her a seltzer and himself a rum and Coke. "You'll have the seltzer and maybe some coffee and you'll sober up. You're a funny girl, Denise." Flora withdrew her hand and worried one of the edges of her handkerchief. "I don't know what's coming next," she said. "I don't know what's in store for me. I don't want to go." Peter nodded, his attention straying to the Billingsleys, who were doing push-ups onstage. "You don't have to go anywhere," he said absently. "I hear she's got a concert violinist coming on next."

Her throat was the driest it had ever been, and was being violated by something inorganic. She couldn't open her eyes if she wanted to.

"I can stay, can't I?" Ariel-called-Arlo said, to which Ava responded, "No, honey. We need you to leave for a second. I'm sorry. Can you just get some food from the vending machine down the hall?"

Ariel-called-Arlo shuffled moodily out of the room and Dr. Intantola said, "I know this may not be the information you two want to hear, but your mother is being kept alive by the ventilator right now, and really, for a woman of her advanced age, this can put an immense strain on the body."

Ava was quiet in a way Flora recognized: the moment she realized their dog had run away, the moment she hung up the phone after a boy had broken her heart.

"OK," Alan said. "And what about recovery?"

"Well, that's a good question. She's showing brain activity, but it's been rather compromised by the strokes. She's been—I'm sorry to have to say this—taking turns for the worse all week. I'm ethically obligated to suggest a do-not-resuscitate order, though of course it's your choice."

"As in, if she begins to die?" Ava asked.

"Do not attempt to resuscitate—exactly," Dr. Intantola said. "Though, again, it really is your choice as power of attorney. We're just here to carry out your bidding."

"And what if my sister decides not to put in the order?" Alan said.

"Then we do everything we can to keep her alive."

They were gone: it was night, Flora was looking at the ceiling but seeing stars. She was outside, maybe, though she could still hear nurses in the hall. There were no mechanical things in her body, nothing forcing her chest to rise and fall—she was just tired, really. She simply needed to rest. And next to her was Dickie. He was tired, too.

"How is he?" her mother asked, still in her Easter gloves. Her father stood next to her: the tall provider.

Flora turned to Dickie and then back to her mother. "Tired," she said.

Her mother nodded. "Of course. He's had a long day."

But there was something strange about Dickie's body. It seemed denser than usual, and somehow otherworldly. His heart beat erratically.

"He's had several long days," her father said, and put his hand across Dickie's forehead as if to take his temperature. Flora did the same, and found he was cold. "Let him rest. Let him get a handle on his heart," her father said, and smiled. Then he kissed her on the forehead and pulled her mother close and the two of them left to get dinner, her father calling back to Flora that they'd come visit again tomorrow after lunch.

Nearly nine months to the day after their afternoon on the beach in Saugatuck, Arthur was born. And two years after that, Ava. Alan, born six years after Ava, was a surprise, though Flora and Dickie never told him. Ava became a gallerist, Alan a day trader and eventually a CFO. When Dickie had to have coronary bypass surgery and Flora realized he'd spent their small nest egg on repairs to the Orland Green house— whose patio was being reclaimed by ivy, whose basement had suffered multiple floods, whose kitchen was outdated and would never attract potential buyers—she asked Alan to pay for it, and he did. They were never able to sell the house, and Alan began to finance their retirement. When Dickie's heart failed for the last time, Alan paid for the funeral. Ten years later, he paid for Flora's retirement home, paid for proper repairs to the house, and paid a real estate agent to sell it to a young family of four.

"You're thinking too much about the past," Peter said after she told him all this. "You're too young to have a past like that." Onstage, the concert violinist played Beethoven's Violin Sonata no. 9. A hush had fallen over the club. Even the man smoking the Cuban seemed to have settled into himself, and was watching sleepily as the violinist swayed to her own music. "You have your whole life ahead of you," Peter said. "And everyone loves you. Loves people like you. Loves lucky ladies like you." He hadn't looked at her for the entire conversation—he hadn't looked at her in a long time, for a matter of fact. She leaned forward to see if he was actually as bitter as he sounded, and what she saw instead was Arthur's face, clean-shaven except for his sideburns. He turned to her and smiled, pointing at the violinist. "Ma, isn't this great?" He was older than he'd ever been—he was Peter's age. He was the age she was now, in the size 9 dress with the pumps and the clutch. She bit her lower lip, and he rested a hand on hers. "What's wrong, Ma? Don't be upset. Do you know how hard it is to get a seat at a Joan Daniels broadcast? And here we are!" She shook her head and managed, "My love." Then she pulled her hand away, thinking that it would be better to maintain decorum, and said quickly "Have you seen your father? Or Ava and Alan?" Arthur laughed as though they were at Niagara Falls and Flora was too busy buttoning her raincoat to enjoy the once-in-a-lifetime view. "They're at home!" he said. "Remember? This is your birthday gift. We had to pay out the nose for plane tickets." Flora shook her head again, and Arthur's eyes widened. "Ma, you're joking with me, aren't you? This is your favorite show." She would have been insulted by this had it not been Arthur alive and talking. "Darling, it's my friend's favorite show, not mine," she said. "You'll have to meet him. I think he's stood up." She scanned the room for Peter but it was useless. "He'll come back," she said. "But don't you think your father should be here with us, at least? Because the three of us?" Arthur turned his head to the side like an inquisitive dog, a habit of his she'd always adored. "The three of us what?" he asked. She abandoned the line of questioning and grabbed his hand, just in time for the violinist to finish the adagio and stand up to applause. "A most talented specimen, don't you think?" Joan Daniels crowed. "It really makes you wonder about all the magnificent souls we pass on the street. Which one of them may be an artistic genius? Which one of them may be a true savant?" Arthur sat forward in his seat. "Now this next guest is someone truly special, I must admit. He has lived a life of risk-taking and adventure and heroism, and he's here to tell the tale." Once again, the spotlight swiveled to Flora's table, and Arthur stood up, beaming. "Young Arthur Fells, everyone. Come tell us about your adventures!" Arthur paused to kiss Flora on the cheek, which elicited some applause and cooing from the audience—and which mortified Flora, as the two of them looked the same age—and then bounded up onstage, straightening his skinny tie. "Arthur, do you prefer your full name, or Art, or Artie?" Arthur laughed sheepishly. "Never been much of a nickname fellow myself," he said. "Arthur is fine."

There he was in that Chicago apartment he had left Flora for, on the floor with John, who had wrecked his parents' car in high school and spent the night in the drunk tank, and two other boys she didn't know. They were grizzled, all, and vacant-eyed, and laughing. They looked up at the ceiling, hands folded over their chests. "Sharif," John said, and one of the two other boys lifted up his head. "We could swim." Arthur started to laugh, and then the others laughed, and Arthur managed, "So just you and Sharif want to swim, dickhead? Just you two?" And they all laughed harder, and struggled to their feet and disappeared behind different doors. And when they emerged, they were wearing swim trunks and T-shirts, and the boy whose name Flora didn't know said, "There's like . . . this is like love." Sharif and John ignored him, but Arthur nodded. "Yeah, it is." She followed them: she couldn't tell who she was, or even *if* she was, but what mattered was her son was in her sight. They got in Arthur's van, and she was in there with them, and John said, "Time to re-up." He produced a package of tinfoil with tiny paper squares, and handed one to each of the boys, and each of the boys placed their paper squares on their tongues. Then the nameless boy fished out some kind of little vial and they passed it around, snorting what was it? Snuff? It was white— Flora squinted. Opium, maybe. Or cocaine. She'd never seen anything like it, nor the paper squares. Arthur drove. He drove for a long time down strange streets—Flora didn't know much about Chicago other than that it was where Dickie had gotten a job—and stopped at a beach. It was summer, but Lake Michigan still looked frigid. Flora looked down at where her hands should be: no hands. Her feet: no feet. The boys got out of the van and tore off their T-shirts and ran to the water's edge, stumbling back to avoid the weak tide, and then trying to shove each other in. Eventually John waded in up to his waist and Sharif tackled him, and the nameless boy dove under and then burst to the surface, shaking his soaking head. Arthur was wading in carefully, hugging his sides, avoiding the other boys' splashes. From farther down the beach guitar music played—the kind of music Dickie called "shaggy haired." Arthur dropped under and then popped back up, yelping. The nameless boy tackled him. They waded around, dunking one another, half-swimming, and then it was night and there

were more of them, girls and boys now, and they were drinking beer
and there was a bonfire burning and people were dancing to the same
guitar music, closer now. Flora found herself next to her son. He was
admiring the dancers without dancing himself, and whenever the
focus shifted to him, he would down the rest of his beer in an instant
and smash the can underfoot to applause. The nameless boy, thin and
too young-looking in his swim trunks, challenged Arthur to some
kind of drinking contest and everyone cheered them on. This was
how Flora learned the boy was called Darren. Darren and Arthur
must have chugged five or six beers apiece, the flames' glow soft on
their unlined faces, and then one of the girls said, "OK, so now if you
two are so *manly* you should have a swimming contest and see who's
manliest." Arthur laughed and spit on the ground and Darren, who
Flora could tell was already losing his balance, said, "I can beat this
guy with my eyes closed."

They swam, and Flora floated with them. Arthur swam confi-
dently, athletically, replicating perfectly the front crawl he'd learned to
do at the Y in Orland Green. Darren, by contrast, swam like someone
half his age, slapping the water with stiff arms and jerking his head
up to gasp for air. They made it far, surprisingly far, before Darren
swallowed some water and began to flail and choke. Arthur didn't notice this until Darren had gone under. Flora recognized the panic and
adrenaline in Arthur's eyes: he'd missed a fly ball and his Little League
coach was yelling at him; he'd come home late and Dickie had stayed
up to punish him. He swam back a few strokes and dove under desperately. After a matter of seconds, he was back to the surface, wiping
his long hair out of his eyes, and then dove under again, and again,
and stayed under longer each time. And just when Flora thought she'd
gone to another corner of hell where her son died by drowning, he
burst to the surface with Darren's arm over his shoulder. He swam
back quickly, wrangling Darren onto his back, and finally allowed a
wave from a passing motorboat to propel him to shore, where Darren
detached from him and coughed and spat water and the others rushed
forward to attend to them.

She saw many things after that. Four-year-old Ava accidentally cracking an egg she was trying to dye. Seventeen-year-old Alan posing for his prom photo with that nice girl who grew up to become a botanist. Dickie shirtless, calling up to the window of her sorority at midnight: "Wake up, my beautiful future wife!" And then Arthur on the balcony, the man holding him by the shirt collar. The man's fist made contact with Arthur's gray face. A strange, sunken face. Arthur did nothing to retaliate. "I'm going to fucking kill you if you don't tell me where it is," the man said. And Arthur said, "I swear I don't know." And the man said, "All right, junky fuck," and brought him to the railing, and Arthur said something in protest, something pleading, and the man said, "We've been doing this for months, and I'm done." And then the man grabbed Arthur and shoved him over. Flora looked at the sky, which was full of city smog. She didn't want to see how her son landed.

Teenage Ariel-called-Arlo, short-haired like their mother, was sitting on an ottoman in front of Flora. Sunlight came in through the tall windows in the house Ava and her husband had bought with the sale of one of his life-sized sculptures to a private collector. "Grandma," Ariel-called-Arlo said, and Flora said, "What is it, sweetheart?" Ariel-called-Arlo's face was set with a child's righteous conviction. "Grandma, if you could live your whole life over, like not have to just stay home and take care of your kids and make food—like if you could do *anything* or become *anyone*, what would you have been?" Flora felt light, almost dizzy with lightness. She laughed. "The only thing I wish I could have been was someone who loved more," she said. "There are things and people I don't think I loved enough. Do you understand what I mean, sweetheart?" Ariel-called-Arlo shook their head, clearly disappointed.

Flora sat up in the bed. There were no nurses in the hall, no doctors. Everything was quiet, and she felt light still. She stood up, the treads of her socks sticky on the linoleum, and left her room. Empty, the entire hospital. She walked down the hall, slow and stiff from so much lying down. Every single room was dark except for one at the opposite end of the hall. She walked toward it and stood at the door. Inside, Peter's wife strained and sweated, a team of nurses and doctors surrounding her, encouraging her to push. Peter stood at her side, holding her hand, promising her that it would be over soon. He looked up and saw Flora. "Thank god you're here!" he said, and nodded at his wife. "She's having trouble. The baby's stuck on her tailbone." The doctors and nurses turned to look at Flora and stepped aside. The room was cold: she was cold in her gown, her feet already growing numb through her socks. Peter's wife looked up, hair matted to her forehead, wincing in pain. Flora stood between her legs. She brought one hand forward to catch the baby and palpated Peter's wife's stomach, feeling the baby stretching her uterus, feeling him hooked on a part of her that couldn't move with him. She said, "Push yourself up. Can you push yourself up?" And Peter's wife pushed herself slowly backward in the hospital bed. "No," Flora said. "I mean raise your back and your behind off the bed. Do a bridge." Peter said, "Denise—" but Peter's wife did it, straining and groaning the entire time, and the baby's powdery, bloody, jaundiced head emerged. Flora looked at Peter, who looked in sweaty disbelief back at her. She said, "My real name is Flora. I'm sorry I didn't tell you sooner." The baby was halfway out, then all the way out, and Peter was laughing and crying, and Flora placed the baby on Peter's wife's chest and Peter's wife was laughing and crying, too.

Alan and Ava were having a conversation that was difficult to follow. Flora had heard them send their spouses away, presumably to bring them something from the cafeteria.

"She would want to be kept alive," Alan said. "She would want us to do everything."

Ava was pacing, feet close and then farther away.

"Where is she in there?" she said.

Alan scoffed. "What are you talking about, where is she? She's there. She's thinking. She's perceiving."

Ava sighed.

"OK, you can't decide what to do, I don't blame you," Alan said. "But consider her wishes."

"She never made a living will," Ava said. She was right—Flora had always thought things like that too morbid.

"Right, but consider how she was. She loved life. She was always smiling."

"Sure," Ava said. "That's true."

"She's hardy," Alan said.

"She could be. She may be different now."

Flora was onstage, under the spotlight. Next to her, Joan Daniels— warmer than she'd been before, beneficent. It took a moment for Flora's eyes to adjust, but she could see the audience, the women in cloches and men in suits replaced by everyone who'd left some trace of themselves in her life. There was Dickie, Alan and Ava, Arthur, all looking as she hadn't seen them look in forty years. And crowded behind them: childhood playmates, sorority sisters, their next-door neighbors in Orland Green, the dog they'd had that had run away, her sisters. Her parents sat at their own table apart from everyone else, holding hands, her father's face peaceful. "Flora Fells," Joan Daniels said. "We are positively honored to welcome you onstage tonight. Did you know that you're our last guest this evening? Our headliner?" She wondered where Peter and his family were—she almost asked aloud, but then realized they must be at home with their newborn. Joan Daniels sang the first few bars from "When You Wish Upon a Star" in a way that Flora found beautiful despite the vibrato. After enthusiastic applause from the audience, she turned to Flora. "What do you want to tell us, my dear?" she asked. "Tell us whatever you want. We're here to listen."

What did she want to tell them? She motioned for the microphone and Joan Daniels gave it to her. "Thank you all," she said. "All of you who are here, and all of you who couldn't be here. Thank you all, really. You've done so much for me." Her parents stood to applaud, then Dickie, then the children, then the hordes in the back. All of a sudden, the band was behind her, playing an instrumental she didn't recognize, and the spotlight had turned less severe—it had turned to sunlight.

"So you've made your decision?" came Dr. Intantola's voice from somewhere. Ava said, "Yes." Alan was nearby, Flora could feel it, and Ariel-called-Arlo, and they were quiet. "For what it's worth, I think you've chosen right," Dr. Intantola said.

"Flora Fells, everyone!" Joan Daniels said. And there was more applause, and Flora felt a tingling in her limbs, and then a gush of warmth in her chest, and then the sensation of an overwhelming love, the greatest love she'd ever felt in her life.

Acknowledgments

This book owes a lot to a taste-making group I'll call Extremely On-line Queers, who gave the title story so much support when it initially debuted in 2020. Their enthusiasm made me even more excited about writing the rest of this collection.

I have so much love and admiration for Luke Neima, who has been publishing my writing for years, and whose publication of "Fugato" in *Granta* got everything started. A big thank-you to Jordan Ginsberg, who published "Bugsy" in *Hazlitt* and has zero compunction with the wonderful world of kink.

I am hugely indebted, as always, to Zack Knoll and Carina Guiterman, editors extraordinaire. To Barbara Jones, who is an amazing agent, and to Ross Harris, who was an amazing agent and is now crushing it in the startup world. To Hannah Bishop and Alyssa DiPierro, who do their jobs with alacrity and poise. And to Lashanda Anakwah, who saw me through the sometimes-tedious process of making this book A Thing in the World.

"Like and Subscribe" owes so much to Adrian Rojas's encyclopedic knowledge of online gaming and Twitch, as well as to his hilarious Twitter presence. I'm lucky to have friends like Vivian McNaughton and Corley Miller, who kept reading these stories as I wrote them and encouraging me to keep going.

I feel fortunate to have a family that understands my need to write about things like celebrity e-girls and queer porn. Thanks to my dad for reading "Bugsy" and not judging me, and to my mom for providing inspiration for many moments in "On the Inside" and "The Last Show." Thank you to my extended family for loyally buying my books and embracing my weird interests.

Fig Tree: thank you for loving this collection and loving me with your tender and beautiful heart.

My grandma would have been flummoxed by these stories but supported me nonetheless. She has inspired so many wonderful things in both my writing and my life. I love you, grandma—I'll see you on the other side.

About the Author

Rafael Frumkin is a graduate of the Iowa Writers' Workshop and the Medill School of Journalism. He is the author of the novels *The Comedown* (2018) and *Confidence* (2023). His fiction, nonfiction, and criticism have appeared in *Granta, Guernica, Hazlitt, The New York Times, The Washington Post, Virginia Quarterly Review,* and *The Best American Nonrequired Reading,* among others. He is a professor of creative writing at Southern Illinois University.